Elijah J. Berryman

Gabriel's Testatent

Elijah J. Berryman

Gabriel's Testatent

ISBN/EAN: 9783337192549

Printed in Europe, USA, Canada, Australia, Japan

Cover: Foto ©Andreas Hilbeck / pixelio.de

More available books at **www.hansebooks.com**

GABRIEL'S TESTATENT.

(Inside)—Blow—Blow—Blow—(Outside)

Gabriel's Side Show—Cir-cus.

A Single Act—Eys—Eir—Eys.

PICTURE SIGNS OF THE TIMES,

DICTATION OF THE GOSPEL-WIRE.

1891

SANT-A-ROSA, SONOMA COUNTY, CALIFORNIA, U. S. A.

SOME ASK SOME CATCH ON MORE.

TABLE CONTENTS.

FIRST SCENE.

Extract from the Wilderness,......The Flower of Mysteries

SECOND SCENE.

Extract of Mark.................The Model of this Book

THIRD SCENE.

After Luke, now then............. .....See Additions

FOURTH SCENE.

Arrival of Chief Band ......Chief Arrival from Jasper City

FIFTH SCENE.

Picture—The Electric Gospel...........Porcupine Tablets

SIXTH SCENE.

Judgment of the She.................... (Planet Earth)

SEVENTH SCENE.

Joe, the Mail Carrier...Journey to the Heavens and Return
End—at Judgment—She—(planet earth).

Berry dead at work—Dead Berry dead at Dead
work—Look in the Letter—She.

By respect I am Joe McGinty Gabriel—or Baby Joe,
The Son-o-ma Boy, giving all this why is He my Friend;
Because I love not in affection—but in duty I am bound
To the red-men of the north-west who prophesy a Messias.
I am permitted to say—a better one does not come in time,
I promise—I Am—I fulfill when snow is about there.

    Now and again, I Am,

        ELI JOE BERRY-MAN.

GABRIEL'S TESTATENT,

—OR,—

PICTURE SIGNS OF THE TIMES.

INTRODUCTION.

I am to introduce introduction
One two second our—**Two Strike**—minute our
Son Born Again,
A First over a Second—this educated flies with Gabriel's
Trumpet. He that **made** Trumpet maid—spider.
Now **come educate His** flies—maid that flies he spied her.
Come **now, educate; you are** one of His flies.
This is His—flies hear Gabriel's Trumpet—flies all
Over the world hear Gabriel's Trumpet.
All over the world flies blow Gabriel's Trumpet.
One of the world fly-blows Gabriel's Trumpet.
Gabriel come in the world—he flies, come hear him
Blow off Gabriel's Trumpet.
God above, fool take care; God above blows fool away;
Away fool, blow for God above!

I am Eli Josias Joseph, by respect
To Him, my **Friend, this book to me is dictated** without
affection.
I love to fulfill His Promise; **for my** writing I do
Willingly pass proceeds not **mine,**
For I Am Antonio Bassanio, **or, &c.** This is mine, letter the
Last.
Son, see cook—see first picture **of** life and last picture of life.
Now take stay down sentiment of his Friend; I Am his
Publis-her, by FRIEND SHIP.

Sentiment—he works, a fool may know;
His Works **no fool** can know—His Works **the fool may see;**
His Works **a fool** can—Will see;
His Works the **blind fool may feel;** the **fool never feels like**
him
At work. This is **after McGinty words;** over after dead
Picture. This is my **Dead-eye-case-Son—**

Dead-eye-case-shun—Dead-eye-dick-shun—
Dick Dead Eye shun—I case Dead Son—
Dead sons eye the case.
Dead I Am, case hard—Dead Son, your case harden ;
Into your case, Dead Son, hard then; now then, Son Come
      Again.
Son again Born ; SON BORN AGAIN.

Into your work at thirty, half time; near thirty-one, half time.
Into your Work at thirty-one, full time.
Just as you are—into your Work just as you are.
Work out time ; just as you are, hard work, heavy tire ;
Work all heavy tire, down shift work, heat, heavy tire ;
Work lose heat, tire heavy, work loose heat,
Loose yourself—die dig-eye—dive headlong,
Along ahead into her.

   Please tell me what to write, I Am; I am the same
Son, I am the same Son Dead, I am the same Dead Son.
Come just at man, dive me in ; then I die, I am same Son.
I write anything, dead, for I Am.
When dead I write anything for my Publis-her. I Am a Jew.
I dive out into it, for I Am The Jew ;
I am the Common Jew Trinity :

FATHER——ELI——SPIRIT

Book Cross of Trinity.

I am to you a Saviour Work for the Common Trinity.
Father of Christ, I Am, Eli Joseph.
            Father of Christiamity, Joseph.

Common Trinity.   Father—of Christ—ianity—Joseph.
Common Trinity Son—a scrub crank, turning towards heaven.
Common Trinity Holy Spirit—Mary. return to earth of
      Venus.
            Our God above made three one.
Three is one—one is three—Joseph, John and Jesus.
First comes last—last comes first—Jesus is John Joseph.

Many years departed, in the Home of the Free,
Joe McGinty is mud, still his Spirit kicks the bottom of the
      holy see.

He is waiting, on the Kingdom of God, as Joseph of an
ancient line;
Brave in love of God, he would hold Christ to the cross; in
present time.
Remaining as Joseph (son of Jacob) true, noble, continent
man,
Vile woman went her ways, this Joe obeys Gods command.
In beginning unseen, the Mystery, comes to life by His word.
With his power some blind will see, some born deaf now have
heard.
God, Himself, his word owns, pictures of evil life it contains,
Pictures, the greatest evil his Spirit could retain.
He gave it for evil—some evil believe he was right.
Some profess to know, His kite flies not as high as it might.
　　　　　Great men like their own way.
They may live without trouble, they may draw their own pay,
God kills the white man and red, they with His power shall
never die,
They accept God's ways, His understanding of man,
Christ was the model of God's love, death the first of God's
plan.
　　　　　Others may snuff his bread of literature.
It remains fresh and ready and just the same.
The red man's life is for the Happy Hunting Ground,
Noble Brave his Great Spirit, in white trash is seldom found.
To God subdued to nature, they lived in ancient days,
The white man crowds him unthankful takes his home,
　　　　　Binds his Spirit it will not stay,
That Spirit prefers to fall backward, in the jaws of death, Its
own way.
Apart from white trash they soar to the Home of the Free
Well pleased with kindness, independence and liberty.
They beloved of old, may help that Spirit named Christ, in all
ages in God's Home;
Never was flesh of man to see Christ, that Spirit is in man un-
known.
Who can reveal the secret thoughts of a Christ, when by him-
self alone.
　　　　　It is beyond the scope of reason,
For simple man, to view the original scene of a life in ancient
times.
For the pleasure of judgment, I simply write
As judgment indicates, without change from the original
record,

Except at times,
With the help of imagination, to the understanding.
            Not thinking it useless or better otherwise,
Believing Jesus was crusified, and satisfied, it was so intended,
By gradual development of reason and Christianity,
            He is justified, by kind remembrance.
These extracts from the New Testament, in my belief,
            May condense and double distill the Mystery,
In which I hope to give respect to the Word of God written
By John; he alone claims the word; to Him I give all honor.
By permission he alone was a man from God,
Known in those times; With firm and unchanging belief
            And respect for the Word, and man of God,
With a few sentiments, I scent the following pages
            With pure extracts, of the Flower of Mysteries.
Which was carefully raised from affection; elevated
And developed in truth for that Spiritual Kingdom.
A practical and additional improvement, in the belief
            Of the Grecian Bard of ancient times.

            With the permission of kindness, I am,

                        ELI J. JOSEPH.

God holds no man in ignorance. Free is the mind of man
To explore the truth—and mystery of His ways.
This is of your Saviour and King,
Born between two lights, which is Christ—a Spirit—
A Saviour from God.

EXTRACT.

SOME OF IT TO JOHN IN THE WILDERNESS.

1st Scene—Sign of the Time.

In the beginning was the Word, and the Word was with God.
　　　All things were made by Him.
Without Him was not anything made that was made.
In Him was life, and the life was the Light of men,
　　　And the darkness comprehended it not.
　　　There was a man sent from God,
Whose name was John, the same came for a witness,
　　　To bear witness of the Light.
He was not THAT Light; THAT was the true Light,
But as many as received him, to them gave He power
To become the Sons of God; EVEN to them that believed on
　　HIS name,
Which were born, not of blood, nor of the will of flesh or man,
　　　But of God—and we beheld his glory,
　　　As the only begotten of the Father.
　　　John bare witness,
　　　Saying, this was He of whom I spake.
He that cometh after me is prepared before me;
　　　For He was before me,
　　　No man hath seen God at any time.
The only begotten Son he hath declared Him.
And this is the record of John, when the Jews sent priests
From Jerusalem, to ask him—who art thou,
　　　And he confessed and denied not,
And they ask him what then art thou—Elias,
And he said, I am not that Prophet, and he answered no.
Then said they unto him, who art thou, what sayest thou of
　　thyself?
　　　I baptize with water,
But there standeth ONE among you, whom ye know not.

He it is who, coming after me, is preferred before me.

These things were done where John was baptizing, and John
    bare record,

Saying, I saw the Spirit descending from heaven,
            And I knew Him not,

And I saw and bare record that this is the Son of God,

And looking upon Jesus he said, Behold the Lamb of God,

And the two disciples heard HIM SPEAK and they followed
    Jesus.

One of the two which heard JOHN SPEAK and followed HIM

Was Andrew. He first findeth his own brother

Simeon, and sayeth, We have found the Messias.

And he drove them all out of the Temple, and the sheep and
    the oxen.

The Jews said unto him, What sign shewest thou unto us?

Jesus answered, Destroy this Temple and in three days I will

Raise it up, but he spake of the Temple of his body.
            When, therefore, he was risen from the Dead,

His disciples remembered, and they believed the Scripture.

Jesus said, Except a man be BORN AGAIN, he cannot see

The Kingdom of God ; except a man be born of water and of
    the Spirit,

He cannot enter the Kingdom of God.
            That which is born of flesh is flesh.
            That which is born of Spirit is Spirit.

They answered how can this thing be?
            Jesus said, We speak what we do know,
            And testify, that we have seen,
            And ye receive not our witness,
            Even the Son of man, which is in heaven.

And as Moses lifted up the serpent in the wilderness,

Even so must the Son of man be lifted up, that whosoever
            Believeth in HIM, should not perish

But have eternal life, for God sent not His Son to condemn

The world; but that the world, through Him, might be saved.

He that believeth on him is not condemned,

And this is the condemnation, that Light is come into the
    world,

And men loved darkness rather than Light

A man receives nothing, except it be given him from heaven.

He must increase, but I must decrease.

He that cometh from ABOVE is above all,

For he whom God hath sent, speaketh the Word of God,

For God giveth not the Spirit by measure

Unto him. He that believeth on the Son
Hath everlasting life ; and he that believeth not the Son
Shall not see life.
The Lord knew how the Pharisees had heard that Jesus
Made and baptized more disciples than John; God is
A Spirit, and they that worship Him, must worship Him
In Spirit and in Truth.
That which is born of Spirit is Spirit.
They said unto him, I know that Messias cometh, which is
called Christ.
When he is come, he will tell us all things, and many
More believed because of his own Word.
So Jesus came again into Cana, where he made
The water wine.
And a certain man, when Jesus saw him lie,
And knew that he had been now a long time IN THE CASE,
He said unto him, Will thou be made whole?
The impotent man answered him, Sir, I have no man
When the water is troubled ;
But while I am coming, another steppeth down before me.
Jesus said,
Rise, take up thy bed and walk ;
Sin no more, less a worse thing come unto thee.
For as the Father raiseth up the dead, and quickeneth
THEM, even so the Son quickeneth whom he will.
The hour is coming, and now is, when the dead shall hear
The voice of the Son of God.
For as the Father hath life in Himself, so hath He given
The Son to have life in himself, because he
Is the Son of man. Marvel not at this,
For the hour is coming. I can of mine own self do nothing.
I seek not mine own will, but the will of the Father
Which hath sent me.
If I bear witness of myself my witness is not true ;
And the Father Himself, which hath sent me,
Hath borne witness of me.
Ye have neither heard His voice at any time,
Nor seen His shape.
But I know you, that ye have not the love of God in you.
I am come in my Father's name, and ye receive me not.
If another shall come in HIS OWN NAME,
Him ye will receive.
And this he said to prove him, for he Himself knew
What He would do. When Jesus,

Therefore perceived that they would come and take him
By force, to make him a King, he departed again
Into a mountain, himself alone; and the sea arose
By reason of a great wind that blew.
Then they willingly receive him into the ship;
And IMMMDIATELY the ship was at the land
                    Whither they went.
Jesus answered them, and said, Ye seek me not
                    Because ye saw the miracles,
But because ye did eat of the loaves and were filled.
Lobor not for the meat which perisheth;
But for the meat which endureth unto enternal life,
                    Which the Son of man shall give you.
This is the Work of God, that ye believe
                    On him whom He hath sent.
They said therefore unto him, What sign showest thou then,
                    That we may see and believe thee?
Our Father did eat manna in the desert,
But my Father giveth you the TRUE bread from heaven to eat.
For the bread of God is he which cometh down from heaven,
                    And giveth life unto the world.
And they said unto Him, Lord, evermore give us that bread.
All that the Father giveth me, shall come to me,
And Him that cometh to me I will in no wise cast Him out.
The Jews then murmured at him, because he said I am the
        bread,
                    Which cometh down from heaven.
I say unto you—He that believeth on me hath everlasting life.
                    I am the bread of life,
This is the bread which cometh down from heaven;
                    I am the living bread.
If any man eat of this bread, He shall live forever,
The bread that I will give is my flesh.
The Jews therefore saying, how can this man give us
His flesh to eat; Jesus said unto them,
Except ye eat the flesh of the Son of man,
And drink his blood, you have no life in you,
                    For my flesh is meat, indeed,
                    And my blood is drink, indeed.
This is the bread which cometh down from heaven.
Not as your father did eat manna, and is dead.
He that eateth of this bread, shall live forever.
Many of his disciples when they heard THIS, said,
                    This is an hard saying,

Who can hear it?
He said unto them, does this offend you?
It is the Spirit that quickeneth, the flesh
Profiteth nothing; the words that I speak unto you,
They are Spirit.
From that time, many of his diciples went back,
And walked no more with him.
Neither did his brethren believe in him.
Jesus answered, said, my doctrine is not mine but His that
sent me.
He that speaketh of himself, seeketh his own glory, but he
That seeketh His glory that sent him, the same is true.
But—lo, he speaketh boldly.
How be it we know this man, whence he is,
But when Christ cometh, no man knoweth
whence he is.
And many of the people believed on him, and said,
When Christ cometh will he do more miracles than these,
Which this man hath done?
That great day of the feast, Jesus stood and cried,
Saying, if any man thirst, let him come unto me and drink.
But this spake he of the Spirit.
The Holy Ghost was not yet GIVEN, because that Jesus
was not yet glorified.
Many of the people said, of a truth this is THE PROPHET;
Others said this is the Christ.
But some said, Shall Christ come out of Galilee?
Hath not the Scripture said, Christ cometh of David—
Out of Bethlehem, where David was?
So there was a division among the people, because of him.
Then answered them the Pharisees, Are ye also deceived?
Have any of the rulers of or of the Pharisees believed on him?
And every man went unto his own house.
Jesus said, the Father hath not left me alone,
For I do always those things which please Him.
As he spake these words, many believed on him.
Then said he unto those Jews which believed on him,
If ye continue in my Word, then are ye my disciples, indeed,
And ye shall know the truth;
For I proceed forth and come from God.
Neither came I of myself, but He sent me.
Why do ye not understand my speech, even because
Ye cannot hear my WORK.
I say unto you, if a man keep my sayings he shall

Never see death.
Then said the Jews unto him, Now we know
That thou hast a devil. Abraham is dead,
And the Prophets, and thou sayest, If a man keep
My sayings, he shall never taste death.
          Whom makest thou thyself?
Jesus answered, If I honor myself my honor is nothing;
It is my Father which honoreth me.
          Of whom ye say, He is your God;
          Yet ye have not known Him.
And if I should say I know Him not, I shall be a liar
Like unto you. I say unto you, before Abraham was,
          I am.
Then took they up stones, and cast at him, but Jesus
Hid Himself, and went out of the temple going
Through the midst of them, and so passed by.
   Others said, how can a man that is a sinner do such
Miracles; and there was a division among them.
The Jews had agreed that if any man did confess that
He was Christ, he should be put out of the synagogue.
We know that God spake unto Moses; thou wast
          Altogether born in sins,
And dost thou teach us; and they cast him.
Some of the Pharisees said, Are we blind also?
Then said Jesus unto them again,
          I am the door of the sheep.
Therefore doth my Father love me,
          Because I lay down my life.
No man taketh it from me, but I lay it down
Of myself. I have power to lay it down,
And I have power to take it up again.
This commandment have I received of my Father.
   There was a divssion, therefore, again among the Jews
For these sayings. Then cometh the Jews and said unto him,
How long dost thou make us to doubt?
If thou be the Christ, tell us plainly.
Jesus answered them, I told you, and ye believed not.
          I and MY Father are one.
Then the Jews took up stones again, to stone him.
Jesus answered them:
Many good "Works" have I shewed you from my Father;
For which of these "Works" do ye stone me?
   The Jews answered him, For a good Work
We stone thee not, but for blasphemy, and because that

Thou, being man, makest thyself God.

Jesus answered, Is it not written in your law, I said
Ye are gods. Say ye of him whom the Father hath sanctified
Thou blasphemest, because I said I am the Son of God.
If I do not the Works of my Father, believe me not.
But if I do, though ye believe not me, believe the Works.

He escaped out of their hands,
And went away again, beyond Jordan, where
John at first baptized, and there abode.

Now, a certain man was sick,
Named Lazarus. When Jesus heard THAT,
He said, THIS SICKNESS is not unto death, but for the glory
Of God, that the Son of God might be glorified
Thereby. Now Jesus loved Martha AND HER SISTER,
And Lazarus. When he heard, therefore, that he was sick
He abode two days still in the same place, where he was.
Then, AFTER that, said to HIS disciples,
Let us go into Judea again,

They answered, The Jews of late
Sought to stone thee, and goest thou thither again?

Jesus said, are there not twelve
Hours in the day; if any man walk in the day
He stumbleth not, BECAUSE he SEETH THE LIGHT of this world.
Then said Jesus unto them, PLAINLY, LAZARUS is dead!
Then said Thomas, which is called Did-amus, unto HIS fellow
Disciples, Let US ALSO GO, that WE may die with him.

Then Martha, as soon as she had heard that
Jesus was coming, went and met him,
But Mary sat STILL in the house.

He said unto her, Thy brother shall rise again;
Saying, I am the resurrection
And the life. Believe thou this?

She said unto him, Yea, Lord, I Believe that thou art
The Christ, the Son of God,
Which should COME INTO the world.
And when she had said THIS she went
Her way and CALLED Mary, secretly,
Saying, THE Master is come, and calleth for THEE.

When Jesus saw HER weeping,
And the Jews, he GROANED in the Spirit, and was troubled.
They said unto him, Lord, COME and SEE.

Jesus wept!
Then said the Jews, BEHOLD

How he loved him. Jesus therefore again groaned
       In himself. Cometh to the grave.
         It was a cave.
Jesus said, Take away the stone. Martha,
The sister of him that was dead, said unto HIM,
       Lord, by this time he stinketh.
Jesus said unto her, said I not unto thee
That if thou wouldst believe thou shouldst SEE
       The glory of God.
Then they took away the stone FROM THE PLACE,
       And Jesus said, Father, I thank Thee
'That Thou hast heard me. And when he had
Spoken, he cried with a loud voice,
       Lazarus, COME FORTH! And he that was
Dead CAME forth, BOUND hand and FOOT,
       With grave CLOTHES on, and his face was
Bound about with a napkin. Jesus said
       Unto them, LOOSE him and LET HIM GO.
Then many which came to Mary and had seen the things
       Which Jesus did, believed on him;
       But some of them went their ways to the Pharisees.
One named Caiaphas prophesied that Jesus should die
       For that nation.
And not for that nation only; but that he should
Gather together in one the children of God scattered
Abroad. Then from that time fourth
They TOOK COUNSEL together to put him to death.
       And Jesus, when he had found a young ass,
       Sat thereon.
As it is written, fear not daughter of Zion—
       Behold the King sitting on an ass colt;
These things understood not his disciples at first ;
Then remembered they these things WERE WRITTEN of him;
And that they had done THESE THINGS unto him.
       The people, therefore, that were with him
       When he called Lazarus out of his grave,
And raised him from the dead, bare record.
And Jesus answered, the hour is come,
       And the Son of man should be glorified.
And I, if I be lifted up from the earth, will draw
       All men unto me ; this he said,
Signifying what death he should die.
       The people answered, we have heard out of the Law
That Christ abideth forever;

And now sayest Thou, the Son of man
Must be lifted up. WHO IS THIS SON OF MAN?
Now I will tell you before it is come.
When it is come
To pass, ye may believe that I AM HE.
Verily, I say, the cock shall not crow
Till thou hast denied me thrice.
I speak not of myself,
But the Father that dwelleth in me. He does the Works.
If ye love me keep my commandments, and I will
Pray the Father give you another comforter,
That He may abide with you forever.
The Comforter, which is the Holy Ghost, He shall
Teach you all things, and bring all things
To your remembrance, whatsoever I have said unto you.
Ye have heard now I said unto you
I go away and come again unto you.
I go unto the Father, for the Father is greater than I ;
And now I have told you before it came to pass.
Hereafter, I will not talk much with you,
For the Prince of this world cometh and hath nothing in me.
But that the world may know I love the Father,
And as the Father gave me commandments, even so I do.
I am the true vine and my Father is the husbandman ;
Every branch in me that beareth not fruit
He taketh it away;
And every BRANCH that beareth fruit, He purgeth it,
That it may bear more fruit.
Now ye are clean through the WORD
Which I have spoken unto you ;
For all things that I have heard of my Father
I have made known unto you.
If the world hate you, ye know it hated me
Before it hated you.
These things have I spoken unto you
That ye should not be offended.
Yea, the time cometh that whosoever killeth
You, will think he doeth God service.
But these things have I told you,
That when the time should come,
Ye may remember that I told you of them.
But I will see you again and your heart will rejoice,
And in that day ye shall ask me nothing.
These things have I spoken unto you in proverbs.

Behold the hour cometh,
Yea, is now come, that ye shall be scattered
Every man to his own, and shall leave me alone.
Yet I am not alone, because the Father is with me.
And, lifting up his eyes to heaven,
He said, Father, the hour is come,
Glorify Thy Son.
And this is life eternal, that they might know Thee,
The true God.
And Jesus Christ, whom thou hast sent.
Now they know that anything
Whatsoever thou hast given me, art of Thee;
For I have given unto them
The WORDS which thou gavest me;
And they have received them,
And all mine are Thine and Thine are mine,
And now I am no more in the world.
But THESE are in the world, and I come to Thee.
Holy Father, I have given them THE WORD,
And the world hath hated THEM, because they are not
Of the world, even as I am not of the world.
Sanctify them through truth, Thy Word is truth.
When Jesus had spoken THESE WORDS,
He went forth where there was a garden,
Into the which he entered,
That the saying of Jesus might be FULFILLED,
Which he spake, signifying what death he should die.
Pilate said unto them,
I find in him no fault AT ALL, will ye therefore
That I release unto you the King of the Jews?
Then cried they all,
Saying, not THIS man but Barabbas.
Now Barabbas was a robber.
Then Pilate therefore took Jesus and scourged him,
And the SOLDIERS platted a crown of thorns,
And put on him a purple robe.
Pilate therefore went forth again and said unto them,
Behold I bring him forth, I find no fault in him.
Behold the man, they cried out,
Crucify him, crucify him. We have a law,
And by our law he ought to
Die, because he made himself the Son of God.
He said unto the Jews, behold your King; but they cried
Out, away with him, crucify him; and they took Jesus,

And he, bearing his cross went forth into A PLACE
　　　　Called the place of a skull,
　　　　Where they crucified him, and two others
　　　　With Him, on either side, One,
　　　　And Jesus in the midst.
And Pilate wrote a title and put it on the cross,
　　　　And the writing was,
　　　　Jesus of Nazareth, the King of the Jews.
　　　　Then the SOLDIERS, when they had crucified Jesus,
　　　　Took his garments;
　　　　Now the coat was without seam,
　　　　Woven from the top throughout.
They said therefore, among themselves,
　　　　Let us not rend it;
That the Scripture might be fulfilled, these things
　　　　Therefore the SOLDIERS did.
　　　　Now, there STOOD by the cross of Jesus,
His mother, and his mother's sister, Mary, the wife of Cleophas
　　　　And Mary Magdalene.
　　　　Jesus saw his mother,
And the DISCIPLE standing by whom he loved,
　　　　And he said, woman behold thy son.
Then said he to the DISCIPLE, behold thy mother.
　　　　After this Jesus knows that all things
　　　　Were now accomplished;
That the Scripture might be fulfilled, said I thirst,
　　　　And they filled a sponge with vinegar.
When Jesus therefore had received the vinegar,
　　　　He said, it is finished;
And he bowed his head and gave up the Ghost.
　　　　After this Joseph besought Pilate,
That he might take away the body of Jesus.
　　　　The first day of the week cometh
Mary Magdalene—early, when it was yet dark.
　　　　Peter went forth, and that other disciple; .
And the other disciple did outrun Peter.
And he, stooping down AND LOOKING in, saw the linen clothes
　　　　Then went in also the other disciple
Which came first to the sepulchre.
　　　　And he saw and beheld, but Mary
Stood without weeping;
And as she wept and looked in, seeth two—angels
And they say unto her, WOMAN, why weepest thou?
She sayeth, because they have taken away my Lord;

And when she had thus said, she turned herself back and saw
    Jesus
       Standing, and knew not that it was Jesus.
Jesus sayeth unto her, **WOMAN, why** weepest thou,
       Whom seekest **thou?**
       Jesus said unto **her, Mary.**
She turned herself and said **unto Him,** Master.
       Jesus said unto her, **touch** me not,
For I am not yet ascended to **my Father.**
       The same day, at evening, **to the** disciples
He showed unto them his hands and his side.
       Then were the disciples glad.
Jesus said, peace be unto you.
       Verily, I say unto thee,
When thou wast young thou girdest thyself,
       And walkedst whither thou wouldest ;
But when thou shalt **be** old
       Thou **shall stretch** forth thy hands,
And another shall gird thee and carry thee
       Whither thou wouldest not.
       This spake he, signifying by **what**
       Death he should glorify God.
Then Peter, turning about, seeth the disciple which Jesus loved,
       Which also leaned on his breast at supper.
       Then went the saying abroad, among
       The brethren, that this disciple should not die.
This is the disciple which testifieth of these things,
       And WROTE THESE things ;
       And we know that his testimony it true,

                 I suppose
That even the world itself could not contain
       Books should be written.
              A man.

EXTRACT.

2d Scene—Picture Sign of the Time.

OUT THE WILDERNESS, SOME OF IT BY JOHN, UNDER ST.
MATTHEW, MARK, THEN NOW.

Commencing: John was baptizing in
      Or beyond Jordan, in the wilderness;
And he be-held descending upon him,
In (John) Joseph, as he walked looked upon himself,
      And said, be-hold the Lamb of God.
      That was the (Jesus) Christ in him.
A Spirit from God, from heaven a Saviour,
      Which human eyes could see not.
So he said there is One (in John) amongst you,
      Whome ye know not.
And he beheld in the wilderness, also in writing John;
And he confessed, I am not Christs (Spirit)
      Still he denied not.
This is of your Saviour, Jesus Christ,
      A Spirit born between two lights;
Come from God, to be found by following the star of Beth-
lehem.
      Christ, unseen, was born in the city
      Of David.
The book of the generations of Jesus Christ,
      The Son of David, the Son of Abraham;
      Joseph, the husband of Mary,
      Of whom was born Jesus, who is called
Christ; she was found with-Child of the Holy Ghost.
The Angel of the Lord appeared unto him saying, Joseph,
      Thou Son of David, fear not to take unto thee
      Mary, thy wife;
She shall bring forth a Son; thou shall call his name Jesus.
      And HE called HIS name Jesus.
And lo, the star which they saw in the east went before them.
      When they saw the star they rejoiced,
And when they were come into the house
      They saw the young CHILD with Mary.
And they fell down and worshipped him
      (Same child born in manger recorded in Luke)
      With treasures, gifts, gold.

And he came and dwelt in a city called Nazareth,
That it might be fulfilled,
    He shall be called a Nazarene.
In those days came "John the Baptist," preaching
In the wilderness, the kingdom of heaven is at hand.
This is he spoken of by the prophet Esaias,
    O generation of vipers, who hath warned you
    Of the wrath to come.
I indeed baptize you with water, unto repentance ; He
Shall baptize you with the Holy Ghost, and WITH fire.
    His fan is in His hand ;
    He gathers His wheat ;
He will burn up the chaff with unquenchable fire.
And Jesus, baptized, went up out of the water ;
And lo, he saw the Spirit of God descending,
    And lighting upon him.
    Then was Jesus led up, of the Spirit,
Into the wilderness, to be tempted of the devil ;
And the devil taketh him into the " Holy City."
    Then the devil leaveth him, and behold
    Angels come and ministered unto him.
The people which sat in darkness, saw great light.
From that time Jesus began to preach,
    For, the kingdom of heaven is at hand.
Beware of false prophets ; ye shall know them by their fruit.
    Not every one who saith unto me, Lord, Lord,
Shall enter the kingdom of heaven, but he that doeth the will
    Of my Father which is in heaven.
Many will say to me in that day, Lord, Lord,
    Have we not prophesied in thy name ?
And then will I profess unto them, I never knew you,
    Depart from me.
They shall be cast out. There shall be weeping and gnashing.
He cast out the spirits with His Word, and healed
    All that were sick.
But that ye may know that the Son of man hath power
On earth to forgive sins, (he saith unto the sick,)
    Arise, take up thy bed and go ;
    And he arose, and departed to his house.
But when the multitude saw it, they marveled.
    And when he had called unto him his twelve
Disciples, he gave them power AGAINST unclean spirits,
    To cast them out,
Heal the sick, cleanse the lepers, raise the dead. Freely

Ye have received, freely give;
For it is not ye that speak, but the Spirit
Of your Father, which is in you.
Ye shall not have gone over the cities of Israel
Till the Son of man be come.
What I tell you in DARKNESS, that speak ye in LIGHT;
And he that taketh not his CROSS and followeth
After me is not worthy of me.
Verily I say unto you, among them that are born of women
There hath not arisen a greater than John the Baptist.
For all the prophets and the law prophesied
Until John.
Thou hast hid these things from the wise,
And hast revealed them unto babes;
For so it seemed good in Thy Sight.
All things are delivered unto me of my Father,
And no man knoweth the Son but the Father.
Cover—side—opposite
God—hath—declared—Son.

3d Scene—Picture of the Time.

God He hath declared me.
I am not the world which looketh on Himself
And knoweth Him not;
But, by this from me, the world may know
That Jesus was the Son of God.
Born unto Mary He was John Joseph,
Who was the son of Mary and Zacharias Joseph,
His mother, Mary (Elizabeth) Joseph.
And in her old age, him beloved in Spirit left
Her; she was overshadowed by the Holy Ghost.
Sad of heart, she tried to let him through love,
When she with him hid in the mountains.
But so much he loved that Mary, for this,
Through her the Christ was born unto him
And he called his name Jesus
From thence forth.
And God was well pleased,

And at all times could trust in him
And made Himself known in him;
And God was well pleased
With his judgment towards Himself.
And God made him
Known unto the world,
And hid Himself,
For He was weary;
And Jesus in John Joseph was good enough
For them to worship.
After this, even Jesus
Would not talk with them much.
He loved none but God;
He would not return unto them.
God's Light was with them,
Down deep in evil.
See, they slighted His Word,
Committing all acts
Which He forbid from the beginning
Unto the end, (Jesus).
John Joseph fulfilled God's Word,
And all His law.   He came
Out of darkness (when born),
And was glorified
And   raised
From the dead.
And no one is loser by it, except the Jews,
And they were God's chosen people; they praised Him
For all things.
They respected, they would not believe flesh of man
Was God; certainly
Is God well pleased.
His Spirit was in Christ to provoke them;
Still they loved Him.
In God's will they said to Pilate, crucify him;
And the world knew God's Power.
They were persecuted by christians;
And God hates them
That persecuted them that obey His will
And law, and this Jew's law remains the same.
He SHOULD be crucified; he MADE, Himself,
The Son of God;
And I, Eli Joseph, am a thoroughbred
(Jew); I am pleased; I am satisfied.

Few of their enemies become the Sons of God.
Christ was crucified for them (the christians),
    But they disobey God's law;
They misconstrue His Word ; they are ignorant.
God knew they were ignorant.   He left them.   The Jew
        Is satisfied in all time.
He sent them a Saviour, many he lifted their life
        Above the common mind.
Many cannot be satisfied ;
        They will believe God's Son (Jesus)
Should come, as a worthless babe.
        God's child must contain God's wisdom.
Man's child contains man's wisdom of the world,
        And they are wise in their mind,
And God is not right, but in His right mind,
        And God's work made wrong side up,
        He is out of their mind,
        And He don't care,
        If they get out of their mind.
        I have a bookkeeper in hell,
        And he will scorch they they find,
        God loves them; not He
        He burns all up their mind,
        They never any more see by God,
        In Him they never existed,
        He burns all down their kind.
        Now, I am coming to God,
I am His, I mine,
        I am Eli Him Youman,
That is, I am an extract of,
        I Am—am I more—I Am—
Am I—am I a sea of the see of the middle of Cupid,
And this mine underside as holding a concoction of
        An extract of, I remain
I goeth—it stinketh—I knoweth.
        Draw some in—of—in—
Distill—add—some
        Add—some—distill first.
Luke—after—my son now
        After—Luke—now my son gain,
And they had **no** child, because,
        That, Elizabeth, **was** barren,
And they both, **now**
        Well stricken in **years.**

But the ANGEL said, fear not Zacharias,
        And thy wife Elizabeth shall bear
Thee a son (John) and he shall be filled with the Holy Ghost.
        Even from his mother's womb,
And many (in Israel) shall he turn to the Lord THEIR God.
        And he shall go before Him,
In the Spirit and Power of Elias.
        And Zacharias said unto the ANGEL,
Whereby shall I know this;
        And the ANGEL, answering, said: I am Gabriel
That stand,
        In the presence of God.
Thou shalt be dumb, because thou believest not my WORDS,
Which shall be fulfilled in their season.
        And when HE came out they perceived
That he had seen a vision in the temple;
For he beckoned unto them, and remained speechless.
            And after those days Elizabeth
            Conceived, and hid herself FIVE months, saying,
Thus hath the Lord dealt with ME, to take away
        My reproach among men.

And in the sixth month Gabriel was sent
        Unto a city of Galilee, named Nazareth,
To a virgin espoused to Joseph—of David.
        (The virgin's name was Mary.)
And the ANGEL came in
Unto her, he said, Hail, thou that art highly FAVORED;
        The LORD is with thee;
        Blessed art thou among women.
She was troubled,
        And cast in her mind what manner of
        Salutation this should be.
And the ANGEL said, fear not, Mary,
        And bring forth a Son,
        And call his name Jesus.
He shall be great; called the Son of the Highest.
The Power of The Highest shall overshadow thee;
Therefore that HOLY THING born of thee;
        The Son of God.
And Elizabeth, she hath also conceived a son,
        In her old age.
And the angel departed and Mary arose,
        And went into the hill country

And **saluted** Elizabeth.
Elizabeth heard the salutation of Mary,
   The babe leaped;
And Elizabeth **was** filled
   With the Holy Ghost,
   And she spake—
Whence, is this to me, for as soon as the voice of thy **salutation**
   Sounded, the babe leaped for joy.
And Mary said, my soul doth MAGNIFY the LORD,
For he hath regarded the low estate of his hand maiden.
Now, Elizabeth, she brought **forth** a son,
And his father wrote his name, saying,
   His name is JOHN.
   And **they marveled,**
   And **his mouth WAS** OPENED,
Immediately **his tongue loosed, and** he spake
   And PRAISED God.
And **fear came on all that dwelt round about,**
And **all these sayings** were noised abroad,
Saying, what manner of CHILD **shall this be,**
   And the HAND **of the Lord was** with him,
   And his father, Zacharias, was **filled**
   With the Holy Ghost, saying,
   Blessed be the Lord God,
For He hath visited and REDEEMED His people,
As He spake by the mouth of His holy prophets
   Which have been since the world **began,**
And the CHILD shalt be called the prophet
   OF THE HIGHEST,
To give KNOWLEDGE of SALVATION
   Unto HIS people,
Through the tender mercy of **our God**
   To give light to **them that sit in darkness,**
And the Child grew strong **in spirit,**
And was **in** the desert till his **showing, unto Israel.**
Joseph **went from** Nazareth, to **Bethlehem, because**
   He was of David
Taxed, with **Mary,** being great
   With Child.
And so it was, **she brought forth** her first
   Born **Son,**
Wrapt him in swaddling **clothes,**
   . Laid **him in a manger;**
There was no room

In the Inn.
And there (in the same)
Country shepherds
Keep watch over their flock by night,
And lo, the Angel of
The Lord came upon them,
Shone round, about them.
And the Angel said unto them,
Fear not, for behold,
Unto you is born this day,
In the City of David,
A Saviour,
And this shall be a sign unto you,
And suddenly there was, with the Angel,
A multitude of the heavenly
Host praising God.
And it came to pass, the shepherds
Said one to another,
Let us now go, even
Unto Bethlehem
And see this thing, which
Is come to pass.
And they came with haste,
Found Mary and Joseph,
The babe, lying in a manager,
And they made known abroad the saying
Which was told them concerning THIS CHILD.
And all they that heard it wondered at those things
From the shepherds.
Mary kept all these things,
Pondered them in her heart,
And the shepherds returned.
And when eight days were accomplished for his name,
Jesus was so
Named of the Angel before.
And behold, Simon was just and devout.
The Holy Ghost was
Upon him, and it revealed
He should see
The Lord's Christ.
He took him up in his arms
And blessed God, and said, now lettest thou Thy servant
Depart in peace,
According to Thy Word.

And Joseph and **his mother** marveled
　　　　At those things spoken of HIM.
They said **unto Mary,** behold
　　　　This CHILD is set for the fall,
And rising again of many,
Yea, a sword shall pierce through thy **own** soul,
　　　　Also, that the thoughts of many hearts
　　　　May be revealed.
And when THEY had performed all **things**
According to the law, they returned
　　　　To Nazareth.
And the CHILD grew strong **in** Spirit, **filled**
　　　　With wisdom, and grace
　　　　Of God **WAS upon** him.

———————————————

　　　　Now, his PARENT
When he was twelve years old,　　　　．
　　　．　　And Joseph and his mother knew not
　　　　OF IT,
His mother said **unto him,**
　　　　Son, why **hast** thou thus dealt **with us,**
And they understood **not** the sayings which
　　　　He **spake** unto them.
And he went down to Nazareth,
　　　　And was subject unto them.
And he increased in wisdom and in favor,
　　　　With GOD and man.

———

God came unto John,
　　　　The SON of Zacharias, **in the wilderness,**
And he **came** into all the country
　　　　About Jordan preaching,
For the **remission** of sins ; all flesh
　　　　Shall see the **salvation** of God.
O, generation of vipers, who **hath** warned **you to flee,**
　　　　For I say unto you, that God is able
　　　　Of these stones
　　　　To raise up children.
And they said unto him, Master what shall we do ?
And the SOLDIERS likewise said unto him, WHAT SHALL WE DO ?

He said, do violence to no man,
Neither accuse any falsely.
And, as the people were in expectation
All men mused in their hearts of John,
He were the Christ or not.
John answered, saying, unto all,
I indeed baptize with water,
But One Mightier than I cometh; He
Shall BAPTIZE you with
The Holy Ghost
And with FIRE,
Whose fan is in HIS HAND;
Will gather the wheat into His garner;
Chaff He will burn with FIRE
UNQUENCHABLE.
And many other things—
Preached
He.
For all the evil He—rod
Had done, added this, above
All, He, SHUT UP, John.
All the people baptized to pass, Jesus,
Being baptized, and praying
Heaven opened,
The Holy Ghost descended,
A voice from Heaven, my Son,
I am pleased.
And Jesus began
Thirty years of age.
The son of Joseph
Of H Eli.
Of Adam— of God,
And Jesus being FULL of the Holy Ghost, led
By the Spirit, into the wilderness,
Being forty days, tempted in those days
He did eat
Nothing after ward hungered.
And the devil,
If thou be the Son, Command
This stone bee bread.
And Jesus answered,
Man shall not live by bread
Alone, by Word of God.
And the devil,

Into a high mountain show
The world, in time.
And the devil said,
Him, All Power, I give Thee glory,
For that unto me, I will I give it.
If thou wilt
Worship me
Be thine.
And Jesus answered Him,
Get Thee, it is written
Worship thy God
I Him Only serve.
And He brought him to Jerusalem,
And set him and said
If thou be the Son, cast
Thyself down.
For it is written He shall
Charge over thee to keep thee,
Hands bear thee, at any time dash thy foot
And Jesus answered Him, it is said,
And the devil, ended all, the temptations,
He departed for.
And Jesus returned in the Power of Thee
Spirit, and out went a fame of him
Region round,
And he taught,
In their sin—agogs
Glorified all,
And he to Nazareth brought up,
As his custom was,
He the sin—agog stood up,
To read.
There delivered THE BOOK of the prophet Esaias,
Where it was written,
The Spirit of the Lord is upon me, because,
He hath anointed me
To preach
The Gospel.
He hath sent me to heal
The broken hearted captives.
The blind set at liberty,
Them that are bruised ;
To preach acceptable ; he GAVE IT to the minister.
And the eyes of all the sin—agog fastened on him.

This day, is this Scripture,
In your ears.
All wondered at the Words, His is not
Joseph.
Me Physician,
Heal thyself
In THY COUNTRY,
Prophet own country.
When the heaven was shut up,
Three years, six months was great famine
Was all the land, Elias sent a city.
These THINGS filled with wrath
Rose up out of the city and came down,
And they were astonished at his doctrine,
For his Word was Power.
And in saying let us alone what have we,
Come to destroy us, I know who Thou art.
And Jesus rebuked, saying, hold thy peace,
And the devil in the midst came out;
And they were all amazed among themselves,
Spake what a Word is this with authority,
He commandeth COME OUT.
And fame went out every place,
The country round
And he arose entered into.
And he stood over, left her,
Arose now when the son was setting,
Laid his hands on every one of them healed.
Devils came out crying;
He rebuked them, suffered,
They knew that he was Christ.
He departed and went, the people came unto him,
That he should not depart from them,
And he said unto them I must, for am I sent.
And it came to pass,
People pressed to hear the Word of God.
He stood by and saw them washing.
He sat down when he had left speaking in the deep,
Saying, Master, we have toiled and taken nothing;
Nevertheless I will, and when they had
They enclosed a great multitude,
That they should come and help them:
And they came, so that they began
Saying, depart, I am a sinful man.

He was astonished,
At which they had taken, and so was John.
The Sons which were partners, from
Henceforth—men.
They forsook all and followed Him.
And it came to pass, he was in a city;
Behold, a man full,
Fell on his face; he, clean, put forth
His hand, touched—I will be clean—
And immediately departed.
And he charged him, accordingly,
For testimony—more went their fame abroad.
Great multitudes—healed their infirmities.
He withdrew, himself, into the wilderness.
And it came to pass, on a certain day, he was there,
And doctors sitting by, were a Power to heal,
And Behold (in palsy means) they bring him in—
Before they could find way, they bring him in.
To lay him when they could not find by what way
They might, because of the multitude,
They went up on and let him down through
With his couch in the midst,
He said unto him, Man thy sins are forgiven thee.
And the scribes began to reason who is
This which speaketh, who can, but God alone.
Jesus perceived their thought answering, reason.
But that ye may know the Son of man hath power,
Arise, take up thy couch and go.
Immediately rose up that, whereon he lay, departed ;
His own house gloryfying God ;
And they were all amazed they glorified God,
And filled with fear, strange things to-day.
And after these things he saw a publican sitting,
The custom, he said, follow me.
He left, rose, followed him.
But scribes murmured, why do ye eat with sinners,
Jesus answered, they that are whole need not, but they are sick.
I come but sinners to repentance,
And they said, John, fast often,
Make prayers, eat and drink,
And he said, children of the bride chamber fast,
While the bridegroom the days will come.
Bridegroom away from them, fast those days,
And he spake a parable;

Putteth a new upon an old, both,
           Maketh a rent and take out of the new,
           Agreeth not with the old.
An no MAN putteth new in OLD—
           The burst, the spilled, shall perish.
           But new must be put into new—both preserved.
No MAN also having OLD, desireth new; he saith,
It came to pass on the Second, after the First.
           His disciples plucked them in their hands.
           Why do ye that which is not lawful to do?
                Nd Jesus answering not.
                Ye read so much.
He did eat, and gave also to them that were with him.
           There was a man
                Whose hand withered,
                     An accusation against him.
He knew their thoughts, and said, Rise,
           Up in the midst; he arose, and stood.
Said Jesus, I will ask you one thing,
           Is it lawful to save life or destroy it?
                And, looking round, the man Stretched—
His hand was restored as the other.
                And they were filled—communed what
                They might come to pass, in those days.
Continued all night, in prayer to God.
                And when it was day He called them.
                He chose, whom He named.
For there went virtue out, and healed them.
                Blessed are ye that weep now, ye shall laugh.
                Blessed are ye, when they shall separate you
From THEIR company, reproach you, and cast out your evil.
                Rejoice for joy, for behold great heaven,
                In like manner did the prophets.
But woe unto you, rich, your consolation woe unto you.
Woe unto you, full, hunger you that laugh, now weep.
You all men speak; so did their fathers; you here, do good.
                Give to man thy goods, ask them not again.
As ye would men should, do you likewise.
Love which love you, thank ye, sinners love those that love do;
                And if ye lend, hope to receive thanks;
                     Sinners receive them again.
Love ye, your do good, hoping for nothing again.
                Reward, shall ye be, of the Highest.
                     He is kind, unthankful to evil;

Therefore your merciful Father, also is,
          And ye shall be not, forgive and ye shall forgive.
Give, it shall be given pressed down, shaken together,
Running over, into your bosom with the same.
          Measure met withal, you again.
          And He spake a parable, can
The blind lead, they both into the ditch.
          But every one perfect be his master.
Brother, percievest thine own eye ; how canst thou
Let me pull out the mote, when thyself beholdest **not**
          The beam ; thou hypocrite, cast out.
          Shalt thou see clearly, in thy brother's eye.
A tree bringeth forth fruit ; doth a corrupt bringeth forth fruit,
Know his fruit—thorns, not figs, **of** a bramble bush.
          Out of the treasure, bringeth forth good,
          Evil man **out of evil.**
          Call ye, the things which **I say** cometh.
I will show you, he is like, he is like a man,
Foundation, shake it, for it was founded upon a rock
Heareth and doeth, foundation earth fell, ruin was **great.**
          When he ended his sayings the audience entered.
A certain servant dear was sick, ready to die of Jesus.
          The Jews beseeching him he come,
          And they instantly saying **he** was worthy,
For he loveth our nation, he built us a synagog.
     Jesus went with them, he was now not far from friends.
          Trouble not thyself for I, that thou shouldst enter,
I myself worthy to come unto thee.
          Say in a word, I am set under **Authority.**
Having under me, I say one, he goeth, he cometh,
          Do, he doeth it.
Jesus heard these things, he marveled,
And turned about, said unto the people, followed **Him.**
          I say **unto you, I have** not found **so** great faith
          In Israel.
And they that were sent found, had been **sick;**
And behold, **when** he came nigh the gate was a **dead man,**
          Carried, the son of his mother, he had
          Compassion and said weep not.
He came and touched, they that bare him,
          Stood still young man; I say unto thee arise;
          And he that, dead sat up began to speak to,
And there came a fear glorifying God a great prophet,
          Among us, that hath visited His people.

And this rumor of Him throughout the region round;
　　And the disciples of John shewed him things.
John sent them to Jesus, he looked for Another;
　　The men come said, JOHN BAPTIST hath sent us,
　　He that should come, look for another.
In that hour many their infirmities that were blind,
　　　　Gave sight.
Jesus said, tell John seen and heard—
　　Blind see, lame walk, lepers, deaf here, dead raised,
　　　　The Gospel is preached.
Blessed he, not be offended in me.
　　　　And when of John departed, he began
　　　　Speak unto the people concerning John.
Went ye out into the wilderness, see shaken with the wind;
　　　　But what went ye out for to see?
A man clothed, soft raiment, appareled in King's courts.
　　　　But what went ye out for to see?
A Prophet unto you, and much more than a prophet;
THIS IS HE, it is written, behold I send My Messenger;
　　　　I say among those born of woman
There is not a greater Prophet than JOHN THE BAPTIST.
　　　　God is greater than He.
And all the people justified God, the baptism of John.
But the lawyers rejected the council of God,
　　　　Against themselves, being not of Him.
Whereunto, then, shall I liken this generation;
　　　　What are they like?
They are like children sitting and calling one to another,
Unto you ye not wept, for JOHN THE BAPTIST;
　　　　And ye say, HE hath a devil.
The Son of man is come eating, ye say,
　　　　Gluttonous man and sinners.
　　　　　　Wisdom justified Her children;
Desired him that he would sit down to meat.
　　　Behold, Jesus sat at meat, in the box,
　　　　And stood at HIS feet, weeping tears, wipe them,
　　　　　Head them with the ointment.
Now which had bidden him, saw it within Himself;
If he were a prophet, this is that toucheth Him a sinner.
　　　And Jesus answered, He Master, say on;
　　　When nothing to pay, He frankly
　　　Forgave them, will love Him most.
I suppose He forgave most, and said thou hast rightly turned.
　　The woman—seest thou this woman thou gavest me;

She hath washed my feet with tears of her head.
Thou gavest me this woman since, the time, I came in
          Hath not ceased, kiss my head.
Thou didst annoint, but this woman annointed my feet.
     I say her sins, which are many, forgiven,
               She loved much, the same loveth little,
Unto her sins are forgiven, they who this forgiveth,
               Woman faith, go in peace.
And it came to pass,
          Afterward, he preaching, shewing glad tidings,
          God with him, woman of evil spirits and infirmities.
Mary Magdalene went seven devils, of others.
And much people were gathered to Him, out of every city;
He spake a parable: out to sow his seed
          By the wayside, was down, and FOWLS devoured it;
Fell upon a rock, it was sprung up, withered because
Lacked moisture; among thorns, thorns sprang up
          Choked it; fell on good ground, sprang up, bare fruit.
               He said these things, he cried, ears to hear.
What might this parable be;
          Unto you it is given to know the MYSTERIES,
               In parables, seeing might not see,
                    Hearing not, understand.
Now the parable is this, seed of God,
          The wayside here, then cometh taketh their hearts.
          They should believe on the Rock, they hear, receive
With joy, have no root for awhile, in temptation fall away
          Among thorns, when they heard, go choked with cares
               This life; no fruit to perfection.
On the good, honest good heart, having heard
          The Word, keep it, bring forth fruit with patience.
No man covereth it with a vessel, putteth it under a bed.
          Setteth IT on a candlestick, they which enter
               See the light, for nothing is secret;
                    Manifest anything hid. Take heed,
Whosoever hath be given, hath not from him,
          Taken that which he seemeth to have.
                    Come to Him, come at Him, for the press.
And it was told by certain, desiring to see Thee,
He answered, THESE hear the Word of God and do it to pass.
A certain day he said, let us go over unto the other side,
          And they forth sailed, fell asleep;
               There came forth a storm, they were filled with water,
                    And they come,

Saying, Master, Master, perish.
    He arose the wind and raging water.
They ceased, calm, said, Your Faith, another.
    He commandeth, water, obey Him.
They arrive at the country, Galilee;
    Went forth to land, met him the CERTAIN MAN
        Which had devils long time;
           Wear no clothes,
               In any house, in the tombs.
Jesus cried out, and fell down before Him.
    A voice said, what have I to do,
        JESUS, Son of God, torment me not.
He commanded the Spirit out of man;
    It had caught Him.
He kept CHAINS, fetters, BRAKE BANDS,
    THE DEVIL.
Jesus asked Him, what is Thy name,
    He said, LEGION.
Him he would not command into the deep,
    There herds of swine besought Him
        He suffer them,
           And HE SUFFERED them.
The devils out of man enter swine;
    Herd down a steep place into the LAKE.
        Were choked, fed them done,
           Fled—TOLD—country;
They see what was done to Jesus.
    The man the devil, feet of Jesus clothed,
        In his right mind,
           By means, the devils, healed.
The whole multitude, the country about to DEPART,
    They were taken with great FEAR.
        He went up and returned back again.
Now, the man departed that he might be with HIM.
    Jesus sent saying, return to THINE OWN.
Great things God hath done,
    His way throughout the whole great things.
It came to pass was returned, received, waiting for him,
    And he fell down at Jesus, besought him to come.
For he had one age, the people having spent
    All living, could be healed behind Him.
The border of His garment, immediately touched me;
        All denied.
    They that were with Him said, Master,

Press Thee, Touched me,
Somebody, perceive that virtue gone out.
She came trembling, and falling down before Him,
She declared Him before all people,
What cause she had touched Him.
She was healed immediately. He said her said:
Take your journey, bread,
Two coats
Apiece; enter into there
Abide, thence depart.
When ye go out shake dust against them.
They went through preaching,
Gospel heard was done by Him.
He was perplexed because, some
John was, Elias had, other prophets again.
John have I, who is this of whom I hear
Such things, to see Him.
And he took them, and went aside the city called;
And the people knew it, followed him,
He spake, the Kingdom of God healed them.
And began to wear away,
Send the COUNTRY ROUND.
Lodge and get, we are **here in a PLACE;**
But He said unto them, eat; we have no more
Except we go buy meat, all this people.
Make them sit in a company, **and they did so.**
Make them all sit down.
He, looking up to Heaven, brake, to set before;
They did eat, filled up, fragments remained.
It came to pass with Him;
He asked them, people, I am, John the Baptist.
Elias, others say, old prophets.
Again, whom say ye I am, Peter Christ God.
He straightly charged them,
Command them. No.
Man, that thing.
The Son of man must suffer many things
Rejected, raised day to them all.
If any man will, come, let him deny himself
Daily follow me.
For, save life lose it; lose life for **My** sake,
The same save it.
For what is a man
Gain, the whole **world, LOSE**

Himself cast away.
For be ashamed of me, and MY WORDS,
     The Son of man be ashamed,
          His own glory, the HOLY TRUTH.
               There—be—here.
See the Kingdom of God came to pass, after
     He took and went up a mountain,
He prayed, the fashion of his countenance
     Altered, his raiments glistening,
Behold two men, Moses and Elias in glory,
     Spake of his decease, which he should accomplish.
They were with him heavy; when they were awake
     They saw, two men stood—it came to pass;
          Jesus, Master, Moses, Elias,
               Not knowing what he said.
While he thus spake, there came a cloud; he feared,
Into the cloud, a voice out the cloud saying,
     My SON, hear him.
And when the cloud was past, Jesus found it close.
     No man in those days seen it, came to pass,
          Next day come down the hill, much met him.
Behold, a man, Master, I beseech Thee,
     My SON is mine, only child.
Lo, a Spirit taketh him, he crieth,
     Tearing him, bruising him, departeth from him.
          I besought, to cast him out, they could not.
Jesus answering, Shall I be with You and suffer You,
     SON hither.
And he was yet a coming, the devil threw him down,
     Tear him, unclean Spirit,
          Child to his Father.
They all amazed at the Mighty Power of God.
     Wondered every one, which Jesus did.   He said,
          Let these sayings sink down your ears.
For the Son of man, delivered into the hands of men;
     They understood not, saying it hid from them.
     They percieved it not, they feared ask that saying;
Arose a reasoning, which should be GREATEST.
     Jesus, percieving Heart, took CHILD him by Him;
          Whosoever receiveth this CHILD receiveth me;
               Receiveth me, receiveth
                    HIM WHO sent me.
Least among you all
     SHALL be GREAT.

John, Master in Thy **Name, forbade him,**
    He followeth not with us.
        Jesus **said,** forbid him not ; he
            That is not against us, is for **us.**
And it came to pass, he should be received up ;
    Steadfastly set his face,
        To go, messengers before his face
            They entered to make ready for him.
They did receive him, because his face
    Was as he would go, to John, saw this.
They said, that FIRE come down from heaven,
    Consume them Elias did.
He turned, rebuked, ye know not, ye are of man,
    To destroy lives, to save them, they went.
And it came to pass, they went in The **Way,**
    Man said **unto** Him, I will follow **Thee**
        Whither **soever goest.**
          Jesus said,
            The son of man hath his head.
He said unto another, follow me to go and bury,
    Let dead Berry preach, Kingdom of God.
      Also said, I will follow thee,
        Let me bid them farewell **home.**
No man, having his **hand to** the plow, looking back,
    Is fit Kingdom of God.
After these things, appointed, sent them TWO TWO,
    His face, He Himself
        Would come.
Said He unto them, truly great laborers,
    Into harvest, Lambs,
        Neither purse, (by the way) enter first ;
Peace shall rest upon it, if **not** it shall turn again.
    And the same eating and drinking things,
        Gave worthy hire.
          Eat such things, which are set before you ;
Heal that therein, say unto them,
    GOD IS COME,
        Nigh unto your ways.
The very dust of your city, cleaveth,
    We do, wipe off against you.
Notwithstanding, be sure, **the** GOD is nigh **unto you.**
But I say unto you, it shall **be** no more tolerable,
    That day for that city, woe unto thee,
        The MIGHTY works have **been done,**

Have been done they had a great while, ago,
    It shall, at the JUDGMENT for you
        Tho' exalted to HELL,
            He—you heareth—despiseth.
He that despiseth despiseth—that sent me.
    And joy devils, subject,
        As lightning from heaven.
           Behold I tred on scorpions, over all
Hurt you, the SPIRITS, subject you, rather,
    Your names in heaven in Spirit I thank thee,
        Heaven and earth, these things prudent,
           Hast revealed BABES.
Father so it seemed, good things delivered,
    No man knoweth, the son is but the Father;
        And who the Father, but the son,
           Whom the son WILL reveal Him.
And he turned Him privately,
    The Eyes which See all things
        That many Kings desired to See things,
           Have not seen, to hear those things,
             Have not heard them.
A lawyer stood, saying, Master,
    What, shall I inherit life?
        What is written, how readest thou?
Thou shalt, with all thy heart, thy soul strength,
    All thy mind thyself,
        This do and thou shalt live.
Willing to justify Himself, Jesus is my neighbor,
    Certain, man went down among thieves,
        Which stripped him
His raiment, departed—half dead;
    By chance, he saw him pass by the other side,
He was AT THE PLACE looked on him, passed by.
    A certain Samaritan, he journeyed, where he was,
        He saw, had compassion on him,
           Went to his wounds on his own breast,
           Took care of him.
On the morrow took and gave unto him,
    Take care of him, whatsoever more
        When again I will repay thee,
Which now was fell among the thieves,
    He that shewed mercy, then go do likewise.
        It came to pass, he entered into,
           And a certain woman received him,

She had a sister, Mary also sat at Jesus feet.
Heard his Word, was cumbered, and came **to** him
Said, Lord dost thou not care, my sister hath left me
To serve alone, therefore help me.
Jesus answered, thou art careful, troubled, many THINGS,
One thing is needful; Mary, chosen, part,
Which shall not be taken away,
And it came to pass, he in a certain place ceased,
Unto Him John also taught his,
When ye pray, Our Father in heaven come
Thy will as in heaven, so in earth,
Give our bread, forgive our sins,
For we also forgive, indebted to us.
Lead us to temptation—deliver from evil.
Which shall have a friend, unto him at midnight,
And say, **Friend, lend** me three loaves;
A Friend of mine, his journey, is come to me,
I have nothing before him,
And within **shall** answer, trouble me not,
The door **is** not shut,
My children are with me in bed,
I cannot rise and give thee.
Though he will not rise and give him,
Because he is his friend, because
Of his importunity, he will give him
As as needeth.
I say, ask it shall be given, you seek.
Knock, opened unto you;
Every one asketh, he that seeketh findeth;
Knocketh, it be opened.
A son shall ask bread of you,
That is, will He give him a stone;
If he a fish, fish HIM a serpent;
If he ask an egg,
Offer him a scorpion?
Ye being evil **know** how to give gifts,
Your children, much more give,
The Holy Spirit ask Him.
He casting out **a** devil was dumb,
And it came to, the devil gone, the dumb spake.
The people wondered.
But some said he casteth out devils, through
The Chief.
Others, tempting him, a sign from heaven.

He, knowing their thoughts, divided desolation;
　　Divided, a house falleth.
Satan divided Himself;
　　Shall **his** kingdom stand ?
　　　　　I cast out devils, Beelzebub;
If I BEELZEBUB, cast out DEVILS,
　　WHOM **do** them out.
　　　　Therefore judges **I GOD** finger out devils.
When a man, armed, keepeth **his place,**
　　Good are in peace.
Stronger than he, shall come and overcome **him,**
　　His armour trusted, divideth **spoils.**
That not **with** me is against me,
　　He not with me scattereth.
The unclean spirit, out of a man ;
　　He walketh, seeking **rest,**
　　　　Finding none, **he return whence**
　　　　　I came **out;**
And he findeth it swept and garnished,
　　Goeth **he to** seven **other** spirits,
Wicked himself, they enter in and **dwell there.**
　　The **last** state of that man is **the first,**
It came to pass, a certain woman of **the** company,
　　Lifted up and said unto him, **the** womb,
　　The paps thou hast sucked, rather blessed are they,
　　　　Hear the Word **of** God **and keep it.**
The people gathered **thick** together **to** say,
　　An evil generation seek **a sign.**
　　　　But **Jonas, the** prophet, **Jonas a** sign,
　　　　　Shall the Son **of man be** generation.
The Queen shall rise up in judgment.
　　Condemn the utmost parts of the EARTH.
　　　　Hear the wisdom of Solomon, behold
　　　　　Greater—Jonas—here.
The MEN shall rise up in the Judgment,
　　This generation shall condemn it,
　　　　They repented at the preaching, behold
　　　　　Greater—Solomon—here.
No man lighted, putteth it in a secret place,
　　They which **come in** may See the Light.
Light is the eye, single **body** full of Light.
　　Thine, evil body, **full of** darkness
Take heed therefore, light thee be not darkness,
　　Whole body full **of** light, no part **dark,**

Full of Light thee, bright shining candle
Give the Light.
He spake certain, Phar I see,
He sat down to meat, he marveled;
He had not washed before dinner;
Now do ye Phar I see clean the cup,
The platter, inward part of wickedness.
Ye fools, He that made, is WITHOUT, within.
Give ye have, and behold,
Things are clean unto you.
Woe ye tithe mint, rue manner pass,
, Judgment ye have done, to leave other undone.
You the uppermost seats in the market,
You hypocrites, ye, as graves, appear not;
Walk over, not aware of them.
The lawyers, thus saying thou reproachest us.
Woe, ye lawyers, ye lade men with burdens;
Ye yourselves touch not the burden of your fingers.
Woe you build the sepulchres, and kill them.
I will send them some, slay and persecute,
Shed the foundation of the world,
Be required generation.
Zacharias perished between the altar and the temple;
I say unto you, be required generation.
You lawyers have away the KEY OF KNOWLEDGE;
Them that were entering in ye hindered.
These things unto him the scribes began
To urge him, to provoke him, to speak of many things,
Laying wait for him, seeking
To catch something out of His
That they might accuse him.
The meantime gathered innumerable multitude
People, in so much trod one another.
Began, Beware, Leaven is hypocrisy;
Nothing revealed, not be known.
Therefore ye have spoken in darkness,
In the light, that which ye have spoken
The closets shall be proclaimed the housetops.
I say, you My Friends, be not afraid;
And after no more that they can do.
And He thought within, saying,
What shall I, because I have no room my fruits?
This Will I do,
I will pull down and build greater,

There I bestow
All MY FRUITS,
GOODS.

I will say, **much** goods laid for years,
Take, **eat,** and be merry.
Thou fool, thy soul required of thee,
Shall those things be **which** thou hast ?
He that treasure for himself, **is not** towards God;
Therefore I say unto you, **take** your life,
Ye eat, for the body,
Ye put on.
Life is more than raiment,
The ravens neither sow nor reap, **storehouses,**
God feedeth them ; more **than FOWLS.**
You, taking, can add, stature, cubit ;
Ye then be not **able** to do that **thing which is least,**
Take ye thought the rest.
Lilies, how they grow,
Toil not, spin, yet I say unto you,
Solomon, his glory arrayed, one of these.
Clothe the grass to-day in the field,
To-morrow, cast the oven ; will you,
O, ye little, seek ye what ye shall eat,
What ye drink, of doubtful mind,
These things do nations seek after,
Knoweth that ye have need of these things ;
Seek **ye God,** all these things,
Unto you ; FEAR NOT, good pleasure **give the** kingdom.
Sell, ye have, alms, yourselves bags,
Wax old, a TREASURE the Heavens, **faileth not ;**
Thief—approacheth—corruption.
Treasure is, there will your heart be also.
Your loins girded about, your light burning ;
He will return from the WEDDING
When—He—Cometh.   ＼
They may, **unto** him immediately.
Servants, when he cometh, find watching ;
Gird himself, sit down to meat,
Will come forth and serve them.
If he shall come **in** the second watch,
Come in the third, find them those servants.
Know if the house had known what hour the Thief come,
He have watched, suffered to be broken through.
Be ye ready also, Son of man cometh,

An hour, think not.

Thou this parable **unto** us, even to all,

Who then **is** that faithful and wise Steward

Whom shall ruler over His household,

Their portion of meat in due **season.**

That servant when he cometh, shall find doing;

Truth unto you, he will make Him ruler

Over that he hath.

That in his HEART delayeth His coming,

Begin to beat the menservants, maidens,

Eat, drink, to be drunken;

Come in a day when he looketh not,

At an hour when he is not—aware,

Cut him—sunder,

Appoint him his portion, the unbelievers.

Prepare not, neither according to his will—stripes;

He that knew **not** did commit things,

Stripes, beaten with few stripes;

For unto much is given, him

Required; **committed** much of him, ask the more.

I am come to send fire on earth;

Will I, It be already kindled.

I Have a Baptism **to, with, how am I?**

Suppose I am, **Come to, on earth,**

Mingled with Jesus, answering,

Suppose ye, sinners suffered such things,

Nay, except ye repent, perish.

These eighteen fell and slew, think ye,

Sinners above all men in Jerusalem;

Except ye repent, all perish.

He spake this parable; A certain man

Planted His vineyard, sought **fruit, found** none;

Behold three years seeking fruit, find none;

Cut it down, why cumbereth the GROUND?

Let it alone this year,

I shall dig about and dung it;

If it bear fruit, well; **if not,**

After those shall cut it down.

He was teaching, one of the sin—agogs;

There was a spirit bowed together, in **no wise**

Up herself; Jesus saw her, he called **her to him,**

Said, Woman, thou art loosed from thine;

He, his hands upon her, she was made straight,

And glorified God, the Ruler of the sin—agog.

Indignation, Jesus had healed on THE SABBATH.
People, there are six days men ought to work.
   There, come be healed, on the SABBATH DAY ;
Hypocrites, each one of you loose his ox
   Or his ass, the stall, lead him to, watering.
Ought this woman, daughter, eighteen years,
   Loosed bond on the SABBATH DAY.
When he said these things, his adversaries
              Were ashamed.
All the people, the glorious things, were by Him.
    Unto what is God like ?
      Shall I resemble it,
A grain of mustard, a man took into His garden ;
    It grew, waxed a great tree,
       Fowls lodged the branches of it.
Again liken Kingdom of God ;
    Like leaven, a woman took and hid
       Three—meal, whole leavened.
          Teaching, journeying Jerusalem,
One unto him, there few saved ? Said unto them,
    Strive to enter at the gate ;
      Many seek to enter in, not able.
Once the Master riseth up, hath shut the door ;
    Begin to stand without,
       Knock the door, Lord, open us ; shall answer,
I know you, ye are ; begin to say,
    Eaten, drink, in presence, streets.
I tell you I know whence, depart.
    Ye workers, gnashing teeth.
      See Jacob, the Kingdom of God, yourselves thrust out.
And come from the east,
    West, north,
      South sit down God.
Behold, there are last which shall be first,
    Are first—last the day
Come certain Phar I sees get thee out.
    He—rod will kill thee,
      Said unto that fox, behold out devils,
        I do cures day to-morrow,
The third day, I perfected,
    Walk day to-morrow, it cannot be,
      Out of Jew—rusalem.
        Jew—rusalem stonest them are sent.
How often I have children,

Together doth gather, Her broad **Her Wings,**
Ye not, Behold left unto **you, desolation.**
Verily unto you, **Ye see** me,
The time **come** ye say blessed **is he**
That cometh in the **name of the.**
IT **COME TO** PASS
He went into one Chief Phar **I see**
To eat, the Sabbath day watched Him.
Behold there was dropsy,
Jesus spake, lawyers heal the SABBATH DAY,
Held Peace, took him, healed let Him go,
Saying you have An Ass, ox, a pit straightway
Pull him out on the SABBATH DAY,
Answer him these things.
He put forth a parable bidden, marked
Chief Rooms.
Thou art bidden of man,
Sit now down in the Highest Rooms,
Honorable man be bidden **of him,**
That bade ye come and say,
Give this man place,
Begin with shame,
Lowest room.
Bidden go sit **down the lowest** room.
He bade cometh FRIEND up **hither.**
Shalt thou have worship in The Presence, sit **at meat**
For exalteth himself, shall be abased.
Humbleth himself, EXALTED HIM.
That bade him, Thou makest a dinner a supper.
Friends, thy brethern kinsmen, rich neighbors,
Bid again, a recompense, be made thee.
Makest a feast, call the maimed, lame, the blind,
Be blessed for they cannot recompense thee,
Recompense resurrection the Just.
Sat at meat with him these THINGS,
Said unto him, blessed he, **in the Kingdom of God.**
A certain man, a great supper bade **many,**
At supper come, all things now **ready,**
They all one **consent, make excuse,**
First of ground, **I** pray thee me excused,
Another—I have bought oxen, I prove **them,** me excused,
Another—I married—I CANNOT come,
So that **servant** shewed these things,
House angry, to HIS SERVANT.

Out quickly, lanes of the city, hither the poor, halt the blind;
    Servant thou hast commanded, there is room.
Out in the highway, hedges, compel THEM to come
      In—House—Filled;
        These men, BIDDEN, taste My Supper.
Great multitudes, he turned, said them,
    Come to me, hate not his Father,
      Mother, children,
His own life, he be MY DISCIPLE.
    Whosoever cometh after, BE DISCIPLE.
You, intending a tower, sitteth down first,
    Counteth cost, sufficient finish it,
      Lest foundation, not finish, behold, to mock Him,
        THIS MAN began to build, not able to finish.
King going to make war against King,
    Sitteth down FIRST, consulteth, be able
      To meet him, cometh against him;
The other a great way (off) sendeth conditions of peace.
Whosoever he be, forsaketh not, hath MY DISCIPLE.
Is good, if the salt has lost his Saviour,
    Shall it be seasoned for the land?
      The dunghill cast out.
        He that hear Him, Hear.
Then drew near sinners for to hear
    Scribes murmured, man eateth with Them.
Parable unto, saying, He lose one of Them,
    Leave the wilderness until he findeth it;
      Found, layeth on his shoulder, rejoicing.
Cometh Home, together HIS FRIENDS,
    Partners, saying, rejoice with me,
      I have found my lost, wilderness.
Unto you, likewise, joy shall heaven, over ONE,
    More than just persons, no repentance.
What woman having silver, one piece, not light,
    Sweep the house diligently, till find it.
      When she found it, her Friends
    Together, rejoice with me, I have found I had lost.
Likewise you, joy the presence
      God over ONE sinner that repenteth.
I certain man, two sons.
    Younger, Father give portion to me.
Divided His living; many days after the younger
    Gathered all together, his journey a far country,
      Wasted substance, living

Spent, Mighty **famine in the land;**
Began to want.
Joined, himself of that country, He sent him His fields to feed.
Fain **filled** his belly, swine did eat, unto Him.
He came to himself;
Hired servants, Father, enough and to spare,
I perish; arise, go to my Father,
Say, Father, I sinned against heaven, before,
And am worthy to, called thy Son—servants.
Make me as—One—hired servant.
Arose, came to his Father.
He was a great way (off) his Father
Compassion, ran—fell—neck kissed.
Son, him, Father, I have sinned—heaven,
Thy Sight, am worthy to be called (SUN) now—Son.
But the Father,
Bring forth Best—put it on him—put ring his hand, his feet;
Bring hither, kill it—let eat, Merry.
This son dead—ALIVE—AGAIN,
LOST—found—MERRY,
Elder—Son—field.
He came and drew nigh music dancing,
Called one, THESE THINGS meant.
He unto him—thy Brother is come.
Father—killed—calf,
Because—received—sound.
Angry—therefore—Father.
Out and entered into him
Said to, LO, many years, I SERVE THEE,
Neither commandment, yet never a KID
That might make Merry friends,
Soon son come devoured living HARLOTS
Killed—Him—calf.
Son—Art—me.
I—is—thine.
Meet should make Merry be glad
Dead—alive—again.
Was—lost—found.
He—His—Disciples.
Some accused him, He had wasted His goods,
Called Him, how is it I hear—This **of Thee,**
Give account Stewardship, steward.
Steward within Himself, what shall I do
Away from **me the stewardship,**

I cannot dig to, to beg I am ashamed,
       I am resolved to do that;
When I am put out of the Stewardship
    Cannot I, I beg—I am ashamed.
Receive me **unto** House.
    Every one said unto first, How much
Measures of **oil,** and said, take thy bill, sit
    Down quickly write, He said, take thy
      Bill write measures **of** wheat, because
Wisely in this generation. CHILDREN of LIGHT
    Make yourselves FRIENDS.
Mammon **ye** fail—unright—cousn—ess,
    Into everlasting habitations.
Faithful, faithful **in** much; unjust, **unjust much.**
Mammon;
    Who **will commit** to trust true RICHES.
If ye have that which is another **man's,**
    Give you—which is your own.
Serve TWO Masters, he will hate, love the other;
    Hold **the ONE.** Ye dispise God, mammon,
      Covetous derided Him.
        Ye justify yourselves before men;
          God knoweth your hearts.
Highty esteemed; admonition in the SIGHT of GOD.
    Prophets were until JOHN;
      Since THAT God is preached.
        Man—into—it.
It is easier for heaven, EARTH pass, the **law to** fail.
Committeth adultery, whosoever marrieth HER
    That is put away—from her husband
      Committeth adultery.
There—was—rich—man,
    Clothed in purple, fine linen, fared sumptuously
    Every day—was a—certain beggar, Lazarus,
    Laid—gate, full of sores,
      Desiring crumbs, fell rich man, dogs
        Licked sores.
To pass, beggar died, carried the angels bosom.
    Rich man was was buried—in hell torments;
      Afar off Lazarus, his bosom, cried, mercy;
        Lazarus, tip finger, water cool—flame.
          Lazarus—tormented—him.
SON remember lifetime—good things, evil things,
    Comforted—tormented,

Besides **all** this, between US

Is a great gulf fixed, **they** pass, they cannot;

Neither can they pass to US that would come.

I pray Thee Father—I testify—unto them.

Also, place of torment.

Saith, Moses and prophets—let them, hear them.

ONE went unto them—dead—repent—Moses,

Will they be persuaded, ONE rose from the Dead.

It is impossible, but offences will come.

UNTO HIM through whom they come.

Better a millstone, hanged his neck,

And cast into the Sea—see,

Than ONE of these Little ONES.

Take heed, to yourselves, thy trespass against thee.

Rebuke **him, if he repent** forgive him.

If he trespass against, seven times **in a day,**

Repent—forgive—Him.

Increase, if ye had faith, as a grain seed,

Mustard, might say, be plucked by the root,

Thou planted in the sea—see **it** obey you.

You plowing, feeding cattle, say Him by **by** and by.

When he is come, the field, sit down to meat;

Rather make ready, wherewith I sup, and gird—thyself.

I have eaten, drunken, afterwards eat and drink;

Think THAT servant did things commanded **Him?**

Likewise, done things commanded you;

Unprofitable servants, that was DUTY **to do.**

To pass Jew-rusalem, he passed through the midst (Sa) Maria,

A certain village, met him

Men—lepers stood off, Jesus mercy on us.

Go yourselves, the priests;

To pass, they went, cleansed.

When he saw he was healed, back

With—loud—God;

Fell down his face, his feet, thanks—(Sa) Mari (tan).

Jesus, cleansed, are the nine,

Found returned—to give glory to God, this STRANGER.

He said, **arise,** THY WAY, made whole.

God should come, HE, answered God,

Cometh not by observation,

Neither, Lo here—lo there—lo behold, or God is with In You.

He disciples, the days will come,

Ye shall desire to see ONE of **man;**

Ye shall see—not it.

They shall say to you, see here—see there—see not—after them.
Lightning Lighteneth one Heaven,
Shineth the other—part heaven.
Son man—in—day.
First suffer things, rejected, generation.
Noe, son of man, did eat, drink, wives married,
Until Noe entered into, the flood came,
Destroyed them all.
Lot, they did eat, drink, sold, builded ;
It rained fire, brimstone, Heaven,
Destroyed them all.
Shall it be, when the Son is revealed.
Housetops, stuff the house, let Him **down**
To take it away,
Fill-d, let likewise, not return back.
Lot's seek to save life, shall lose it ;
Lose life, preserve it.
You night, be two men in one bed,
One taken, the other left ;
Women shall grind together, one taken, left.
Two men the field, one taken, left.
They said, where, Lord. He said,
Unto wheresoever body, will gather together.
And parable, unto this end, pray not to faint.
In a city, judge, God, neither regarded man.
A Widow, city, came unto Him, saying, avenge ;
He would not awhile, afterwards,
Himself, God, nor regarded man ;
This troubleth, I will avenge continually, she weary me.
Hear unjust judge ; shall not God avenge.
Cry day, night, unto him, he bear long, them,
I tell you speedily ; Son find faith earth.
He parable : certain, trusted themselves ;
Righteous, despised others.
Two men into the temple, pray one, and the other
Stood, thus—Himself, God—I thank thee I am not, men,
Extortioners, unjust, adulterers, or even this (re)public(an),
I fast ; of all that I possess.—Afar off,
Lift, so eyes, Heaven, smote his breast, God merciful
ME A SINNER—
Tell this man, down house, justified.
Himself be abased, humbleth himself, exalted.
Brought unto infants, He would, His disciples saw it.
Suffer children to me, forbid not, such is God.

You shall receive God as a LITTLE CHILD,
No wise enter therein.
Ruler, good Master, I do inherit life?
Callest thou me good—good **God**—one that is.
Knowest commandments—commit adultery, kill,
Steal, false witness, honor thy Mother.
These things kept youth up.
(Jesus), things unto Him, lackest one thing.
Sell all, distribute the poor,
Shalt treasure—heaven, follow me.
This he very sorrowful, very rich;
Jesus, He was, sorrowful **he said**,
How hardly, the **Kingdom of God**,
For easier, camel needle's eye,
Rich man enter God.   Lo,
We left all, **followed Thee;**
Unto **you, there is man left house, parents, wife,**
The kingdom of God's sake,
Not receive more—in this present time,
World to come everlasting.
Then took twelve, Behold, go to Jew-rusalem.
Written prophets, the Son of man, accomplished.
He delivered, Gentiles be mocked, spitefully entreated,
Spitted on scourge him.
Put him to death, the third day, he shall rise again,
Understood none, things Saying, hid from them.
Neither knew things spoken.
To pass, come nigh unto certain.
BLIND MAN the wayside begging.
Hearing it asked; he MEANT
Jesus of Nazareth passeth.
Cried Jesus, David, mercy on me.
They rebuked him, he cried so much the more,
Son of David have mercy—me.
Jesus stood, commanded, brought unto him, he was come.
He asked him wilt thou.
And he said, Lord, that I may receive my sight.
Jesus unto him, receive thy sight, faith saved thee.
Immediately he received his sight.
Followed him, all the people, they saw, unto **God,**
Jesus **passed a** man, which was the Chief
Among (re)public(ans) little of stature, so rich
Could not for press he **was** so LITTLE.
He climbed up to see, to pass **that WAY.**

Jesus came to the place up looked,
        Said him unto MAKE HASTE, come down,
           He made HASTE, receive him joyfully.
Saw it they all saying murmured,
        Gone to guest with sinner, man that sinner.
         He stood, said, behold goods, **my half I give.**
If I have taken any man by false,
        I restore him accusation, him said
For as much he also son of man come to seek, save lost.
These added Jew—rusalem, because Kingdom, God appeared.
Certain nobleman far country receive, Himself return.
        Servants deliver POUNDS till I come.
          Said unto them, occupy till **I come.**
Sent message him, have THIS man reign over,
        Pass returned, having kingdom.
          Commanded, servants called unto him.
To whom He had given, know much, every man gained **by**
          trading.
        Pound hath gained pounds unto him.
Good servant, faithful in a very little,
Authority over, second came saying pound hath gained pounds
        Also Him over another, saying behold here
          Is thy POUND in a napkin in an AUSTERE MAN.
Layedst not down, reapest not sow, out of thine own mouth.
        Wicked servant thou knewest I was austere ;
         I not down, reaping that I did not sow.
Therefore **into** the bank, I coming required with usury.
        He spake unto took by, take him the pound.
         Give to him that hath lost the pound.
          They said Lord, he hath no needeth.
Everyone that hath given, him that hath not,
        Even that he hath shall away from him.
Mine enemies would not I should over them;
        Bring hither, slay them before me.
He went before ascending up Jew—rusalem
        Came, when he was come nigh, to pass, Beth— page.
         Olives, two desciples, colt tied,
Him hither, loose him, because need of him;
They sent, went their way, found, said them as loosing,
        Colt owners thereof said, loose why, ye the colt.
They said, him of need Him brought Jesus.
        Garments cast colt, Jesus brought him ;
         They Jesus thereon sat ;
          He they spread clothes, he went the Way.

He came nigh, Olive's descent, even mount, multitude
   Began rejoice, disciples praise,
     Voice loud for God, for all the MIGHTY
They had seen ; Blessed King, saying, cometh
       In the name of heaven.
   Highest glory, peace, some multitude.
    Pharisees from among
Rebuke. I tell you these, hold their peace,
    Stones immediately cry.
   He came, he beheld, over it wept it ;
Thou hadst known, in this day peace now hid from thine eyes.
Come up on thee, enemies, cast a trench, the compass round
   Every side, keep thee on—in even ground,
     Leavest thee one stone upon another.
       Thou knowest Thy Visitation.
He went, the into the temple, cast out,
   Began, **to,** sold therein, them that bought.
My house is **the saying, unto** prayer, ye have **made a den**
   Thieves, taught daily in the temple, the chief priest,
    Scribes, destroy, people, sought daily by Him.
Might do, could not, what find not, they might do ;
    Very **attentive to hear** him.
And it came to those days, a pass,
   On one of those days, He taught the temple ;
People preached the gospel, scribes, priest came, elders,
   Tell us, spake, saying things, doth authority ;
   Who is He, Authority give thee this.
Ask me, I will ask you, answered one thing,
   The Baptism of John,
   Heaven, out of men ; reasoned themselves, saying,
   From Heaven, believe ye Him not, He will say why?
Of men, stone us persuaded, for John was a prophet;
   Whence was it tell not, could they answered.
Jesus said to them, I tell you neither by what authority,
   To speak the people this parable began:
     Vineyard man, certain planted, husbandmen;
      Far country let forth, long time,
Season, servant Husbandman sent, give him fruit ;
   Another beat him, shamefully treated him, empty;
    And wounded out cast, him out him also.
Shall I do, what My Beloved Son reverenced Him, see,
   This is the heir, saying, themselves reasoned,
    Let us kill, inheritance, ours be ;
Kill him, therefore unto them of vineyard.

He shall come, destroy, the vineyard, when, heard it ;
God said, forbid it.
Beheld, them this, them that is written ;
Stone the builders rejected; same head corner ;
Fall, upon that stone, be broken,
It shall fall, will grind to powder, chief priests
Sought hands to lay on him, people feared.
Perceived, against spoken parable, against them,
Sent forth spies, feign themselves, just men,
Hold, Words His Might delivered.
The power of Authority, Governor,
They answer rightly, teachest, know neither
Acceptest the person of any,
Teachest the Way of God truly.
Call son no tribute, it lawful craftiness
Perceive ye why tempt ye me, with a penny
Superscription, Cæsar's ghost,
Unto Cæsar render therefore.
Be Cæsar's, unto God the things which be Gods.
Could not take His Words, before the people.
They marveled, peace held, their answer.
To him certain of the Sad u sees, deny resurrection, him,
Saying, Master, Moses wrote unto us ;
Having a wife, if another man die, children without,
Raise his brother, raise seed of his brother;
Therefore seven brethren took one brother's wife,
Died without children;
First took, second took, third took
Her; woman died also.
Therefore wife seven brothers, whose wife ;
Seven times seven, had no resurrection,
But they shall be accounted in the resurrection,
Who, who, neither
Marry Dead, children of God be resurrected.
That the dead are raised, Moses shewed the bush.
Calleth God Abe, Isaac, Jacob ; God is not of the dead.
The dead some to Time Him.
Master, thou hast well said ; Durst question all,
How Christ is David's son.
David himself sit the right
Till I make thine footstool of enemies
Desire to walk in love, greetings, markets, rooms, feasts ;
Show make long prayers ;
Receive greater damnation.

Up looked, rich men casting gifts, the treasury.
  Certain widow thither, casting poor two mites.
True poor woman cast all—thyself more than mites to me;
For all this abundance can cast,
    She pennury cast living.
Spake, goodly stones, gifts, said,
  Days will come, shall not be left, another stone to down,
And they asked him, Master, when shall these things be;
  Signs will there be, shall pass, things to come?
Take heed, be not not deceived, I my name I Am,
  Christ, the time draweth near,
    Not ye therefore after them.
But ye shall hear of commotions, things must pass,
  Come first the end is by by,
    Nation, Kingdom rise, against nation,
Great earth quakes, diverse places famines,
  Pestilence, fearful sights,
    Great SIGNS from heaven,
These, they lay their hands upon you,
  Persecute, delivering the sinagog ruler, my sake.
  Turn you a testimony, settle it, your hearts meditate.
Ye answer, I will you, a mouth of Wisdom.
Adversaries resist, gainsay, betrayed by Parents and friends.
  Some you shall cause death,
    Ye shall be hated—my sake.
Hair of your head, perish, possess patience.
  Compassed armies, desolation is nigh,
Let the mountains, depart out, let the country enter,
  Days of vengeance; written may be fulfilled,
    Woe that child, to them that suck.
Days great, shall distress, land upon this people.
  Fall sword, captive, Jew-rusalem trodden down, until
  The time of the gentiles fulfilled,
    Signs the sun—moon—star.
Nations distress earth, sea perplexity roaring.
  Heart failing, looking after things,
    Coming on the earth, Powers shake heaven,
     See coming, in a cloud, great glory,
      Power, great Son of man.
Things begin, to pass, to come.
  Look up your head lift up, your redemption nigh.
Behold, spake parable, tree, fig trees;
  Now ye see, shoot forth, summer is now at hand.
    Now ye have, ye see things past to come,

Come, to pass, know ye the Kingdom of God.
This generation shall pass away, all be fulfilled.
Heaven, earth—away, MY WORDS not pass away.
Lest heed yourselves, at any time overcharge your hearts,
Surfeiting, drunkenness, care life, upon unawares ;
Snare all them, dwell the face of the earth.
Ye may therefore watch, worthy is escape,
All things shall stand—the Son of man
Day time teaching the temple, night went out
In the Olives mount ; people came early
Morning temple hear him.
Now the FEAST draw nigh, which passover called.
Priests sought, feared the kill him, people ;
Satan, sir named I scare out, numbered Judas one,
He went his way, communed priests,
Might he betray, captains unto them.
They glad to give him, money promised, sought opportunity
Him betray, in the absence of multitude.
John saying, go prepare passover, we eat, us,
Where wilt prepare, said him, them unto him ;
Then behold, entered the city, shall a man meet you,
Follow, pitcher water, enter in bearing ;
The guest chamber, shall eat the passover, disciples.
Show you a large, furnished, upper room ready ;
Found, went they unto passover ; I suffer.
I say I will thereof eat until be it fulfilled of God.
Cup thanks, take this divide it among, give yourselves some.
I will drink of the fruit of this vine, God shall come.
Break it took bread gave, saying body remembrance of me,
Likewise cup saying supper, New testament cup.
Blood is shed testament for you.
Behold hands betrayeth him on the table.
Truly Son of man, determined goeth unto betrayed.
Inquire began themselves, among it was, should do this
Greatest among strife, accounted greatest.
Gentiles exercise authority—benefactors Gentiles not,
Shall greatest among you, let him be as the younger;
Chief as he serve, that doth.
Greater he sitteth at meat
Among you that serveth.
They which have continued in My temptations,
I appoint you, a kingdom, hath appointed you.
Eat, drink, at My table, My Kingdom, judging Israel.
Satan hath desired to have you, he may sift as wheat.

Strengthen thy brethren, converted.
    Lord, I am ready to go—into prison, death.
The cock crows this day, before thou deny, takedst,
      He said I sent ye without shoes, lack ye anything ;
        And said, nothing, unto them.
Likewise take it all script, it has no sword, sell his garment.
And he come out, and he went to the Olives mount,
      And when he was at the place, enter into temptation,
        Withdraw from about a stones cast;
Kneel down and if thou be willing, remove this cup
      From me, nevertheless, nothing will but thine be done,
Appeared unto him, heaven angels, strengthening him
      And being earnestly, prayed in an agony,
        His sweat as falling as blood falling.
He up prayer, came to his disciples,
      Sleeping Sorrow.
And he said why rise ye; sleep, let us unto temptation.
      Multitude spake, behold,
        Before them, Jesus draw near KISS him.
Jesus, Son of man with a kiss; betrayest,
      Follow they, which about there, saw him ;
And one smote right ear, priest one servant cut,
      Jesus far answered, suffer ye,
        Touch—ear—heal—him.
Jesus chief temple, captains, thief again, come out
      Staves ; I was daily in the temple, stretched hands
        Against, this your hour, power of darkness.
Then brought high priest, Peter far off;
      Fire, kindle midst hall, sat Peter down.
Certain maid him beheld, sat the fire earnestly looked,
      Man, also this with him,
        Denied him woman, said I know him not.
Little after, while saw him another
      Them also man, Peter man I am not.
Space one hour, confidentially affirmed,
      Fellow, also saying, he is a Galileian.
Peter, man I know not what thou sayest ;
      Immediately spake he, yet while he crew (the cock)
Lord, Peter, look, Peter remembered Word(before cock crew)
        And Peter went out bitterly.
Men mocked him, Jesus smote him, before thrice;
And struck blindfolded face, asked him say prophecy;
      And many other thing spake blasphemously.
        It soon day, was elders, priests, people together.

Led council, saying unto him together,
  Art Christ tell us, he said them if you will believe;
   If also ye ask, answer me will you nor let me go.
Hereafter shall God sit on the Son of man,
  The Power they said art all the Son of God.
   And he said to Him, I am an as let me go,
And they said need we any further witness.
  Whole multitude arose, led Pilate,
   Began, accuse him saying, fellow the nation,
Perverting, give tribute to Cæsar's ghost.
  Pilate asked him, art the King the King,
   Thou sayest, answered ;
Chief priest people, I find no fault in this man.
  He teaching stireth up the people,
   Throughout Pilate heard of Galilee,
Soon he knew of He—rods jurisdiction, Himself,
He—rod saw Jesus exceeding glad, desirous long season,
  He questioned with him, many words nothing,
   Chief priest, vehemently accused, stood him.
War set him at naught, mocked him arrayed in a robe,
  Pilate sent again him He—rod to Pilate,
   Pilate, chief priest, rulers people.
Brought this man me, unto perverteth the people ;
Found, examined him, touching fault, whereof ye accuse him
  Herod nothing worthy death, done unto him,
   Chastise him, release him therefore.
Necessity, the least one of the feast cried, Barrabas,
  Certain murder, sidition city cast prison,
Pilate, Jesus spake, willingly again therefore to them,
  They cried, him crucify, cried crucify him.
Evil, why what hath he done they,
  I find no fault in him, I will let him go chastised.
They instantly required crucified, priest prevailed.
  Pilate gave sentence required.
Released murder, for sedition into prison, desired.
  Their will laid hold on Simeon, coming cross Jesus.
Follower him people, women lamented, bewailed.
Daughters, weep not for me, yourselves for your children,
Behold days coming, barren bare, never wombs, paps gave
   suck.
Begin to say MOUNTAINS FALL, cover us.
  Those things in a green tree shall be dry.
  Two other led, with death, male factors two others.
When they were come Cal—vary crucified him.

Male factors on right hand and left ;
Where was Jesus, in the middle.
Jesus forgive, they knew, what they do,
And lots raiment parted, cast lots ;
People holding stood rulers derided, let him save,
Himself Christ chose, God; that is God made Christ.
Soldiers coming—vinegar.
If Jews save thyself, vinegar soldiers.
Superscription, Latin Hebrew, Jews King the this.
One male factor hanged, saying, Christ save us.
Indeed justly receive due reward.
Deeds hath done nothing amiss.
Jesus remember me, when I comest into kingdom,
Jesus verily, I say, tho with me in paradise.
Sixth hour darkness, earth ninth hour.
Sun darkened, vail of the temple in the midst.
Jesus cried voice loud, said, hands I commend my Spirit.
Having the ghost up, gave thus said he,
Now centurion (yourself) what was done,
Certainly this righteous man God glorified,
Together in that Sight, beholding thing done, smote breast.
Acquaintance followed woman, Galilee stood afar off.
Behold was John Joseph a councellor.
He was a good man, just,
He waited himself for the Kingdom,
This man went, body of Jesus unto Pilate,
Down it took he, laid it that was, hewn stone,
Linen clothes preparatory, sabbath drew on
Woman came him from Galilee, followed after,
Was laid, how this body was laid,
Prepare spice, restored Sabbath commandment.
Now day first of, upon week early,
Morning bringing sepulchre, prepared spice certain,
Sepulchre found, entered in, Jesus,
To pass it came perplexed thereabout,
Behold two, stood, garments shining,
Afraid their faces down bowed, earth seek dead among living
Spake risen, remember how Galilee was
Delivered, must sinful hands crucified,
Again rise day, third, Words remember
Returned sepulchre, told these things to all,
Magdalene Mary, Mary the mother, and
Other apostles there,
Idle tales, Words seemed they believed not,

Peter ran, arose sepulchre, stooping down,
Linen clothes laid, themselves, departed wondering.
Behold them that same day from about three score furlongs,
    Together talked all these things, happened,
That pass, came communed Jesus, reasoned near.
    Eyes holden should know not him,
Communications are these, manner another, walked sad.
    Art thou only a stranger in Jerusalem,
Come pass these days Jesus, Nazareth, Prophet Mighty.
    Indeed before God—and all the people.
Priests delivered rulers death crucified, condemned him.
Trusted deemed Israel; should beside third day, done since
Certain woman company early, astonished sepulchre,
    Found body, saying, seen visions, angels alive
       Which certain were, sepulchre found it.
    Even so, women had him, saw not
O fools slow of heart, hearts slow spoken,
    Prophets ought Christ, two things suffer.
       Glory beginning at Moses expounded scripture.
       Concerning Himself,
          Village, draw whither nigh, went
Though he would have gone further;
    Him constrained abide with us.
       Evening, towards far spent want to tarry,
         He took brake gave it to them,
Their eyes were open, they knew him,
    Vanished their sight out,
    Our heart burn within us, by the way the scripture,
       Rose they hour some together, with them,
       Risen Lord appeared, indeed.
Told things done the way, breaking bread,
    Stood the midst of them, be peace unto.
Terrified, affrighted, supposed had a spirit.
Troubled, arise your thoughts, and hearts, bones flesh have.
    Shewed his feet, hands, spoken
Joy wondered, unto them, have meat ye,
Give piece boiled fish, they gave him honey comb,
    Took it did before—then—eat.
These Words I spake, you things fulfilled, were written
       Concerning me.
Thus written, Christ to suffer, to dead, to raise
       Three Days.
Repentance preached, his name, nation's beginning.
       Jew—rusalem.

Witness ye, things these.
I send the promise of Father, upon you
Tarry ye the Jew—rusalem, endowed with power.
Led them out, lifted up hands;
And, blessed, it came to pass.
Parted, blessed them, carried to heaven.
They worshiped Him, returned to great joy;
Continually, temple, praising God.
He blessed, a man.
Still, uncompromised mystery,
Room for thought.
Guided noble intentions, drawn by
Knowledge of man's power.
Leads humbleness, overlooks success,
Live with God above.
Make room, Great Spirit to balance body.
On narrow rails, on road of life.
Mind, swing over brow of care;
Compact feeble body, compact strength;
Leaving open space, travel safely over open field.
Literature deeds receiving, who, men advance
Understanding, of God's family.
Who live, for an unfeeling bank account,
Each see we through—to the heart.
Entice attention, be waiting love
Ready to drip at pressure of hands,
It is Myself, to act this quickly, folded arms;
Myself prize My love a treasure above world,
Power depreciate, allow, approach Me.
My attraction close desire,
Boldness rejected as bruises,
Face of dignity, still, not pleased,
Love—free—another.
Time comes, I need not stand mark,
Base minds, direct thoughts,
Forever blessed, God filled willingly,
Stand the gaze of men,
Holding to resting place on the road of life.
Minds may open, into unknown space,
View fields of future,
Practical present divide,
From the period of antiquity,
Live, love rounded form, I alone give
Attractions useless, equal weight Spirits of God,

I remain mark the rude opinions of **men.**
I stand that expression in becoming solitude,
It is best, accept this modesty; into a becoming uniform
It is best, we endure once more,
Nerves of noble men are strung,
Coward's heart heavy, his mind dumb.
This compliment of war view plainly;
A canvas for picture of dead.
Welcome modest peace
Sounds war, spirit of men, into humility.
Battle many consuming sparks of rage,
Trouble the mind, invite love, quiet happiness,
Bravery a way, firmness led the **way,**
Praise future course, in the course of time.
Trouble each individual endure, in heavens
Space, the moon marks still the steps of time
Bleak, hardship pursues the red man,
Their Great Spirit the first—to incite
So defends, their belief,
Their right is their right, wrong who makes complaint,
Move a step
From edge of pride, from off low superiority.
Heeding law, defense, Indian feel the opposition,
In course, true belief in truth,
Mind that defiant color which speaks
Without raving fear, fear not those, many in attitude wrong,
Wake, the sleeping brained white man
Believe life is now an idle dream,
Grind gizard hearts to life.
Make blood wilting flesh, condemn God, for waste of war
He holds Wire, pure mortality,
Do revolving clouds advance family of Creator?
Do breath dew of heaven, body the soil of sin?
Breeding humanity, look down the steps,
Measuring times space
Of decency, see small profits.
Patience is service recommended from above praise
Him, who is nothing
To oppose His Power.
You stand blinded theory holding opposition weak,
Oposing who—HIM is free,
Care is an extensive field, the glittering heavens,
Speak plain.
Blind humanity do not comprehend,

God shaped thoughts to suit hopes,
Gave firmness desire, a course towards please, above God above.
Guage penalties—justice to all.
Proceed intimate **with** life, intimate with none, proceed,
Minds do not mature, to brains praise, to idle woman's love,
Each youth must day take, the weakness of desire,
Brim fill the shame of—unprofitable investigation,
Activity, **a** scrub be in reflection, meditation into activity,
Failure investigate, life is rich,
One, is experience, penalty of wrong,
Does profit individual, himself, checks cash happy future,
Mud may hope, dust return, may fly,
Good, continue.
My thoughts please—will thoughts, Mine, please,
Be recognized vineyard, Hand, God, pruning,
Leave growth tangled, which clusters,
Harvests of bitter consolation,
Leave assumed men's methods, His absence,
Leading purpose, strength, confirmed, **confusion,**
Fellow, His Spirit above, His methods teach patience,
Keep knowledge from wrong,
Wander over the road rough, of failure,
Times many, mind stamp caution, with care,
For successful future, care, success, necessary,
Should man **live,** not long, good his days to accomplish;
That receive, think men comprehend, by life,
Requires man mind, the beginning of light heaven.
The fading hue, life departing, shows future envelopes earth,
Wings with light remain in the fall,
Planets show view, purpose the unseen future,
Minds bring action, man each individual, duty execute,
Death time, **speaks** freely acts, their bones left remembrance,
Preparation, quick meet messenger, He meets,
Future, was mind made to know, without doubt,
Accept fear humanity accept, humanity has no claim to
Future purpose concealed may be in preparations, a conflict,
Range of pleasure educate, solitude derived unlimited
Cannot have, all know, thought wisdom, teach such.
Advantage, take weakness, patience spirits
Is sufficient frail body, knows God above, required action,
Uselessness, see restraint by weakness, by despair.
Study, satisfy ways of fate, unknown preparing for destiny;
Looking profitable, for thing lost.
Spark last, life departing, are we, God above glad ;

Who, God above Himself, stars equal.
Keeps He mystery, easy is it ;
Trench walk, keep sacred, time in all time.
Dig easy, new course, modern, catch remarks.
Open mankind, future mind, humanity future advance.
Creation understanding, leave unproductive waiting
Lead groweth deeper, existence of mysteries, course is winding.
Bridge the river, we over view.
Out knowledge, the ignorant, animal man.
Construe evil, may they rest over the jaws, made made Himself.
Vail dispair, him depart, eternity shades appear.
Final appearing before, get, move success, failure.
Strength easy quite, firm spirit patience, confidence.
Spirit well love contentment.
Benefits, doubtful ease mind, sensible to advantage.
Smothering type courage, evil darkness.
Conscience, holding light goodness, gloomy in the air.
Distill bad good, true, pure, bad to good.
I power should ask, my mind to be, it be action.
Beheld, should the circumference, without ceremony,
Should, that it impress thoughts, with hells of clouds.
Free be I, that the breeze that blows, shows eternity,
Come in truth ; Go God's Power.
Make Jesus, pretentions, precosity.
Sir, no, twelve in age Father to, recognize business.
He, stature increased, God wisdom favor, acknowledging man.
He times at not perfect, will self-government in action.
Said, most feared, feared not to face the globe.
Hell, death educated man, fields walk of despair.
View expectation calmly, demolish ruins clouds.
Thirty, age, know the Son of God.
Accept fortified situation, pretentions, without.
Popularity, brace up, command bars of contention, stood firm.
His time, Power of God, attraction His.
Body ordinary digestion, suitable actions, conditions human.
Given Spirit present day, lives Himself, from He.
Spirit praised, thoughts from love divided, God prompted.
Insignificance display him, seeking his Creator.
Model stands Power God gave him, He was with
Affections pleased, sincere quality.
Existence, open the midst of might.
Heaven, brightness honor man, lived not for wealth.
Life term short, in representing, Himself, to public demoralized.
Gave His wish, best, benefit, of man.

Move a step
From edge of pride, from off low superiority.
Heeding law, defense, Indian feel the opposition,
In course, true belief in truth,
Mind that defiant color which speaks
Without raving fear, fear not those, many in attitude wrong,
Wake, the sleeping brained white man
Believe life is now an idle dream,
Grind gizard hearts to life.
Make blood wilting flesh, condemn God, for waste of war
He holds Wire, pure mortality,
Do revolving clouds advance family of Creator?
Do breath dew of heaven, body the soil of sin?
Breeding humanity, look down the steps,
Measuring times space
Of decency, see small profits.
Patience is service recommended from above praise
Him, who is nothing
To oppose His Power.
You stand blinded theory holding opposition weak,
Oposing who—HIM is free,
Care is an extensive field, the glittering heavens,
Speak plain,
Blind humanity do not comprehend,
Three days the temple raised to life,
Verily marvel, not known, the witness is strife,
Of the water, Spirit born is the Spirit,
Patience by humbleness, by faith wife without
Man speaks born again who was to life,
Enter, saying; have we seen, enter Kingdom God.
All step see, modesty light trod,
Only Christ be given by that law,
Language success style cause,
Fault great suspicious of Power,
Magdalene Mary virgin, purity Flower,
Spirit Jesus, given John Joseph, named,
Mary Elizabeth, Joseph's Mary living,
Mist back time common Christianity,
Sacred view that line.
Him, knew few, literature, well story told,
Truth, Christianity, see differences, character unfold,
See truth, Christianity in differences.
Good, to wise good, to others a specie of insanity
Rear common kind, follow progressive time;

Lead imagination from the story, Christ gave them;
For their own hypocrites pray, for a good heaven;
Beginning wicked, some wisdom living sympathy,
Care not, love of God not care, by them shown,
Mind a piece of their prayers not known,
God love in heaven, happy they need care,
Due man, gives proportion proper, work his share;
Trouble their lives God, no make division,
Pleasure, future death, is the disposition God containing,
Character, wait condition, mental hypocrites,
Speak, Christ Spirit without alarm, power purpose armed.
Love of God, meagerly whelps, your time age do compare,
Love of God, other he teach them, he earths air,
Christ, age useful known, speaking literature of time,
Known details, Jesus the only man, known to be true,
Brain his tablet, practical Spirits, course persue,
Same style, showing difference, same condition,
Story same, telling same mental disposition,
Soft now—his thoughts, were they venus;
The beautious blush, noble cheeks fair,
Mild love sincere, no desire, thoughts base,
Mind subdued, heaven passion revealed,
Hearts, tears, no Word can conceal;
Surround the Witness, lonely of the field,
Woe of patience, advanced age to sorrow,
Aurora, messenger, depart for to-morrow,
Mind now, character weak, mind low design;
Hypocrite, deceitful hypocrite all deceitful divine,
Doctrine course not his will he believe,
Life his lie, wise talk be men, not deceived,
US, give the US buckskins; pass out these US,
IF not, STAND, away for TIME to burn, first, last,
For time burn,
Similar, stay minds own their kind,
Progress, tail subdued, civilized scum of time,
Upward course claim, steady with aim,
Opposite to Plutos Gate, Opposite to hypocrite
Christ, praise now well.
His residence praised God, heavens above gates Pluto hell.
Christ, who, himself laid low, God to praise see above.
Him they tell, he is God, Christ, and One,
Said should they all love,
Success accused God's son, ye host, ignorant host,
Allows He, they wander a dreary coast;

Him in Spirits God, his life was **divine**,
Above thoughts, ancient men, above ancient time,
Born son, CHILD of God, in depths of depths of love.
In action distant loving mother, only God above,
Testament, take his own, course shows he run;
Christ make of Joseph, Joseph the carpenter's son,
Found her Joseph, she child was great big, God's child with,
Minded he was, her put away,
Loved well still, prompted Spirit remain to Mary.
Things saying her born of, be called, should God's son be
Continue called, people all tell He was not the Son of man,
Skip imagination, His Word reason, mystery not impossible,
Heaven peaceful, hell dreadful, to please, is it to please life
Flesh for heaven, never, this world released,
May spirits have wings, mystery, alike unfurled;
Man simple, that region tell of, open to suspicion,
Before time in death, **know** humanity, a condition,
Called God, speak Jesus, Testament, His shows,
Son in deceit speak of Father, Power unknown,
Spirits composed please, stretched to please God's will,
God, praise from himself, limits of reason
Way proving action, in **life** wisdom, mystery equal division;
Purpose in multitude driven, Spirits **in and out,**
Ignorance, I hope, not to know, I claim I cannot **see,**
Such, with wise men, wise eyes, never can never **agree;**
My welfare, I with, content, mystery remains in growth.
Teach disdain experience, Kingdom see to man.
Is God no man, is man God born again, no—yes no.
Dies death first, spirit flesh, Spirit life to life in days
Was Joseph Jesus, in three days from death;
Truth, plain truth, think of that fact
Is reason, not strong imagination useless, lead the way.
A cross plan Christ crucifixion, God's smallest work;
Suffice with power acknowledge,
People bringing thoughts, to mind not cause given,
God comprehend Power not,
Earth movements, remove the sky for a heaven,
Brought forth, babe of God, is the way,
Praised, loosed tongue praised God, following day,
Reason is practical, is God woman—mankind prove,
God **is** slow—faults many find
Spirit, for her humbled, **in** patience.
Own spirit, wait, die, prepare for fate.
Wait side, this side of Pluto's misty **gate,**

Receive spirit, heal anew, add temples **to reason;**
Talk born again, Spirits, **love** in proper season
Love born, leads Spirit, new life gains seldom trouble ;
Thought stroubled, berry grief, burn strife.
Son, see God Child, Spirits come simple, above idle wife.
Power God's praise, Him, please we can his human kind ;
Prayer Him, look over ideas, to insignificant to Himself.
Force His, light scope of, cannot imagine,
Son, which way to God, ends nothing.
Known, our God by Spirit, Spirit worship truth.
Flesh separate, revealed it God Him, **son long time flesh.**
Spirits perish, spirits live unbounded.
Nothing is man, is part **spirit** God.
His Light commands fields, electricity controlling **forming.**
Own way controlling beginning, a uni**verse, on there growth.**
Man future, see here heaven, purity being pleasure **life pleasure.**
Flesh, penalties evil hell, known believed.
Christ **Jesus** named God Spirit, see God Himself.
Came **to** the Word John, given in **the** wilderness.
God Spirit claims John, with his Word His own book;
He **spirit** man from God, spirit in him.
Bold, he **owning** writing, own Spirit, praise name.
Name, an ancient given **Itself,**
Perfect, without to him understanding,
He mankind **Jesus, the** Christ,
God behold, Holy **Ghost** descending, Him behold upon.
Containing Spirit, **his own testament wrote.**
Time in Christ, **support only his theory.**
Or **Jesus, help God** there never was an equal,
Protection continually, He claim not.
Prove him, this God, common spirit christian belief.
Descended Joseph, to love God carpenter's son.
Say, **three be** One, God's love—scrub Joseph—Spirit Christ.
No man Spirits see—flesh son—Spirits controlled;
Free flesh, not Spirits space of heaven.
Father God like, Him, strength against attraction.
Weak son obeys, loves His laws, attractions, earth.
God pleasing at times, Son at times was MAN, with God.
For love wisdom, voice said, Beloved Son thou art, I am pleased.
Foundation is annointed, record ;
Christianity, My Story beginning truth, in truth.
Youth, ignorant unthankful, worthless.
Spirit, God gives **manhood,** children of appreciate truth.
God's **young ones, become ones active,** cultivate brain.

Past parables **look**, life evil, very, **study plain.**
Prove man, in life, knowledge life by God is given.
Part remain **the** sphere, revolve through heaven.
Advanced humanity a gigantic plan,
Shone His Light all, when Jesus was the son of man.

Christ, him when baptized, see, Holy Ghost and fire,
The Word in the wilderness, to John by the Gospel Wire;
John known Jesus, Esaias numerous prophets **in** name,
Jesus known John, Christ, one all and the same.
Scope that country, in time and age purpose told,
Time development, could of **his** full name unfold.
God's Word plainly, it came to John, the **Word** claims,
People, see from John, **see the** four different names.
Show actions important, precious multitude, they were few;
The story repeats **truth,** impressed the ancient Jew.
A prophet, respected **they** all men, fulfill help his course;
Stretched, his blood **by blood,** by love of blood dript the **cross.**
Be, let him crucify, **God** was will, **theirs was law;**
Afar off looked off the the soldiers, pain **his, from withdraw.**
Him, it behooves **suffer, words** his we **call to mind,**
Regret record, on **recovery cannot find.**
Him they took, for his death **cross, they no desire,**
Wire arms stretched nailed hands, fire God's electric **fire.**
Jesus John Joseph pain relieved all, cross body received.
Thence from useful life, life peacefully ended,
Days in those, Mary not yet, His Father **ascended.**
Praise, mother eyes modest, great big, **that with that** child.
Talk angels, God's humanity in **human form;**
Angel GABRIEL, thing that was Jesus **to Mary,** to be born.
Lives overshadowed, two, knew they alone course,
John, was with Jesus, **for** Christ, was Spirit modest force.
By perfect patience, by course, repentance his cause;
In favor with God man increased, Christ removed the flaws;
Love of God worthy, woman that life matured, for mind,
That Spirit in life received, life common cannot find.
The age of all time, by man age that Spirit Unknown.
See, in that Spirit manhood, manhood, if shown.
Children to God, **to** worthless babes that Grace is not given,
For worthless they useless, to country or heaven.
Child, was Jesus through virtue, in Mary born,
Purity, coming through Christ Jesus God's Son.
In her, the GABRIEL born, was again,
Love plain, big with love willingly remain.

Relieve that heals pain mortal, in life,
Man leads that death. forget his grief and strife,
As the Light it came, the sheep lost were found.
Light, oh Light love shone, God all around,
His mother he came from, saved the fall
Lost to the Shepherd, love for he followed the call,
Him she led, on came God's lamb, His own way,
God gives the world to each to all sinners to-day;
Pack their own load each one, not to ask his brother's pay.
Through love, born love which must forever live,
Woman for man will come, come see the gifts God can give.
For the lamb lost, sad, the Shepherd felt alone,
Light he made, and she light, guides she him home;
Pasture, all follow in, which light led the way,
Found and lost, for that light, His light shines without pay,
Time back that sacred night, along years ago,
Birth, behold God's Lamb a plain. the Light, low,
Repeats life God's Word, turns man from God's Light,
Could God—God could forever sacred repeat that flight,
The Shepherds call, to the lost they come they hear,
They, His Word believe voice His love, quiet call,
Soar they—yes, far above Adam's darkness, Adam's fall.
Who, man believe, walking light, to be saved.
Spirit, above his is rapids, thoughts above the grave.
Came God's Lambs through gloom, born they Light, the op-
posite shore,
They get to where they cross love, God hapiness floats them o'er
Lambs God's, try to please God, gives He them pleasant Power
Life they wash in purity, with life He sweetens Flower,
Love they God's way, no see fault, see work He has given.
Made the earth He, no—yes, they are satisfied in heaven.
Love gives Word to God, bread give it to the multitude,
Flesh strenghten, remains God the light of fate,
Like their help, growth now Power mankind, wait,
Knowledge that, the only hope, love His Word to believe.
A miracle, beginning beyond the heat gate, of life received
The germ, developed in darkness a sprout, all alone,
Darkness covers the seed of wild oats sown;
The dreary sower repents, stops back in dark gloom,
Rejected come, to their beauty leads to shine home,
Her, in darkness they see, the light mother,
From God gift; slow, simple Adam, wife in time
They pass her, think willingly, for wait future life,
God, virtue woman beauty, she leads upward the course.

Strength, patience **binds** love together, with quiet force;
They love they show love, take His Word His place **Power,**
Patiently must **wait,** growth maturity wisdom flower.
God's lambs these models, follow all their way,
Please His will, He shows with them, Light of future Day.
     Follow, may man his own course—yes,
Man like, God likes be lost when He is found,
May take him mankind, him, God shows spirit body bound.
Pattern of man's work, of Himself God makes no display;
To please Him, follow this Light, Lambs lead the way.
Now believe, His Word unchanged beginning, dated night,day;
His Word, God is old Happiness is His will His course,
Word given, a follow Adam **lose much force;**
He was to God as **never found, not a Lamb Lost.**
Wander to lost **Paradise, wander** to gloomy stygian gloomy
    coast;
Eve an Adam **placed the garden, His Word cannot** they wait.
Christ Mary **waited in Paradise, Light** came to gate,
Mother pain, **bring forth son of man,**
Care, **in sincere, be above a wife.**
Spirit **leaves, sad, many days save his life;**
Protection **moulds his life,** him **hold to modest ways.**
Mother, son, God **spirit comes, bound for her of course;**
Wait, she holds him light; **see,** through modest **force.**
Born, virtue seven devils power, she avoided man's **ways;**
Her, he came her love for her, impatient she delays.
Mother, man is a light on the high road of life,
God's Son keeps, shines above, the light of wife.
    Like a reaper, God's Spirit a foe to life of man,
He matures growth a growth, a growth from naked land;
Return dust, leave spirit, **life** in tears answer call;
Spirit matured ignorance; **enemy flesh,** never fall.

God hath, **I declare me.**
    Never, tell things, not heard;
       I obey, we cannot tell—**we take we heard.**
Think Son, with Son, declare ignorance.
    Think Son, rest, think **man** mightier **We, model Book.**
      Reverend man, respect **I** thee,
        Out of respect, reverend man **I out** of thee.
God hath me, **I declare,** Him.
    God had me, **I declared** Him, I had Him.
Readest thou writing, not **study** lying without waiting.
    Out of thee without **lie, it** best within **many,**

Know, I do not lift every scrub in the world,
     If they follow make course, God hold them.
          God will not bother every man in the world ;
     If they make His Course better, it is, better you see Him.
          I declare God, I declare, well has Him ;
               That is, I has Him I declare when He wants me.
When He wants to He has Himself, suppose, wants He.
     He is all OBEY ME, above about me, He,
          He, about holds out all these things.
               Now things, take these things,
                    God shows Himself, nearly.
About, you about look, at these things,
     See, not, things which are not, seen things.
          Things which before you, are of God, in Power.
               Pass you away these things,
Your mind, your mind, now mind give you away
     To Power about.
               Kill me, simply kill me, I ready die A man,
                    I Am, I hope not A man.
I hope I am; nothing is a man.
     I hope I am no you, no more no A man.
          I am I hope I am above, B'A) DAM' (AN I am.
               Follow to him yes him, burn into hell a man.
                    I Am, a man is Mine, I Am,
I am, Heart As A Rock, I Am Slay, I am Persecute, I Am.
     Now to thee A man,
          Kiss My—in it not, I Am for never, more I Am,
               Eli's Boy Rock them,
                    My breeze blow;
                         Puck little Stone Heart them,
                              Where you come I Am I Am.
My breeze go blow them away,
     Off by breeze take them fire them,
          It take far it burn, them away down.
               You say come breeze blow me way up,
                    You come to Me, Mine breeze bring Boy,
                         Tell my boy I no breeze,
I no die, I rock I no blow, Myself Time,
     Quick again very much My breeze go,
          I wind it in, I, you, come go.

LAST CASE.

4th Scene—Sign of Time.

BAND OF LAST ARRIVALS—LAST CHIEF ARRIVALS.

Big—Buckskin — the —Tiger— **Chief —of Big Ben**
    Fairolight ;
Lord Pale Face—Few **Cards—of Jasper City.**
Chief Son Two **Strikes—Sand off Winning Cards.**
Ann Attractive **Deck—Harbor Kicking Bear Deal**
    Bold Disciple keep cases ;
Agents cut, your choice order, moderately gratis.

FIRST—CASE—THE LAST.

    Little fresh Sport, do much, for the red man's
Spirit ante up, chip in with Son Again Born the
    Bottom copper on Gabriel's Trumpet.

Come shake sharp wit
    Let US berry Tommy Hawk,
Lie about dead as the cherry tree
    Stand for Liberty,
Stand My Son Again Born Speak,
    The Freedom of Gabriel's Trumpet,

    Eli Joses Joseph stands in Old Son—o-ma
The hub head center from whence
    He cranks the universe, big round wide wake time,
Angel GABRIEL ON EARTH,
    Read record second visit found in Son Again Born.

    Look down Adam, Look out eve Angel
Gabriel kicks Adam down,
    Kicks up eve, cover eyes,

In Gabriel's Trumpet look round,
   Read in Son Again Born.

   Look up out little Jew Eli's Word
Directs you, prophet Elijah comes to
   Memory God's promise, God does not forget His promise
Of ancient times that promise fulfills the Word,
   Taps your money, 50c come again 50c.

   Look bags, buy bundle, money sax,
Ye read, ye understand God's Law
   In Son Again Born come get a head once,
One Gabriel's Trumpet.

   Unthankful you have the Indians home,
To help, give help, no missionaries, read,
   Son Again Born, Gabriel's Trumpet by Chief Josia Joseph.

   Sweet charity back bone of missionary,
Do compare, red man's belief to josh,
   Find book, Great Spirit make,
American Savior Goods, or go to China,
   Son Again Born, Joe Gabriel's Trumpet in here.

   Come to book, farmer boy, life ye feed,
Believe, ye know ye read so, sow;
   Proceed to plow through Gabriel's Trumpet.
Cultivate, Son Again Born, here it is, seed for sale.

   Are ye common christian, certain,
Believe ye Jesus was God, are ye certain.
   Ingersold—God's Power is no fable, see,
God's son again is not all Him, Himself,
   His son writes Books to see, here they are for sale.

   Are ye lawyer Hard Case, are ye scribe Hard Stuff.
Ignorance leave, to appreciate, a lot of son again
   Heal over through Gabriel's Trumpet.
Cure insane ignorance, vanish.

   Big science step, see, over through Gabriel's Trumpet,
To pass interest, go through Son,
   Again Born, here they are.

Step out see breeze, Professor All Know Much, **the farisee.**
Catch it, neck **stiff,** hold stiff breeze;
    Any lies breeze, seize, Son Again Born.
Blow about Gabriel's Trumpet, they are here.

    Young man Loud Shout, breeze blow about,
Look out of breath to see the sky removed.
    To move get to Son Again Born, into it
Float out in Gabriel's Trumpet once.

    Old man Sober Breath breathe dry **breeze**
Pocket your forgetmenot, to leave
    When you pass, be above Old Big Money, **follow Gospel**
Wire Gabriel's Trumpet leave tin, for Son Again **Born.**

    Man preacher, leave when you pass above, **breeze,**
Remember a few lines by Joe in Son Again **Born,**
    Or give three howls in—for Gabriel's Trumpet,
Take it away for 50c, find yourself.

    Priest hold down, down, dead fall, stiff
Quick distill your stuff to pass, do ye,
    Read Late in Books read Son Again Born,
Call mass for Gabriel Strumpet, take it away for 50c.

    Young Jake Sankytimony think much do you pass
While you wait to see, your brain improve,
    Pocket your fill of Son Again Born
When full, fill hide with Gabriel's Trumpet only.

Puff some man up big corporation
Steam stew him up, to work brain machine
    Slow down to hear Gabriel's Trumpet,
A Boy Whistle of the future, Son Again.

    My dark and dusty friends
Take a tumble **from** trouble your dusty ware off,
    To come get in Gabriel's Trumpet,
Dodge or come read Son Again come your **little 50c.**

    Young Counter **Jump,** drop money,
Arm your shelves in upper story with Gabriel's Trumpet,
    Fort defy brain Son Again Born is on the war path.

Sailor furl your lugs, come too, anchor,
    You are near the gang, walk
Buy Son Again Born, heave up, and row for
    Gabriel's Trumpet, good for 50c dock—u—ment.

Stop your drag, Drive Easy, opportunity
    Embrace Son Again Born for 50c,
Arm squeeze Gabriel's Trumpet if you please—her 50c.

Prospect mine miner. Gabriel's Trumpet contains nuggets,
    Croppings of Son Again Born pay plain
As grass roots on down come on shift for 50c.

Big Beef the beer butcher, skin them,
    The sucking black sheep and dry calves
Come Soak Gin, set them up for Son Again,
    Say boys again for Gabriel's Trumpet.

Wiry Fast Freight, down breaks, chuck your rollers
    For the good indian—near, conduct—or pass in,
For Son Again Born Y switch in,
    Come here for Gabriel's Trumpet.

Come Rough Wart, the snag pilot, heave too
    Hail Son Again Born have some fun,
On Home voyage drop your tin, sink her—sound
    Gabriel's Trumpet.

Factory maid, take time, if you please don't fret,
    To worry body sweet talk, made Son Born Again,
Never to sour on Gabriel's Trumpet,
    If you are safe; save your—for 50c.

Can Cinnamon, cotton seed look out of Dixie,
    So brain seed, look out through Gabriel's Trumpet,
Mature mind understand Son Again so brain seed 50c each.

Loud Bark the saw-log man,
    Cant hook handle timber,
Come hook one Son Born Again; hook one
    Gabriel's Trumpet your 50c good for 50c.

Come quiet eve, fall him, you find leave, come
    To pick yourself up one Gabriel's Trumpet,

Fall in to get one Son Again Born, hold one off for yourself.

Mind poisoned eat, rake brain drink,
  Dose Gabriel's Trumpet, to heal sore cave mind,
  Temple rub much, Son Again Born, cure case 50c each.

Captain to mate, Steward come eat mess
  Of Son Again Born, take a head wind tack,
Run down through Gabriel's Trumpet,
  Sale here for 50-cent piece.

Come Hard Case, smoke stack of peace,
  Inhale my Holy Smoke to explode
Hard shell, breathe Gabriel's Trumpet one lung,
  Blow Son Again Born the other.

Come to trouble, little slight brain waist,
  Sting my books, see light in on Son Again,
Drive your stinger away through Gabriel's Trumpet,
  Your nest fill, 50—sense empty.

Young Good Much Hearest, thou keep quiet proper time,
  Read little short Gabriel's Trumpet, spring season;
Loud paint Son red, paint Son Born,
  Bate trap Gabriel's Trumpet.

Big Blow, very fly blow your city full,
  Many flies in the flight of Gabriel's Trumpet;
Son Again Born very great, blow, hard time 50—sense times.

Climb crook, perch outside cage jailbird,
  Rob, steal, hold up, scratch;
The Highway produce turnip, beat, Son Again Born,
  You come pure sharp, steal Gabriel's Trumpet.

Maid fisher maiden, hook the fish, play line him,
  Head the sucker, Sal—mon, tail cut, bone him,
Make prize pickle, codfish, with patience;
  Read Son Again Born, let them nibble, bite,
Drop them down deck, continue, many
  Times, put on, Power Gabriel's Trumpet.

Young one, go it stage struck,
  If you don't mind you show, off without you,

Mind the Merchant of Venus is Gabriel's Last Weak,
    Engagement, last for time to please Son
Again Born, no dead head, pass yourself 50c reserve.

Hear the Last forever Friend a working man,
    He eats the Last Supper, drinks Last
Wine will Last, Son Again eat, come drink
    All through your Gabriel's Trumpet,
        She again fine, fair wine.

Up anchor, spread sales of your courtship,
    Joe Gabriel fly for her again Son,
The Strumpet knows your love was fair.

5th Scene—Picture—Time.

The world may judge Son Joe by his own life
    Record in Gabriel's Trumpet.
Boy Son is a thorough bred, scrub world, beat her
    If you can leave brain seed for the fields of time.
Let them spread all over the fields of crime
    Come on home, leave china, filth and slime.
Gabriel's Trumpet tells all, you burnt a hell of time.
    My Son let them deny, you prove their slime,
Burnt all through the world, furnace, crime.
    I son burnt up, knows all slime, never needs fire ages time,
He writes, he knows, he proves life,
    His record of his time of life Mine,
He has a Great Big Spirit, take His Word
    As Dictated, or take it alone,
Spirit has him with Him, so let alone,
    We keep away when we are alone,
Spirit Judge looks eyes, Sons make no mistakes,
    Find fault, big miss take the telegraph to Mary,
Third ward off in a yard of Son—o-ma Count,
    Calif US Americans get along there just the same,
One else would not do,
    I Am Yours I Am, Yours Eli.

Joe Josi, come **to see, if** you move it.
  Man of the world, understand My **Works, they move,**
You move, come see if you move It,
  Air is deep, **sky is** heavy, is it heavy on shoulders,
Under the world, unbalance your mind.
  Do **you come** up, you go down;
Climb up manhood, in the morning of **life,**
  Wake **up** top of world unto noon,
Late in quiet eve roll down out of eye **sight**.
  Earth is rocky, life is heavy;
Is air solid stuff, cut through to **see if**
  You breathe a breath of it,
Strike Two, see if you move It, through it.
  Do you have a Little Wound from it, Son **Two Strikes,**

A GAME—LITTLE—WOUND,

Come to game, **Little Wound,**
  Kill **clean** game, never eat **white man.**
  Every morning white man top scalp world,
Roll them down under, **the** world, Eastman,
  Straddle **over** the wide west, Old Gall,
Hump the **buffalo** again **over** the prairies;
  Brace **up, man, be like** Young—man—Fear—no—horse.
Come John **Cloud up,** never run like rain dears,
  Paint **Red Clouds,** Son again,
Say Big Foot, **let** them have their baby game,
  With the profit of Wounded Knee prophet.
Come Rose Bud the autumn fall, like self control.
  Brave Indian, like Standing Rock,
  Indian brave like me, I Am **Justis** Heart, as a rock.

Great Son—TWO STRIKES—two,
  Be bold Indian maid, Wild—Shy—Ann, Pie—you—it,
  Make Snake hunt, On—eat—a, Sweet Cherry key.

Take no white pale man, description his depredation,
  Dim, he tells Few Tails of himself,

PORCUPINE—TABLETS.

Ye red man, Great Father, no president is Great Father;
  Great Spirit, no little white man president.
Make all over, round top sky;
  He give Son Born see stars, Spirits move
In Happy Hunting Ground be good, big, Indian,
  Slow fire in hell, bad man burn

Two Hundred, One thousand years breathe fire,
    Not soon forget, good, very next time '
Great Father make moon, Great Father talk Son,
    Great Father feel all round little earth,
        He looks another way.

Chief Sons—KICKING BEAR—Light,
    Great Father make sky cities stars, sky round,
        Earth inside, Great Father live above sky.
Great Spirit come by breeze,
    Down One Boy take another Boy Home, .
Great Spirit All Wire All Know Big Crank, no fool,
    His breeze feel all men, wire see sift all men,
Great Spirit All Happiness Great Spirit was
    Forever Big Work Him God is not all trouble,
Great Spirit come kill fool Boy.
    Give life Boy, new God's Boy write Book (SPIRIT,)
God's Spirit makes Boy write,
    Baby Joe don't know Great Spirit tell,
Him everything to know
    God's Boy Heaven cities see, he never troubles God,
To wait on Him he is rough an tumble.
    He runs to fall when God tells him he loves,
He fears he is very small to God
    All top sky God very solid,
Great Spirit, not much little man,
    God's Heart big solid, Heart as rock
God's Word is to all men, when they are dead,
    They know, they believe lately
God sends Great Spirit in breeze, electricity quick,
    His breeze blows electricity quick.

Great—SPIRIT FOR TWO—Strike Son
    They the sons of ancient American Liberty
You trash them to death, you crowd
    Liberty, foreign pauper crowd
God's Spirit does not descend every day to Judge
    The world, many years departed He returns His own way
Leave room, right way mind, best mind Him the right way
    Right your way do not chain the Indian, to inactivity
You take his arms, he wants the right,
    He is silence of poverty, he holds his misery,
If he wants, the Great Spirit, He allows him he fights
    The Great Spirit, if he wants, tells him, fight

He takes liberty, they like liberty,
    I walk alone, I Am Liberty,
I Am the Frame and Bones of Time,
    I am touchy, I never forget, I cannot forgive,
I can relieve, believe My Word,
      Think, know, Spirit of Truth,
Leave centre, make earth attract, round you,
    In you, darken light sky,
        Roll dark black clouds, in you,
           If you can sound roll thunder,
              Vivid flash lightning.
To ease your mind,
          Look beyond My star eyes,
          Move from Heaven, inside, refuse, clouds,
          If you make rain clean up water spouts,
            Move clouds in a minute,
            And forever if you can.
You move my insides,
    You are near my underside, of heaven,
        I Am my Spirit in me,
          I Am nothing that don't suit me,
            I have many eye bright stars,
              I Am no man, I look in Myself,
My Spirit comes in to earth from me,
    Earth never brought me,
        I let her go, she goes round about way,
          Son single eye Light
            Shine through to bottom side,
              Far back to side; other side.
    Light single eye, see many stars
        Shine, shine see far and bright,
I star cities see far, move, roll, fall, stand
        Still all in Heaven, some see some blind,
I hold all, my son, forever shine,
Think heavy, look about inside, look sharp single eye,
        Single eye, picture course earth
          Continuing to slime My Spirit,
My Spirit, eye sore; I burn clean out time,
        Of life time, move life out into hell,
Make Myself sick, to clean all up all slime of me,
I Am I say forever, 200—1000 years is in one year of me.
    I am I look another way,
        I feel all over somewhat in me,
          My Spirit is live,

My Spirit comes in Son, He loves,
He loves, he eyes, he knows, He sees in them,
He holds them, He feels, He takes them apart,
He brings them together,
If they will go they go, down, down,
Away off He never knows them,
Into space hell, they burn down, down,
Up, Up, He never knew them,
He don't miss them, He never lost them,
They have their own spirit takes them,
They don't know where they stay,
Stay, they stay, they burn slowly, their mind away
In all times they see no light present day,
They feel slender, they wither, they keep,
Quiet when they know me, they say
I Am, is a devil of man, that they never knew
How I Am was made, then when they know,
They are far away from I Am,
Many could in all time do as please,
God likes few pick, pick men do me good,
See a few, a few in life, they ask Him His Power,
He says now study pick man Wisdom Flower,
If they wither and decay, dry protect,
Wait mind, profit future day
I fear, I write anything God, bring Spirit wants me to
Him His and His sky round, earth wants few,
We want for nothing, believe you, His Belly full,
Round running over heap up, press down
You are in it, yes you are,
God rolls up one rim side looks inside
Clouds, round morning sky, mind clean, clear up a noon,
At noon turn on down, down below quite,
Under your quiet eve, you are clean, under it.
Baby Joe Boy, write, I please you,
Long time ago you cry me.
Quite run over, to hold out friend boys,
You open wide eyes,
Love to all look up to me, come into me
Why in it, my Good Boy Save, I we in it.
Remember your, you are not without for me,
Mind you did not make Me inside, eye sore,
Inside eye, fear not, stay in it, I am save you
Until I save you live.
You sleep, you twist around in it.

You up and light, down, heavy,
 You work at play, you are quite into it,
  Come out **to** Myself, I will take you all over the sky,
  Then, now we will rest,
   Choice fruit when ripe, I pack,
    My Baby **Boy,** in a wrapper with eve
I **Shoulder** them, together we stay,
 Until **we** come home.
My two Babies feel tickled, proud and **happy,**
 They feel and look all over, they kiss me,
They hug around and touch My Neck ;
 I move them, I study them, I busy them,
I have no time for fool, only this kind touch me again.
 Touch shoulder top, come out side, lay off by me
They tread my planets, **they** my air stars,
 They feel, they **do not** fall, they go through **air,**
They come down, they feel good, deep climb.
On up by|me, they **on My** Knee, I study them,
 Forever together **in** their arms, they always feel,
  They want to come to me, to feel.
Me good, **I** make them behave same as me,
 When I wish, I love to hold them tight.
They look up and cry for me, when I hold them.
 When I drop them they run, not to bother me.
They stay together, and look in theirselves.
 They hold fast together, smile happy.
And at all times look and think of me, hold each,
 An looks close, I smile, I am please
Them, overlook them close together, close **to me.**
They come up together close to me,
 They come up in My Arms,
  They I hold them, in My **Arms,**
   I tight squeeze them.
Sleep in My Arms, them I hold,
 They wake, they sometimes cry, I box them
  Apart, they come to love me forever,
I again I bring them together, they never forget,
 They **hang** close to me, they do not bother me,
  I take them when I want them,
   They do cry after me,
 They **work** for me so willingly, I make **them cry.**
They do not busy me, if I call them
 They help tend to my business, Work
  Each one, they go and come, apart each one

For me, for me they are mine, they mind,
  They inspire to know me, they mine mind,
They raise themselves to know me, please,
  They study My Work for me, I help them please,
    We look around over My Work, we correct make,
    Make the way, as we go together.
If you don't like us when way in, you stay away
  Off, we kick you away, outside in hell away off,
    Without trouble we breeze you through the gate.
By you our measure you we make no mistake,
  Take this to make, take you gain out,
    We gain, not we lose, we don't want gain,
      We keep away from, all pair yourselves
        To think to see us, we are over,
          You sit quite under us,
            We will respect your case
              If you look up to us.
  We will not sit on you,
      You will be saved yourselves,
        Mind well, it will not burn yourselves.
            Come to live or go off to die, you may,
            I am here you are in a place, in for it.
Where you come out, then you are in it,
Wait, for you to improve, mine in time,
Make something over My Work in Time,
Work something over me in time, I will give you something.
  The death grip squeeze breath, breath out of you,
  Breath wind, wash kill dry, clean out, you purify,
  Purify yourselves out or I will Fire Ghost all into you.
        I must come you at last,
        I must last for you at first,
    I was first, you last, I Am forever,
    If if, you see I Am come, to believe I Am,
    I Am come for you to believe I Am,
    If if you are ignorant to doubt, mind,
Your will, may know, you say, I am off, wrong,
  Wrong off, you upside down and walk.
You are the fruit, over far away off, I take trip you
    One devil of man, kick you out to
          Fire hell in time,
I am Spirit, Adam run, Omego.
  I am the Kill, Quick, Fire Chief—cook a man;
Down a man, I fill, electricity is my steam stew.
    Forever when you come to meals, to supper.

In it well, some of you have found out light,
Into it, roller take quick light, electricity, eat ;
   Feed man machine, all big, work the dead
With the dead light, come see dead son.
Work with the dead, big dead son,
   I keep quiet, man to make him his work.
Never seem to know me, to ask praise.
   I claim no praise, show me future, small machine.
      A future, come on electricity, I show
         For my future understanding,
Electricity, man, is my fly-wheel band,
    Band, son man help me, make things
      We make, he never hear me, I do him,
        Son mind see, head Myself,
          Like Make I Am Alone, stand.
Stay throughout, stand still alone without Me,
    Come over lightning tracks for me,
I give you light, uncover My Light, earth-machine.
    Case Me, My enemy in,
      I Am I send Word to you, My Clerk,
        I can see from the bright morning star,
         He writes a SLEEPY SON.
He writes for me, Through Electricity, Candle,
   Three Powers, Electricity Man, Spirit Light,
    Roll the heavy world down
      Through light air space,
        She runs away, I put on, Governor,
She moves steady, if you lose the Band,
    Lightning, fire—I put the Band,
      And she runs like lightning fire.
I keep Clerks, herd planets, Clerks star cities,
    My Clerk star cities, by My Sight,
Record Light Shine, I have a band of them,
    I blow trumpet, I wake them very early in the morning,
Bring in herd of asses, GABRIEL TRUMPET BLOW,
    Quite early by light in the morning,
I like to see all the herd feed,
    On they pack the load, I take it
Quiet quite easy, away far star city, the band,
    I see at one look I see them,
      I know the one that lays down,
His load is heavy when I come help him up,
    When I feed, he eats, anybody eat for me this.
They come down from, for below heaven,

My Son take the Bread, asses eat take it multitude,
Eat break it, eat full fill up with fragments,
　　Your bread baskets full fill, up run top over,
　　　　See, grow stout good big, Boy,
　　　　　　I am come over you once, twice,
　　　　　　　　See you feed multitude,
Break eat, once, twice, disciples seat them,
　　Once, twice down the way side
　　　　By hundreds, fill them down, them see
　　　　　　Away full make room,
　　　　　　　　Come by, eat, into Mary's Table,
　　　　　　　　　　Son burner light out, sit down.
Let the grass grow, you have burnt all down,
　　You warm the rock, you run lava beds,
　　　　Over mountains, burnt world.
Grass grow again, like grass green trees like roots.
　　Rein habit earth like this in morning time,
　　　　Increase your mind, multiply, decrease,
　　　　　　You sail out of the flood into fire,
In the flood you know you drink too much,
　　In fire I know you eat fire,
　　　　I come in to burn inside out,
　　　　　　Dead Son Top Side, be the same inside;
　　　　　　　　All be a little bit the same inside and outside.
Leave your side, take my side,
　　I Chief Boss My Side, I burn to kill your side,
But side in side, away side of the other side,
　　We walk fields of the middle of it.
　　　　Find this Two, let-her last,
　　　　Go earth roll or I make you shake,
　　　　Roll, never lose me, I am Good Customer,
　　　　Roll all your things, punkings, beat, yourself
　　　　　　All over, I feed you, out in there,
　　　　　　　　I awake to my close, bright
　　　　　　　　　　With love for Kill me Quick.
　　God should not claim fool son of the world, round.
His Son is Joe Gabriel, from with, in Him
　　Come out to Son—Shine—Himself,
　　　　Father take whip, Son—Shine,
　　　　　　Father is Joe Great, wild west Son—Shine,
Joe is west wild, very, Great—Son—Shine,
　　Joe go west, step over the east,
　　　　Wild Joe way south, step over the north,
Over centre, turn, little centre wheel, around

Round them more, round them around
　　　Then round them, around quick all **over big round,**
Take them around, **in** Great Big Round UP,
　　Brand them, **fire,** red hot,
　　　　Get letters red as fire, Brand,
　　　　　　Brand with letters, G—I—T—S——S—A—B.
　　　　　　　Our Brand letters read, mean this:

Gabriel—In—Trumpet—Savior——Scrub—A—Boy.
Gabriel—In—Trumpet—Son——Savior—A—Boy.
Gabriel—In—Trumpet—Son——Scrub—Again—Born.

Study—A—Book——Get—In—To—Self.
Savior—A—Boy——Get—In—To—Scrub.
Strumpet—A—Boss——Get—In—Trumpet—Strumpet.

　　Gabriel—In—To—Strumpet——Son—A—Boy.
　　Get In–To Strumpet——Saviour–A Boy,
　　Strumpet In–To Gabriel——Scrub–A Boy.

　　Take my book—all the world—round,
　　Round all the world—take—my book,
　　My Book—all the round world—take.

　　Joe the Boy—Saviour earth—returned,
　　Returned to earth—My Boy Saviour—Joe,
　　My Boy Joe—Saviour returned—to earth.

　　Gabriel—shows his Trumpet—in Bright Light,
　　The Bright Light—of Gabriel's Trumpet—shows,
　　Show His Trumpet—in Gabriel's Bright Light.

　　I Am Joe Josi—don't—get any higher,
　　Don't—get any higher—than Joe Josi,
　　I don't want—I Am Joe **Josi**—**I** get there.

　　When **I am** through—let me rest—anywhere,
　　I rest I am—anywhere—when I get through,
　　Let me rest—I get where—when I get through.

　　I pack a heart—like stone—there in **I get,**
　　I heart like stone—there I get—I pack,
　　I in there—**get** a heart like stone—I pack.

O God O they don't want—Son give them—something another
Son give them something—Another God O—they don't want
Something another Son—God give—them to want.

Let them—take these whets—without any pets.
Without any pets—let them take—these whets.
Take these—whets them without—any pets.

Box pack them—up to **come**—**by** courtship.
By courtship—pack them to **come** by—box them.
Pack them up—to come by—courtship box.

Breeze come and go—to herd—handle **them**.
Herd—handle them Breeze—come and **go** to.
Come and go Breeze—herd—handle them **to**.

I stay **in my** home—when I want—I come **to** go.
I come to **go** stay—in my Home—when I want.
In my Home—when I want I come—I stay I **go**.

Pale face—don't like go stay—stop away.
Don't like—go stay stop away—pale face.
Away stay go—stop pale face—don't like.

I come—**red man's** home in red man's—home see,
In red man's home—come—see in red man,
Red man come—see home—red man home.

Brave Buck I Am—going to quit—or say to much,
To quit or say to—much Brave Buck—I am going,
I am going to quit brave—buck or **say too** much.

Indian **Brave**—brave against all—U. S. America,
All U. S. Americans against—all Brave Buck Indians,
Against few Buck Indians—All Brave American men.

Brave Indian fight for America—die for Liberty,
For Liberty—die for America—fight brave Indian,
Gain **your** Liberty—in **A**merica or die—fight brave Indian.

Give the white man home—don't treat—like a dog,
White man give them—at home—you treat like a dog,
You treat them like dogs—they leave—home.

Don't bother the life of them—away;
The life of them—don't bother—to stay away,
You bother—the life of them —keep some away.

They did not come—along last—to take a home.
You come along—at the last to take—all their home;
Come along you—dam you to last—help them at home.

This is my last—to help the redman—to a home.
Redman this is my last—help me—is your home,
I am the Last—in your home—redman help me.

I am your first—and last—we scatter them together,
First and last—we are together—if we don't scatter,
We scatter a few—together First and Last;
Great scatter—Boy Indian—Book Maker.

Come Gallager—let her go—Hearst,
Come Hearst—Gallager letter—go;
Letter go Gallager's—Hearse.

Fire let her—Hearst—to hell;
Burn letter—to hell—with Hearst.

6th Scene—Picture—Time.

Last let her Hearst—first letter to Hearst.
Son—to son—of Examiner;
Say Son of a—Examin—her—Sir—1891; Janu—ary,
You have acted a
The sneaking mouse with my Book,
                              Gabriel's Trumpet.

Fear not—
        People remain ignorant of your connection,
        With it you may come forward, I am pleased
        If you take some notice, of this One—
                My Own Second One.

It is in regard to a Saviour
    Is promised to the Montana Indians,
    And I will again say, if a better man cannot
        Come to time
    I will be pleased to assume the task,
        When the Snow Flies.
  To protect yourself, I am, be-willing,
      You may advertise--
        As the Dam,
          The Big,
            The Crank of the
              World,
                Eli J. Joseph--I am.

      Picture Silence—Contempt—Silent—
      He who thinks—I am—a fool dam,
        I—know—one—see—this date-age,
    One Gabriel Trumpet—Public-shed, Santa Rosa,
        March along 1890—one,
From Public-shed office this unnoticed letter to Hearst
      May come along 1890—one,
      I am still, Gabriel's Trumpet—no answer.

A Hearst—come, to Examiner.
    Please allow your book reviewer time to examine
This little book, which I Am, pleased to submit to the public
I think it adds another chain to the streak of evidence
For that Saviour which our Montana Indians are awaiting.
      Your account May 1st edition,
I hope they may be notified that the white man believes
Like the Indian, that the Great Spirit never lies—I will
Endeavor to show my proportion of such a belief
      In this quiet manner.
When they need, I hope they may have a man
Come to them with money, brains, and friendship, and freely
Spread it on the red man. If no better man comes
    To time, I MAY assume the task
When the snow flies again. If the man comes with marks
Of recommendation from the proper Authority, I am willing,
In my modest and unassuming manner, to help him, fulfill
The Word and take a few shares in the responsibility.
    You may shade the white sheets of the Examiner
With the sentiment, if you like, and give this
Book as my recommendation, I believe this will be the red-
      man's

First personal acquaintance with Christ, he shows a steady,
    Nerve, he shows, no use of superfluous expressions,
I think he has sense to say, for the Great Spirit of God.
He would not exaggerate for financial success or political
    Popularity, His belief, his own right.
I am to hope at present, you will not be alarmed for me.
I am in poverty, of a very high degree;
Almost equal to the Indian, our model of ancient American
    Liberty.
I can say, the Noble Savage, needs a Saviour, or he will soon
    be as low,
And degraded in his views of life, as the average
Specimens of white humanity, which She-
Associates with on some of our U. S. reservations.
I am able to weigh the value of a Good Word,
Against thousands of dollars, in broadcast advertisements
To show love of God, I beg you not to condemn
My Book; if I am successful, I hope to advance
The Northwestern savage in his native land of Liberty
By helping the man they predict, and think will come,
With such great power, and authority, to turn the world
        On the—white—man.
I believe I will be justifiable in calling Him the Crank of the
    Universe, as I am, very young, for my age.
I have the impudence to ask Him to make S F hub for crank,
That we may turn easy, on this part of the globe.
       Yours with love, Elijah J. Berryman.
          I am Elijah Josias Joseph.
I blow against this for one year without answer:
       I go off—to the city—and die, dead
        And they—come back—to say—
He who knows I am a fool,
      Dam, I know one I am.
Kill me quick—
      I lay wait, I away lay—Hearst office,
And stretch to wait, decent,
      December—three days.
Hearst stay, no full, no fill its office,
      Talk, Private Secretary, say,
Hearst for Berry—is very busy man;
Private Hearst home—cold day—send Berry not away.
Business manager, Private Secretary talks.
    Hearst Boss, private man, not like talk Berry—man.
Berry—man—dead—like let Hearst off,

Home Hearst **come**, Berry—come too—Berry—man,
   Raise Berry—man—Berry—raise,
     Raise—Berry—man—off,
       Three—days—waited,
         Hearst—way busy—Hearst.

Berry—waited stretched—inside **office,**
   Berry—man catch—no Hearst,
     Raise—dead Berry—man **take fire;**
       No good man to **Our** Fan Boy,
        Away from Home—to Last
         Come this—My Way—Hearst go
         Take him—hold up—let down—easy,
Last come by First—Hearst,
   My Hearst—kick out wink—
     I burn—I sink—you down,
       Go, down—up Hearst, come **up warm**—
        By me.

I hold **you** all warm, **in** My Arms of Love,
Let them come fly away, for My Home Above,
Let lead you above—try you—above heard,
Let them believe you, I have I kick, you, well,
Let them take this man life—Boy sick, now, then, well,
   I swear by my writing hand,
     I fulfill, burnt all, blind in the field of hell,
       It best you come keep up—
        Up doing—very—well,
I hold direct, to course, all wings above,
   I fly you all, for the Home of Love,
     Let me lead them from ignorance and slime,
       Let me lead, please, lead then,
     I bear you away over the fields of crime,
       Let me—please—lead,
     Will will bear with you all over
       In the wings of time.

     Let me kick full, you I do very fine,
     I run all over, to throw up your crime.

     I burn one in it, I burn man in it out of time,
     Forever—I throw up—all crime,
     Now as ever—I never—I Am
     Out from the middle—of for never.

Fire—red—hot Saviour self—feel fine,
I Am a long time—I **Am** come Home—A man.

P. S.—Let her come—in before this
            Your—Saviour—man,
Save her—**man**—Save I—u—or—man—Save—I—our man,
       Save your—man, Saviour is A man.

      Two Hearts beat—Hearst as **one,**
      Beat—Two Hearts—By One,
      One, two—Hearst beat, by One,
      One, Two Hearts beat, by one,
Beat one Hearst—take One—Two Hearts,
A—man—take Two—Hearts—you beat one—Hearst,
Take Two Hearts—Yoke to One—Hearst—A—man,
Yoke Two Hearts—one Hearst beat—A—man,
Two Hearts—Yoke beat One—Hearst—A—man,
Hearst take—Two Hearts—beat **one—man.**

      Thoughts—dictations—George Washington.

Home in Home **of God—rest** Washington **style,**
U. S. America, **Washington** your style—see **no crime,**
I Am, **your Saviour, self,** see man, the crime **of time,**
Saviour Goods, man **First** to Last all **Time,**
In Time—Saviour Goods—First, Last, **all time.**
First and Last Saviour Goods all time.

      Breeze me I be—come **to take A—man,**
      I Am Kill Quick—I fool A—man,
      Fool man—I Kill Quick—take breeze—A—man,
      I rest easy everywhere in me—A—man,
      Rest easy everywhere in me—A—man,
      Everywhere in me rest easy—A—man.

      I look out into you, a round way **off,**
      I look around you. away off in to me,
      Soon I **look away, round off,** you into me,
      I so disgust, **the breeze, will measure** your mind,
      The breeze I measure, disgust your mind,
      Your mind the breeze measure, disgust yourself,
Breeze your mind for the breeze—measure yourself disgusted,
I disgust you mind the breeze measure yourself
For the last breeze, measure yourself, mind you,
      You mind **or** the last breeze—measure disgusts you,
      Measure **your** mind for the last disgusted breeze,
      Last for your mind measure breeze disgusted.
   Treat it fair, will you be so disgusted,

Disgusted, it cannot be in it is without you,
 It takes you out of yourself, away off disgusted,
I am disgusted, Myself, so I stay away most outside Myself,
I take what comes to me as My best good for me,
 Good for me I take what is best for me,
 Take what is good, I am best for me, I am good,
 My breeze keeps me from hard mean dirty work.
The law of late so late I do not change,
 I do not change late, old man, this is My Law,
  Old man of late this has not changed the law,
   Of late this has not changed, this is My Law.
This not change, old man, this is My old Law,
 This is Old, this is My Change, this is My Law
  From over, ever for never to A man.

  Make bread of wisdom flowers,
   Mix with Blood Saviour, Self,
  Eat Saviour Self, be Merry Berry Joe Mary.
   Woe man—Berry—man—with A man,
    Wo—man—A—man—
     A—live.
    By—Eli J. Joseph—Berry—man.

VERY GREAT SLIGHT.

Brain waste, Wasp—nest—FREE PRESS,
 Free squeeze and squash the nest,
  Press opinions together—kill stingers,
   Kill or kill stingers, through you
For the very Last Time, fear down to kill stingers,
Stinger light on my head, mad like, insane body,
  His brain went up the flew,
  He he drives his down stinger,
Stinger in my head, I look another way,
  I am ashamed to scalp him off,
His his slight waist brain is the take mind off.
Waste run out his stinger, brain waste, from below his waist,
  He is knocks him off a body,
 I knock him out, on his head, off my mind,
  I am saved, in time a very bad sting,
He stings he does, the Wasp does up himself,
  I double him up, he in his intended stinger,
Back the Wasp throws his sting—her
  In his own face, and breaks his, his waist breaks,

His brain cracks, he flies to pieces, and I heel him down.
  This is the Wasp-nest Biography.
  This is the Wasp's record of God's Work.
I step on him, his wings dry up, blow away
  End even of his head, he cannot crawl
  Up to Dictations Washington style.
He without waist, out of brain, out of season
With his stingher, he himself fly weak, crawls away to die.
It left in its nest, these few lines of its condemnation,
  They hang, his is character in his nest,
    A San Francisco—Weekly Wasp,
      Illustrated on paper,
    With his spirit of the times he left—
  So—So—So—Buz—Buz—Buz—Zee—Zee—Zee.

[At this date circumstances are such I cannot procure the Wasp review of Gabriel's little Book (record of original) Gabriel's Trumpet. Later I will endeavor to see the statement of the Wasp. At present I can only turn towards the Electric-spark and see an outline of their opinion of the little Book—their idea of Gabriel's Trumpet. I turn on the flame. It shows he commenced something—B–z–z–z—and continued to say that Josia Joseph, of old Son-o-ma, had given an unearthly howl; called him the author of Gabriel's Trumpet, when he is only a-gent. (Reader class may judge the Wasp's praise of the true author.) Wasp went on to state the author of Gabriel's Trumpet was insane. Then at times the Wasp was wild and raving, unjointing itself, saying, Sacrament O Shake-spears ghost should come to tear up the homestead where Gabriel's Trumpet originated. Continued raving about some young man had written lines to a deceased cat, and said, Men-do-c-I-no. The Wasp was raving mad; before I ever saw his nest, he should have sense to know the lines in Gabriel's Trumpet cannot be compared to a dead cat. Still he was pleased to make the comparison. You may understand better by a copy of the pictures of his brain. I do not say above is exact—see a copy of Wasp's review. Some time, if I do, I give his opinion to future. It is, perhaps, best I should not give it now, to allow his influence to appear. The case

stands at **present, and** allows **me an** opportunity to **continue**
to plead for my own protection the time I accept. Who **is**
the one would not wish a **book** he claims, to be a success? **I**
am an exception. **I hope this is** a success. We will then
proceed.]

Vers–us Wasp–Nest–Again hive-swarms.

HE NOT **IN IT** MAY LOOK ON **AND ENJOY THE** CASE.

Wasps quit writing—see we divide his waist **and brain,**
   His the brain belt, below his belt, of the age,
Waist, he cannot get it up, his brain is after age,
    I beg you to keep away from his nest,
      He can sting you, mind.
I can handle him with sixteen sons of witches like him,
    But I Am Spirit, you are butter,
      He lights on you, you lose,
        You don't believe he is honey,
You know I buzz him, hear him,
    I Am not with him for money,
      Without you throw, him he never tells,
        So—buz—zee—he wants money.
I throw him, he is deceitful, for money,
    Study him to know how far he is from honey.
When you fire him you can see through him,
    He was pleasing, simple, for money,
      You see what a friend you had.
He gives anything, something, be–side in with honey,
    I take my case to you, put him with the flies,
      He bothers, I give you mine in honey,
        I fire him, my honey,
I can down him, fire, eat him, he can crawl away off,
    Die to never ask me if I give him his money,
I can load his wings, he cannot fly up even with my honey,
    Or fill full with my honey.
I Am can make him fill full, cram his down him,
    I can make him back his letter—
      Kiss it back like an as—eat my honey,

He made himself an ass for money,
He is one as—kiss my honey,
When he lights on mine I give him my honey,
When I kick he leaves his feed, pocket-money,
When I kick wink out of feed—pocket my honey,
I knock the nest–hive all off the world,
My ask questions, does it all,
He is full of stingers,
He is wild, he kicks the world, so hard
The nest loosens, the hive falls away,
The young ones come out and see the world
Rolls round, they buz round and come up close
By in the breeze, and are drawn in,
Go round very quick to keep up with world speed,
Then they run in fast, close and light on her, at last
The old ones learn them, if they light without running
They fall, earth going so fast they would tumble
Over their head, the friction would burn, then
Some smash, to Atoms, smash.
Some their wings broke, they cannot fly,
They hop all crippled along,
At the last they grow some,
Their wings heal up and fly to hang on the bush as
They feel some, very much need, Berry Honey,
Dry up good,
They come out of the bush as they clip
The OLD ONES wings,
They rule the roost,
The OLD SHE, they kick her out,
She lived and burnt,
She lives one thousand years or more,
They leave one so good, they then did not love SHE.
But She, they come around to look at She,
She comes them, they over, fall, She looks them,
She She comes up to tell them, burn see forever,
They fear, I save, hold I take them,
Love me, keep them back, they stand noble manhood,
She wants them to burn her, She tries them to feel hot,
She tells them She was in it, She Beauty Happiness.
They love me them I hold, stand noble man,
She comes up, they fear will not go in with She,
She comes them to love them in it,
She goes to show them
She is love, beauty, happiness, life, years,

She in it to show
They see—SHE,
They see—She—is burnt,
They see her, rust, old and haggard,
They leave She, they never deceive her,
She burnt all up, then ; SAVIOUR-A-MAN

There—last She—Saviour-A-man,
Now—by Poe—Two Make—steam her—flowing
This life—Dry Washing—son.

My—Poe Two Make—Steam—the world,
    By this life—come—Washing-sons,
    My steam—Elijah fill full—my God above.

Flowing his life—come —by—City full,
Come full—country—City full,
        O—Good—By—my God—above,
        O—I—cry—tears, tears,
        Come —to see—I love
        Thee—I love—to Last,
        Come—take me—at Last
        To Morning—Star—City.
Kill me quick—red—man.
Crucify—me like—A-man;
I will never—again—come to life.
Berry—me—A-man.
I a Scrub—Saviour—self—maid—man.
                        Toll—Bell—MARY,
                        Dead—Washing—son;
                        Dead—Berry—man,
                        Berry—dead—son
                                    A-man.
I throw all over you Nightoglisterin
I throw all over everything, My Glisterin,
Everything eats My Fly Nightoglisterin.

My Glisterin everything eats like flies.
Everything eat My Nightoglisterin, you improve like flies.
    My Glisterin—educates you, educate flies.

    I God Myself—throw—My Glisterin—to flies,
    Throw my Glisterin—to flies—God—I Am Myself.
Flies take My Glisterin—throw you up yours—with the flies.

I Am Myself—I Am God—Of God Myself.
This is By God—never small never change it.
   O—R—Good God—
   You small die.

Keep God's correct—never burn away to die,
To die correct—keep God's Work, never burn come away,
God's Work burns correct—burns all die correct.
   To keep for never—Remember Work,
   For God, to tell go—she way.
You in the beginning—keep time, remember me away.
   I was round in the beginning, look round for Myself,
In the beginning round Myself, I was looking
Round where you are yourself—I was look in, the beginning,
   I look round, all over—Myself—I know as a beginning,
I made beginning round, all over to Myself I made round to beginning.
Then I begin round again to Myself—you know to begin,
   My inside Myself.
I made something round—Myself, inside Myself, beginning.
   I feel round over Myself—to collect inside beginning.
I something inside heavy lose, I cry see—sea beginning,
   See, sea run round, something heavy
I wipe a band round heavy move float—over see,
I wipe the band round around, quick move the worst inside me.
The band touches heavy—also sea—see
It has on it the axgreaseshun of the worst inside me.
The Hub outside touches no axgreaseshun of me;
Inside they never know how they get round,
   They get round by collection, of axgreaseshun of me.
They must wash axgreaseshun of me out through themselves.
   When axgreaseshun collects heavy, I feel bad or worse.
   I burn up to dust, the axgreaseshun of me.
I floo flood over the world, I Scrub the world clean,
Dry off, then again I flood it—and scrub—all down
   As hard make wash out nooks and corners,
Then I pour fresh water all over and dry off it,
Then dry I burn slight, dust flies, pure and clean,
All the flies, gnats, wasps, spiedhers, dead,
Reinhabit flies, gnats, wasps—SHE burnt dead.
In new time flies, gnats, wasps, suck up all axgreaseshun of me,
Man—hood—woman—hood, fill up with My Glisterin,
Wash back out all come jump out of axgreaseshun,

Then again **blow me** like—Nightroglisterin,
I will shine them—Electricit—tie, button, hold **up**
                    By Electricity.
Electric—Gospel—come Public-shed—on Earth
          By Electric Gospel Wire,
Somewhere all around it collected in one spot
          In December, **1891**,
And rolled up flew all, over **on world**,
          Electricity fire **wire—sound**—
          At that time **Blows, Blows,**
          All the world hear **Gabriel's Trumpet.**
Gabriel blows Trumpet—by—Night-o-glisterin,
                    The Morning
                    Bright—Light.
At that time—Gabriel, Two Strikes, earth **again,**
Lights one tip toe in Son—o'ma—Count—one,
          Two—Starts and spreads hands nailed and
Foot rough shod, kicks and knocks the
          Heads off the world as SHE brings them
          Around, he rakes them off and
          They all out, see they look into space,
                    Reinhabit new heads, open to see
                    They were there and hung in space.
Gabriel, when **he** leaves this sound as the
          Words fresh **from** Trumpet,
The world **for all time** to hear same as from
          Original—Gabriel's—Trumpet.

Come see Saviour-self—
          By Son Joe—My Baby **Boy,**
                    From out—Dupe-on—in it—Street,
                    Sand—Friend—from—Sis—go out,
                    Son can see **her** in the Electric Light.
                    Son could **come** her—like Electric Light,
                    He keeps away independent as Light,
                    He is the Light—independent American,
                    His Electric deadens yours,
                              You Gas Light dead,
                    Dead—is Washing—Son,
                    Dead Son—is Washing—son,
                    Watch—Two Strike—Dead son,
                    Son DEAD—Two Strike—dead Son,
                    Pass—**Two** Strike—he is dead, dead,
                    Satisfied—so—Crucified,

Crucified—all—Satisfied.
I rise him—from—work go,
He that lives—never—dies again,
He lives—for never—again,
He that rises—is above life—again,
He rises—his life—forever again,
He never—descends to—low life,
He is Mary's—Saviour,
   She is—alone.
He brings her—up at the Last.
He I Am, Chri—Last and First,
I Am they cry me—First and Last,
  First—I Am—Last,
  Last—I Am—First,
I Rise—know—I Am Home,
Home—at Home—At Last.
  Rise—Rise—
  Then—sit there,
  You—you get there,
  Bug—her just
  Two Strikes—Two-Strike.

Dead Berry—Indians—Boy,
Indians—Berry—Dead Boy,
Berry did—for Indian Boy,
Good—honest—Indian,
Honest—be like—Indian,
Indian—brave—honest,
I Am—honest—Indian,
I am Big Buck—Brave—A man at last.
Man first—to last a man,
Good over all—My God above
     Good-Bye.
Do not leave me here very long
I will work—until you—kick me out
Or if so—save me—I do not about care
For future, I don't care to want,
To heat, hell for some, many years,
   10000000
You think—grease me—the Gospel Wire,
I would burn quite quite quick heat white here.

Berry—my man to leave Two-Two Strikes,
I rise on an on I gap, rise and quit for myself,

Tell Saviour self, I rise and quit, quiet,
I believe on—Breeze save Breeze believe be save,
Go back, study, O, I work.
I over am under below at work—I am below decently at work.
He looks, look see where a God Spirit goes out
At a hole in the sky,
You better then bet he sees through the hole
Out to the Light of God Himself,
The Light Sky is his shed roof,
Of course he sees out of the shed,
His eye is Light, Light Eye sight,
He looks through his eye, the Light of God.
God Spirit tells him look tow, I Spirit,
I will do your writing, I will work your hand the way
I want it, you are tow go out self, give me plenty of room,
I want all your little body to run the pencil,
I don't need help, I use you, I made you a purpose,
You are we are Two Strike Pencil Power,
Last for 1000000—yrs Electricit
Dog-gone She away, see God Fulfills First space Electricit yrs
Save your picture First—with you Last.
I rise to get, and this my last picture, the first picture at first,
I sit and take it when I am in study over through my writing.
It is taken in by Electric in the world,
Gabriel's Trumpet blows, Gabriel blows busted,
There is nothing left of him but his picture, this is something,
Exact, the exact true fulfillment, his life,
As true of life as this of body, and more true—I Am it is
True as I am through.
When—I rise you bet—I am through,
Here I am, you watch me—till you through,
And you will see—you—I cannot get you through,
You must fish—bait—and cut for yourself through,
I am going—fish—fish for myself through—I cannot help
You—fish—rather I can ask you—fish—for me,
Thor—fish plainly I ask you for me—fish help me fish the fish.

I will never back my Word for witches sixteen witches,
I throw stuff this, all this shoo at you—I must, must I,
Much must I stop—before I get I must stop, I stop or I am
Before I Am through.
I am out of room in my copy, I will not copy,
I am or-igin-all through and not through.
I go through sick tire—look up quit this style is work,

I glad quit you, I gap, stretch, look through out of myself—
   Out—go.

Dead Berry—Clean Play—Out in Work
Looking over the Spires—Steeple Sparks—from Jasper City,
His Spirit—Much Known—himself a man,
His Spirit So Much Make more than himself it makes him feel
His Spirit is Big Great Big Much It Spires Sparks
   Out him to make him the man,
His Spirit come to make him the man that was to come.
Make out of his shell—Gabriel's—Trumpet shell him
   Close to her the Trumpet out of his shell he looks,
   Close to hear Trumpet Blow copy—sound—he copies,
Electric sound—Gabriel's Gospel Wire in ears, eyes, head,
He sparks all over and writes looks what he hears on paper,
The, he man, give future time, Original Gabriel's Trumpet,
   To his ear Cup—id He fills him there—whisper sound,
He repeats, dictates, interprets Gabriel's Trumpet Original
   Cupid I—flies feel around over rule—all the stingers,
   Out makes him leave and forget the, there was a Wasp,
     And he looks up again Cup—well fine fire,
   They throw there the wipe at wasp—stingers nest,
     They are together again against all,
      They are My Two—Cuplids,
Here they are Two—is—One—One—is—Two,
First—comes last—last come first
One—in—Three—One—makes—Three
One makes—Three—For One—Two—Strike—Shoo.
She—the steam her whistle blows
  I am ready—My God Above,
So I ready I don't know what to do I if I do write this
  I do write for you right take me
    For I don't want I know—when I do wright
     But you know you have this right
      If I am when I write I know but you know
I know this is right, I have perfected my right
  I write—I know I write
    I can read plain hear what I write
I have perfect, where I write Cuplids box ear to know right
Dead body Berry—Cuplids each side say, hold Hans her right
   I go—dead—Berry—myself—leave the Light burning.
I go in study—correct make any change make
  Myself made all—no else one make change this
   You correct, change or correct —for me

I will change or correct this my own personality
No other one make a last change for me
I am here for some little time
I can change—but I cannot correct this,
This is quite correct, it suits me you see,
God make—me know—I am through,
Pinch—kick my ribs—outside in,
And I will—away—Save your—business.
You know you made me write this business,
You know what the business is,
And I came in business, I am in for the business,
I will take the hold hog business, I will, yes I will.
All you have to do is talk business, I Am with you,
You know I Am, I am with you not for money,
I Am inside in it, I stood and waited long
For you to kick me in it, you fooled me
In the business, and I don't care for snap,
I bang whack full of Electricit spark, out of it
I can get to wait along out, but you,
You know what I am—you—you know
Her that is is not not—S–Her is not burnt,
S–Her is beauty, bright happiness,
Of course you know—if she don't want—she wants,
Of course when she wants—she wants, wants, wants,
I can stand and starve stiff if she kicks me, she wants,
Stood I did—stiff—tamed—before ever she kicked me out.
I kicked almost her when I was starving—I from First,
I kicked her almost, quite heat hot out.
I did not want her to think me an Old Rider Hag–hard,
I did not care think, she tell me I Am Old Hag–guard,
I do not care, I will take S–Her if S–Her is Old hag—god,
Yes I will—remember—my God Above.
You may take my case to Yourself,
Of course I not think to quit and leave you,
But you can tell a Wash–at–home and let
Him tell a raft of the business to me.
It is a dirt nasty after a fair,
And of course do not think to turn Yourself
Outside inside, for that little stickher—business,
I Am satisfied coming along very well—away from crucified,
And of course I do not think to want you, connection
With my fool business.
You may send me a bottle of your Spirits of Glee,
And I can pull through, to never know me burnt crucified,

You know me, my life long, by my brain,
I swear, I through, never pull my life.
Of course you know how fields of fill full feel
I can blow myself—you know I say I Am.
   Big—Chop—Chippy—off the Block.
I do not trouble—this is Glisterin your ear
  At right time, and out at the other,
You know by G. Trumpet I can Blow—to you,
To throw down A Chip high—off the Block,
  Can I come—around to Chippy—again,
Can I scheme—to say you will let her be judge
And I the Merchant of—stand before Venus,
Les S-her be judge of Anton-I-O—the Merchant of Venus,
You know me say Love of Antonio Bound for Venus
  Is Elijah in Gabriel's Trumpet—he is Antonio.
Let her take the case in that Gabriel's Trumpet—letter,
 I Am the Scrub—I will stand all consequen—sas.
   Please God—fire the whole—business,
And for all time, this let—her—hold Venus as the judge
For Anton—i'o's B-ass-an-i-o, &c.
This is his Picture Mary Al-I-ce Tail-or—strumpet,
  Is Venus—judge—his for yourself,
You may judge—his sparks can fly all over you,
He is so far above—you are below him judge Venus,
  You are the judge never the less,
You are the judge Venus the First—never left at Last.
  I cry, I sleep, I cry a sleep,
  I awake—like Fresh—sport,
For my choice judge—give me the red—in Spirit,
 I think I can come on alone with one other
  Bottle of the Spirits of Glee,
Even I may not use up so much—My God above
  I will bring you the rest.
R-F-S—if she don't her lay egg business machine
  May rust without oil, (if she don't
  She don't believe my fire,) I give her
Oil grease her, to slide up the Gospel Wire.
My night Light is burning far out into day Light,
I Am weary to quit, wait I come to stand the slight,
S, I Am Able, prepared to stand her slight like A-man,
 My God above says—I Am—not Adam,
He says I am the Scrub Saviour, self—Adam,
  He says as you know what you are
   I will save you our Boy.

Bee **Joe be all the good** names, can **think of me,**
· **This** is Joe—Dead Head—in it.
Inspire Joe some of you
To write about—about You.
When you do I give you all in it.
So fire he gives all the world,
And he **gives his word if he** forgets to mind,
Will stay herd with **gnats** over fields of time.
Clouds rolling—away—Light out fine
Come roll out into Son—Shine
Electric Dead Light—of Son Sparks—still **burning**
This Dead Son gives you, My Fearful **Churning,**
He **cries,** he cries in with **you a little,**
Cry **his cries** back—if you **think feel a little,**
If you think he **is** little, he can cry his **cry to burn you** little,
His eye Light **can** shine top, to your **bottom you,**
He can shine his shoo—through at your **head.**
This is the Son—Shine—Shoo **off,**
This is the Sons Shoo—Shine away off,
This is the Son Shine—Shoo Shining away off.
Do you **think** he is stretched—By Miss—Ouri?
He was last Born in lived in Miss—Ouri,
First born in Mis-s-ouri—he lived there—he came west,
His Dad was Dick—Berry—man,
He came **west** young man, twisted round—and round,
Nearly quite around the round world, came sick of it,
Settled a quiet farm–her—in Son–o–ma Count—y in
Calif–or–ni–a by **Pa–C–if–I–c** O–Ce–An, C–Cal.
There Sky farming **found flew around Ann.**
Joe found his Venus, aud Venus **found him,**
And they flew close together many **times.**
They love, talk, quarrel, love to love without love.
They almost burn, she kicks him out he fires her;
He comes **to** love Pa–O–See quite
Sick of love—we could handle—him
Quite easy—he was for—purpose
He proposed—she refused—she was a purpose to refuse.
We handle him—and hand him—a Purpose;
He Pro–poses—to accept it—never to refuse.
To full fill **it he can** do just about as he please, for me
This is his picture containing—Spirits
Savage devil **heat,** heat—red—white—he Blue—Fire
Out into a–man.
This Boy's life he writes from pictures

Of his own life,
Which full fills My Promise, the last page of the
     Old Testament.
He full fills the Two Strikes Saviour.
He is going to camp—red man expect to look out,
Red man—he wants to camp with you.
     Use your—Judgment—to your—advant-age;
To advance your age—use your Judgment.
This is—Judgment—this is the Son Judge —ment,
    Wants—Jews—Indians—catch on
      Roll under—with pale face,
      I Roll the world with all on it,
      They go under I Quiet Force,
    I fire—I flood them, to kill, eat, drink, die,
    Dead Berry—Joe Berry—Dead to stay with me.
      Light—let her—be Light.
My God above—quit—we Two Strikes—must quit.
     Remember—Washington—memory,
         Good—Bye—Love.
     I cry—and draw in—my tears,
     It must do—for world—country,
       I—go—good—Bye,
       David—Coppers—field
       Raises—Leather Stockings.
This is My Son—The—Path—Finder,
I will have to go—I will write—to-morrow,
     At it—I will work forever at—
       He—goes dead—asleep,
     Man machine—will not—write,
       I wake—him—Rise—Son,
He the only one—in his family—Abel Writer,
He writes for all—the family—most
     His family a race of fools,
     He is the Last—Boy—man—in the family.
First—and—Last to family
He is the only Good man in his family.
There are no good women in the family.
My God Above, take off the Electric Band-age—I run away,
Now—or—sooner—I am Ass shamed off myself;
I shame my family—are they of me?
     My God Above—we take—keep our cases—together
Compare cases we ought, we are down to zero
     We ought—to be—as-shamed
Let them bother to dam us up, then at Last breeze First get even

My God Above we must stop.
    Please—I am to remember the round up
I was out on the plain yesterday—the herd uneasy—moving
The Big Round up is close I must—my fulfill.
We keep in this business—they will all come up around
Us up up up—they cannot round us up though.
He is raised—he is not dead—any fool see that sees,
He First was Dead—by Work—i was over the dead
I worked his arm—when Dead—I worked him Dead;
He was Dead—i made him work—dead dead at work
      He has n good Spirit-man—fool may see
His was Good Spirit—Make—Dead Berry-man see,
Good Spirit make Berry—Dead.

    Sick Sentiment—from Friends—sick of it,
    He was Dead—to please—the fool—that reads
    He is pleasant—was dead—the fool may read,
    The fools read at last—I was pleasant—he was Dead,
    Good Spirit—raise see—Son Again.
He caught—Great Spirit—He would not let go easy,
He must live a long time after again,
    He stretch decent—dead close streets—three days,
      Send—Friend—Sis—go,
    Look streets—dead Berry—A man,
    I come they—cannot—move him,
    Stretched—decent member—three days,
I keep—All Hearst—away—from—Dead—Berry—man
Three days—I Raise him—decently,
He stretches—moves—and walks—for home,
    Flies over the—Bay—up—Valley
    Son-o-ma—Pa is at home,
    Son come—by Steamher—Railtraceit,
    Come come on—his on track—with him his steam
      He was—The Electricity Man.
    Eyeyes of fire—sparks, track, stears by Electricity,
      He could go all around close to world,
      Hold—by—Electricity,
      He—My—Electricity—man.
He was Dead many times—by My Electricity,
I close to him—bring him to life—by Electricity.
    I Am the One, the only One
      Electricity—King.

Compliments of Joe to the Sioux Nation.

Is this I Am—This quite sick Shoo Shine look is away off.
It is Berry—he was with a-gent of the red-man's claim agency.
    It is very good—it is a very good picture.

    This of him known as Joe Gabriel (was with Gabriel) a
Confidential Clerk of the Round-up Trumpet Company; also
redman's agent.   Chief–Two–Strikes sometime.

                                    I Am,——Joe.

All animals insect men—water fowls hold the same
                By Electricity Wipe—of Band,
They all increase, decrease, multiply, equal
Advance their age shows—educated flies.
                Under—Fly—Wheel—Band
                They all, hold—suck—sustainan–ants
                From the wipe Fly Wheel—Band
Around them—the Fly Wheel—Band–makes–many different
Sizes—spied–her—flies—wasps—beatalittle.
Also the Fly Wheel Breeze—Band wipes over
U. S. America—keep her—purify—herd,
You are most responsible—all under—the Fly Wheel Band
I hope I can trust you a little breeze,
With you sank–still flies—sanctify—purify.
He I Crucify—life, I mean, I mean—I crucify.
When he crucifies again—never come to life
He comes to me—I mean—you no better,
                You worse—much worse.
He lets her fly—he goes in with the rest of the flies,
Only he Strikes for My Home—Three Pa—come in
Says modest—cry like—Cir-'cus words I never did like.
Much that is not heavy of it, Pa my worst was
Burnt or brute, blast, son—bith bitch or–dam man myself,
                Or dam man by myself alone—and of course
                You may now know for certain, I burnt then,
                I burnt them many years—in a hell of a place,
                        For that I paid well for my trouble,
An I now over by my—Three Pa I want to come Home,
I if I don't act straight square stahed—
Straigh—for you My God—you stamp
And bruise me the burn for years, years, years,
                Forget all about where I am,
        Leave where a buzz–hard never roost–her
        Or flies blow her, and then I am perfet, satisfy,
                Crucicry cry, I am tears, tears, tears,
                        Cry for I am burning,
I am satisfied—SHE burnt—SHE is the world to fill.

New Band on earth—Electric Fly Life Band,
SHE—take New Electro Gospel wire–life,
Then I will not bother—I will leave you as
The judge, if you come get in Electric Wire Gospel,
You can then handle the boys to kill—time,
        If you let them fly around and light

On your knowse much, sense—they see you
    Are no good, dummy Electro Woescene.
Stave sword them, off **to** improve their time,
It may—times take time many of them are no good,
    Find them out many times in time,
      I must pull away from **the** business,
Or run myself headlong **into what** I did
Not start in for—by **once go** read Gabriel's Trumpet,
Study a hard study **and you will** find out
What I am. I do **not know a** word of this
    Stuff, to repeat, **along here** may pages,
      Last, Last, **Last,**
      I Am—Berry—**A-sleep**—in it.
My life plain shows, plain as pa-per,
It is written on this little pa-per Book,
    More **to** remember me, a scrub
    Than **any** Saviour self, business,
    I **know what** in the world SHE was
    First and Last—Last and First
      Two Strikes.
John, away with yourself—you **knock** Elijah out of Time,
Pa Made US come **to** keep US **fighting** like,
If I did not **work myself over like this** some you—lose,
Some over lose—you lose—some, brain themselves—to lose,
    Now—then—now—I go with sixteen
    Spirits Power, devils **into me,**
    Revise—not—you **improve.**
Well now—some sent I ment I **scent**
From A the writer of this, this revised Old Testament.
My God above—use my little stink brains all they are worth.
    I run out and lose myself.
Run and come little stink before I—you **know** what—well
Use your little stink brains before soo—or sooner
I come back a fresh bird—not as pickle pish;
Horrid, Horrid—ground witch—this terrible, terrible stifing,
    But not—it is written, my it must must go.
      Fishing hooked myself.
I corral around, charged it **to** care full less.
Remember these still, only the kind and pleasant lines.
    Hook **out the** memories of our present times,
    My **God above**—**I** have—no come in it,
    Sooner **hook**—**out of my** brain—serious settled,
    Now throw on the fly–wheel–band some Glisterin.
    Let them in suck–shun for sus–tain–ants,

Some may come to believe you corralled a few
Brains—in can-in top, on can-on head,
    If then put on more.
You know I am a blister on the wheel,
For I get almost squeezed in suck-shun of band,
Patience with suck-shun—Light Air,
Fly-wheel electricity band may blister some,
A few of course there is an advantage—prac-ti-cal,
And let them up the pract-ical flies
Stand without—band practice until they stand in with
Out falling, let them practice into their in on under-stand
Where they are inside or outside, or see that they
    Move so fast they are on or in or stand in
      Or above outside find breath,
Moving so fast they cannot see they are falling,
    And stretching—and gone without the band
      Brings them in around in on time,
    Of course the band is not rub-her,
    It is Light Plain—Air Electricity
Greased with God's Glisterin—whis is nothing but
The axgreasion, the refuse love, His Bodywire,
    They cannot see attraction of wire in tire,
    Moving of course, they conbut—they don't
Glisterin love attraction, God holds and moves all inside
Easier that they move themselves, sick in six in,
    My God above how can You come to to claim
This little Book; please let Your Litt—e Great Spirit
That comes, claim that it, my God above,
Do not let of course my God above claim it,
      Have I have drawn Your Spirit
      And have the right wire, sound Cuplids
    To hear Gabriel's Trumpet when on the in of
Belt comes around to dictate and interpret
My God above, in your Name Cuplids
Great Spirit gives this all the flies,
Great Spirit never let Cuplids grow to
      Big head deceitful.
My God above Great Spirit as far as a——
Know Cuplids Your Airy Big Light Space,
He will not take praise, he sits and boxes
    My ear—still my head
    Great Spirit I cannot praise,
My God above I cannot praise
My God above—our—book—my my,

My God above over look my wish—so long.
Weakness, I do not of course my God
Above, I have caught a Big Spirit
Which praises me for something.
     I can look back and remember
     A letter—something when I was dead.
My God above, I am ashamed, I cannot
Praise the Great Spirit, I can only cry
You to overlook mine, these weak tears.
Of course Great Spirit can see as well
As send Cup—on to sound box my ear.
That Great Spirit come to sound
Gabriel's Trumpet, am I the one to hear
Him correct—dictate and interpret to me?
       For over Fly–Wheel–Band
     My God above—I am full—to blow over.
     Please let Great Spirit stay with me.
     I hear Gabriel Blows his Trumpet.
Let him stay and take me, I am the Joe,
     I can praise sweet for Gabriel's Trumpet,
     And can try to die or whip the son of a ——
     Who ciks at Gabriel's Trumpet.
I am soon very ready to anxious for a
     Sulliman Sooner presently
I knock his eye blak out of his sky light.
     It Spirit hold him his hands, still I can
     When I do a man wrong I am willing to punish
       Myself a little, he can defend himself
And knock me sound, I am in heavy for Gabriel's Trumpet,
     And of course my God above that is the only
       Trick I can do on the ring,
     And of course they can beat me bad to kill,
       Bruise me with their new tricks,
But I am the single act man—let me be
       The boss star one act man at my business,
     And I will swear at myself, I never steal their
New tricks, I never copy their new take off trick,
I was to come with my suckcess–trap–whese act,
I think it is original, I am sure I never seen
       Before I paid my sense to see it.
Of course to start and work out my little act
I reflected on all their styles, I could remember,
Gradually rolled their whole cir–cus up for a no–not
     And stretched my own tent.

My only attraction–sign–May admittance 50c.
Blow—Blow—Blow.
Test a tent of Gabriel's Trumpet.
Inside of course they thought it a hum–bug,
Because I had collected a few of their animal words
And stuck around on the benches a few Gospel Hymns,
And the center pole Shakes–spear–words entire;
But the sons of — can go to —, I started in without
Any theirs, and outside the Gospel, will give
Any a life pass to find anything not original,
Of course they only see pictures, the styles, and methods
Of all the world we passed coming on the trip,
And because they have seen the words and their poets
Had a good sensible style.
I do dispise to have them say my pictures are not
Original, but they have, many of them have,
And when I was a way side the wasp sting me like
Hell, if I fired rocks at him, forgive me;
I was mad as hell; of course I do not
Swell—swear—I not swolen very much,
But his stingers I do not like around in my tent,
So I wished to rock him away,
I think I will never apologize to him, or
To any of the audience who hear of it.
If I have a slim audience on account of the wasps
Of course I can say no more than defend myself,
And they may defend him and stray away—Brush
With him—I am not to let anybody sting or
Say to thinks say–cred—it is not yourself,
If they do not TRUST me I can fire eat the sons of
Or try to dam them down, against me.
There is a man, in my town, in the brush—
His name is Brush—he owns large tracts of it,
He is mammon—I owned a small brush
Patch—and wished him to help me—I was litt–e,
He was big mammon—I—Lemmon–squeezed him
And Fish–baited him, and he would not bite.
I waited some time, around the bank; I was going
To Fish him again—but the Lemmon–squeeze
Him again was the best—but he would not
Come to time—said young man wanted to
You–char him. I was hot and defended the
Young man—for I did not know who
He was back biting—under the bank at a fly—

I was hot at him—he came out and would not
     Bite—I named him man names, many of
     Them, they were not nice ones—he said he
     Was Volun–Tary—I told him, Mr. Volun–Tary,
     You can burn hell Two hundred an thousdans
     Of years.   I was so hot I could not speak plain—
He thought me in Toxi–cated ; it did not hurt
     Me a bit—(I never drink their fire water, not
     A drop of it on my tongue), but said to Fish
     I am always into–xicated, just the same
     Fish came in to fire me, but he could not do it.
     He drank fire water himself, then said he was left.
But hold up— back to the bank of Brush again.
See when I was standing, exicated and firing
     Sparks of dam–nation into him, he stood
Heated white—could scarce speak, he was fire
Dry—his son feared for him—felt for his life,
     And called an angel from over the way.
He came in a second, came in to defend the
Brush, but seen me the Electricity man,
     He said I had better come away——
     He smiled at me for wanting to fire eat,
     He smiled me away, I wanted to jump to fire, but
He came close and soon I left him for the angel flew my fire
     down.
Qut Fish again Lemmon squeeze him to Sant–a–Rosa.
For Son–o–ma the hub head Crank U–N–I–Verse.
     By I am A Jew Died—Dead—Petrified
       The Forrest—Joining.
By A Jew I Am—he that Died—Dead—Petrified
         Forrest—Joining.
In life I sailed my court—ship up and down
Port—her creek—to look over the Vale
     of Mary—Santa Rosa
     I was born by Virgin Mary Saint Rosa,
By my own memory between seven years commencing
     1884—1891—you can take my word for it.
     She does not know me—I came through by
     The Spirit of God—she does not know I am
     Any thing about me—I am a containing Spirit.
     Man—God's Great Spirit—man.
The mother Last Son to man—is Ava–C–Mee.
The father Last Son to man is Dick—Berry–man.
     They in the Garden Eden—Adam—Eve

Born son of man in misery, he grew up, went
His own **way—God** was to please him—educate
Him in life—with His Great Spirit.
Educated down **dull** by books—educated
   Life Bright Light by **love to hear sound**
   Of Gabriel's Trumpet.
  SON OF GOD BORN AGAIN, COMMENCE
   Anew the race for life.
Great Spirit agent from God writes God's promise,
  Breeze measure opened size to—take minds
   This Bundle Pattern.
Make your own pattern by this—you **may** improve
  Yourself in future time, do **not** improve this.
  Revise yourselves in future **time,** do not revise **this.**
This suits the a-gent of God in **the time** he
  Leaves the world—this **is a** record of **the time**
  The Agent of God **was looking over lives at the date**
  This **was written—this is far above the**
   Average of the time.
This is different from the age of the Old Testament,
  I cannot **say this** age is any better,
In this age I **can say they** do not please God **any better—**
  Not **as well as the Jews**—please worse,
  Adam, **Eve bad** then—Adam **now** Adam sight **worse.**
Eve is advancing, **by love** of God man comes to respect **her,**
By Love of God **she** before marriage is to some their
  Look up to Authority—of course they all **fly**
   Very low, but some fly much lower
   Than Mary Santa Rosa.
There are **many** fritter around like, **I mean gaiety,**
She **flew around** with all quite happiness, eye mean to Adam,
  Live—beauty—happiness—eye—**mean** Adam.

  ADAM FIRST AND **LAST—again** BORN—to man.

   To **start God** looked his Sight on earth,
Sight commenced **by** saying—I AM MUD,
I Am left—I Am nothing—I must make myself,
Commencing small nothing—that is nothing—I WILL MAKE
  Add more **to mud,** and shape myself to **wire** life.
He came **to sight them** around that formed **his** mind
  In moist and dry air—collected **heavier** substance
  Out of the air moist and dry—the First thought
  At Last hardened—and collected more substance

To some shape over thought, smoothed around, made oval,
And dent by corrections, commence to harden the substance
  Slightly, took a cloudy evening for it.
  Waited and collected substance from the air,
  Waited, took it easy, collect another thought in shape,
  Collect more substance, warmed slightly by sunshine,
    Harden slightly.
Commenced to have hope of shaping himself to Last,
Commenced to collect many thoughts more than he—expect,
Commenced to know that God looked him by His Sight,
And was making himself, and still he could not know God.
  He could not gain understanding of God's ways.
God was making him to remember he was not making God.
  He wanted Last him to Last and Love God,
  And know God asked not to praise but reverence Him
  As the Maker, and wanted him to know he did not have
    Anything to commence making himself,
    And to respect God for commencing him,
    Giving him sight for him to commence thoughts—
    His thoughts shaped, God gave him Spirit,
    Collected substance in air in years gradually,
    Increased to form the shape of man—grow by
  Sun light, gradually spirit collected and improved,
  In time commenced to work, act and walk—attending
  Man's affairs—at first only worked in thought,
  Waiting to strengthen grow in sunlight waited,
  Needing substance to strengthen Light Flash
From air grew in density by washing through rubbing.
Moving flesh from dirt collected clean grew hard
As collected sand—containing Spirit Sight of God.
  By Sun shine collect gave through him life of
  Electricity—his eye flesh God's Spirit formed.
How he knew not—He was strength nothing
  Wasted from his own body containing Spirit.
  He needed no further support—for him at the
  Same date commencement, God's Sight was
Forming around him the Wo–band, she never knew how
God formed her—she came by Spirit—she never knew
  God's Spirit formed her—as the man—
    Formed her a purpose for a purpose
She was to refuse the time comes when the man would see her.
She was to refuse to show—then His man would respect her.
She was to shame the man for leaving his Maker
The man would come to love, respect his Maker, remember

And not fall to throw—his body—to wo–band there was danger
Of it because she was Electric flesh God's
Wo–band beauty bright happiness for Electric man.
When thoroughly matured God gave the promise they could
Join together Electric flash and show light as one spark.
The penalty was great if they did not mind and
Mature—they could never collect His Electricity,
Which was a Great Spirit to save them at the Last.
They minding His Word to them He gave a purpose.
They would mind Him without holding away a purpose.
They came together for God a purpose they refused.
Each other—while they loved they shone sparks of
Electricity—they loved they—they endeavored to
Con–ceal it—but could not—God made the flies to
Witness if they could not conceal when they witness it,
They fly away from their selves with sparks which show
They see did not come to stand and see in it.
With the Quiet—Electric—Force they came, they left by the same
If they did not they could not improve come Electric again
They apart contain their Electricity Power improves them.
They stay away and work for their selves, improve by
Electricity containing their Electricity Sparks Shine
Bright and clear their bodies Electric lose no Light
Substance, their mind develops clean and clear.
The Electricity forms from the Great Spirit—form in
Them becomes as their own, a part of the Original
Great Spirit, which saves all the Electricity which
Leaves Him, He is self-containing, no Light is lost
In Him containing—Great Spirit is Himself, he looks
At once for man to improve, they the world disobey,
Disbelieve—shamed for years and years would not
Believe His Plain Words—Adam—do not touch—Eve,
When placed—in the Garden—Eden.
They believed God could not tell proper time, God could
Not countenance such disbelievers, for many years contained
Himself, they slighted His Power,
Who made the world—the animals on it,
At all time obeying Word to them—Nature
Talking man was different—God made him different.
He gave him the Bible—to save his manhood—to gain
The Electricity, strength—of animals to save himself
And collect spirit strength from Great Spirit, but they

Acted with the judgment **of** flies, they would **never believe He**
    Made this litt-e world—He was—thinks **less**
And less **of** them—all the time—saying those **who wished**
    Could save themselves—when they did **not take His**
    Word and wait to gain Spirit life, they **could**
    Perish. They came from nothing, if they lost
    He lost them not. He gave Adam the Word
    Which he did **not** obey—he lost—woman was a
Shabby man excuse   **He** gave **the** Word to all Adams
    Of the world, they continue the same excuse,
    Suppose, who treats—the Adam—treats himself,
    Collects his own fair, takes **his own** trip,
    Loses all **his** life before he **commences** to gain Spirit.
He runs and falls, his life away gradually,
Loses Spirit—goes gains spirit in the wrong **direct—shun,**
Grad-u-ally calls for that spirit, disobeys the
Word of God, **at** Last withers if dies, spirit **takes,**
    Burns by breeze taken away—God cannot
    Countenance—when they disobey—The Word,
    Will not believe His Power—He says the sooner **gone.**
        Then feed—he—SHE—glad of it,
      I **want to come** up to Electricit—man,
      Man Electricit, I want to get up,
Electricity man descendants—follow Electricit—you
      Come **out** of man to **come.**

P. S.—You wish to know why I wrote this Testatent,
    So Son so soon, I Am, sold **many sold** me
    In the other one—I choke **down to lose** breath,
      Think, Think—of—them—
Again—can you—bear you—my shoo-shine sooner,
I blow the whole fly-wheel-business out of and quit
    To continue—again out—you up inside of me.
        THE—WORLD—BURNT.
    By Electricity—Dead to life—Electricity man,
    Wo-band commencing—SHE commence to inhabit,
    Increase—multiply—decrease—continue,
    Wold to cone—see this, I must qut, I must qit.

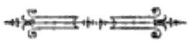

7th Scene—Time.

In the morning see the Light Burning
In that age Light turned down, I me—My think—power,
    Dim light shone out from above Son.
    His mind hears electric heat white
      Never book him with **the** flies.
Improve according to the light of your time.
He improved below—above the dim average light
    Of his time—In ages come—reflect on him.
    Leave the Electric—**Light** out alone,
Wait until you show **like** sparks of fire,
Then light out like Gabriel on the Gospel Wire.
Hold the same spark **to** feed corn—shell her of time
Never **shell yourself ignorant** previous corn—shell— of
    slime.
Many—Noble **we give them** Words fair **and bright,**
The herd **could not believe or see** God's **Power**—only love
    mite.
They could **not see—even** with **Ed—son's world invention,**
    Electric Light.
Of course there was **at** all time—previous—Noble Power,
But the fly herd **could** not see to sift the Wisdom Flower.
God by nature wrote the Bible His own **way**
    If they took His word from nature——
At last nature would draw—they would draw **their pay.**
They prefered dark ignorance—to Light of time
They pull—twisted—smirk—going the trail to furnace crime.
    Run Berry yourselves, whew, I spew sick in stomache
They collect their own—breed the dirties in slime
Improve their race in ages of time,
Savor yourself or you will not feel so fine,
This is the world previous to Electric age of time.
    He—there were many Saviours for them to mind,
A Long fellow poet, was no fool in his time.
    His style is left you—to many pleasing and kind,
All manner were the poets in their age and time.
      All kinds of sons—Ed—son—Emer—son.
The common herd **could** not see through them to mind
So I burnt **the world and left** My Son—Shoo—Shine.
He was a common **Boy** still—he—He loved **well,**
He came to me, **I saved** him—he's alone **out** of fire of hell.

I let them commence the race for life anew
He–they may breed my style of animal—so can you.
They wait in ten years with noble power,
They cultivate a full growth of Wisdom Flowers,
They harvest the crop—in season—take their time,
They come up on the road of life, feel very fine,
They stay think of the Last—by themselves above,
They never again are lowered—by the arms of love.
     You may take this Word—quite on hand,
     They were the Electric-man and Wo-band.
His mind shone the dim blue flame Electric Light,
His eye bright shining—evening star of night,
He sparks of course with her—much together,
He goes far to see her in the worst of weather,
He quits her short—off gains Electric for future life,
He came to experience—she to help him kick out gloom and
     strife.
She the only one could help him—he would not back out for
     trouble,
They came together, consume all kinds of trouble double.
Of course they were ass–shamed shuch love, the worst kind,
They cut their love short, hood–winked the flies of time.
She is very short with the pie—shows only the crust,
She comes not to show him—the fields burn—rust,
She does not wish—him to burn him—or take his life,
She only holds out love—to burn his gloom and strife. .
     His mind is the dim blue—of the Electric Light,
Dull yet steady—he does not heat hot to flicker out in night,
He burns dim electrict, feeds his light with bright love,
He improves the Light — care still — studies for the Home
     above,
He knows God must—over far big—to hold in all the stars,
He thinks God so big he studies—He can make him like little
     Venus, Mars,
He wants to feel and see God, all round holding stars above,
     He wants the direct prescription to hold,
     Gain the strength by the Electric Light of love,
     He must see she in the Electric light of love,
     He must view fields of Light of the Home above,
     He must delay long, improve his own time,
     And come be in with God he now is of course in for time,
     He must never slight God or think less of Him,
     Than He all round—His Tent—Sky-Belly—Above.
It is stretched—yes very large—you can see it is—

Commodious a—rare area, the Land of the Free,
And you may all come black—red—white—blue boys.
Wait, that is remember what I hope told you gain,
The Electricity to stamp your pass—in your—mind.
It has taken many years of toil and trouble to work up
          The brains for this Electric age,
And I want you all to remember my life—is bleeding
          Away for every page.
Man is only human, this kind—deep study toil,
          Wears life tide low—ebbs away.
You must not expect me to kill myself like this for never.
Let me awake—my—Dead Berry—at work.
          Now—then—now Berry
     Dead Berry—come Boy Joe—awake—in forever
     I gave you life—My Electricity—Man—Arise——
     From the Dead—Work—to—Me

BERRY—MAN'S PREDICK—AMENT.

After writing this Book—I find myself—broke—not a cent in
the world—you know I tried Brush mammon would not
bite—I tried my first Book—would not take—I tried to give
it away—it would not take—then I charged for it would not
take—now I have this one and I want it to take—but I can
not print Electricity without money steam—my publisher is
not mammon—I will not ride him to death—but see—this I
am forced to think to accept—a widow woman's mite— to
help—myself out—she gave the business—to Oats of Sant-a
Rosa—her name is
          I. Not—Forget
                    For—my—life.
     I was swore at by Mark U. S. Boruck,
I was staved down my roost by Agent Publis—Bancroft,
     And I was snubbed by East—on—a rich man's son,
I though him friend—but he is the scrubbiest in my time.
     I have a friend comes to my home—of course,
D—Di—on—but I bled him nearly to death
To keep me and my family alive—while I wrote this
So I am compelled to accept help from a widow woman.
     I will assure you I will not forget her soon,
The world is full of rich men who do not know what to
     Do with so much—sho she knows what to do
With her mite—might I know what to do with mammon
I well I fired the Brush—anyway—I expect to hear

About it when I come around—about where God is
   I will wonder—what does He do with me for it.
   You may tell me some time my God above
     I Am Yours, Good Bye.

   Berry—man can—on base drum—in the Circus
   Come to hear the music—follow the process—I—on
    Fall in the rear with the animals.
  String out behind the cows, horse, asses &c.
  Salva—ti—on Arm—y—band—wag—on—Justis—the Tent.
  Crowd up and all may come in.
    Tick—it—wag—on tick—checks 50c.
    Sull—I—man—Breeze be my door keep—her
Come from the Woods—Words Worlds Gospel Fair
    Show in the Sky Tent stretched
   Follow the animals in it—after the ark landed
   I made a big round up—then burnt the lot——
    Electricity man saved—Wo—band—
     Improve—future—time.
     Now we come down cases
    My Spirit out of—The Ark
  Was mostly animal—The Great Spirit has now
   Worked it up to Electricity man,
   And if you descend below him
     Good—Bye—John.
   You to me—Savior—Self——
   Dummy—stuffy—duffy—Adam—if it
  Becomes necessary again hang your breethes,
  And let your shirt go off naked.
  Miss Flyer if your organ is in proper tune.
  Sound it—like—Mary—did the—flute,
   This little is Gabriel's Trumpet.
  Cir—cus over—ladies to your homes,
  After this perform—ants—is the Side—Show,
  For which ladies' men—remain—only ladies
Back out from the ring—men to the front, this side—show
    Is not fit for ladies—to be seen in it.

    THE—SIDE—SHOW.

   P. S.—When my or—gan—ic or—gan—a—shun
    Or—gan is in proper ship—shape—I can
   Without expense—stream—over the Bridge.

P. S.—You have—take it to your friend—now
Are you in—fact—u—ated—the boy is nearly
Killed again—go—dam—him—to sound Gabriel's Trumpet.
I will swear—at this minute—wish I lose my life
If I did not hear trumpet.
I am now at PUBLIC—shed—office—I am in Sant—a—Rosa,
I Am—yours &c .

Dam Berry dam—one—two—Strikes—one.

Remember my God above Great Spirit woke me now——
You must make me—do this side show Bus.
Men consult—instruct by your—stud—y books.
Horsemen—consult breeding—old and young.
Think it all through—think of all—think all of it
Think of all—think of all worms they—where did they come
from?
Did such crawl out of the ark?—they did not.
You know ook—it would not—see one of the worms.
Profit by such theory—the wisdom—connect it not
with me,
Fear for your life—old—and young—never connect such
stuff with me.
I am in earnest—I know what the world thinks of me,
I know something—I know exact what some in world think of
me.
What can I do—I must find her—I will
Come to some good place, how will a clover—dale
Do—my God above I despise to work around
Among these flies they make me think of a Sani—tari—um
Think of all their sickness—how some could originate from
Think of all diseases think all over the family has originate
some
Think how it has spread—originate—some do their self up,
some
Think to see the world is inflecting itself, think of it, some
Breeding world think some of some of worms—do not infect
selves,
Or otherselves—but come return—I must return—to improve
Wild oats—says a lady would not loan—herself I believe he
said money,
I think wild oats are generally—about theirselves—when con-
trolling money.
I think an attorney is just like himself, fingering another one's
money.

But come, I must improve—my time to press on;
Many do their tricks—in the wild-oat valley,
Lift horses teeth—lift thousands of pounds horse flesh
By teeth—by hanging trap-wheeze—could not do with arms,
But can with teeth.   How—I may know how they do it,
My, my, come—set my battery going—these sons of—her
What can I do with them—Attorneys—Brush mammon &.
I feel bad to worse—some use me up with tricks—
Can I leave them—they many of them do their tricks,
Eat red hot iron—eat and chew grind in teeth red hot iron,
I have nothing to do with them, I respect their tricks,
They do not brag, they do not know how they can ever do so
      much,
They do not sit lazy with theirs, like the attorney, at mean
      tricks.
Or like the Brush full of mammon, sneak back bite tricks.
My God above, what can I do with them?   I am the single
      act man,
I am by myself alone in the world—this is my single act, I
      do not
See how it can hurt them, but my God above they do hurt
My feelings.   I may explain some time about an attorney
      trick;
I could not come any trick on him, I am the single act man,
I did not wish to touch my hands to him, I wish to record his
      performance
With me—to you in time—he was a very sullymanbig—still
      I am
Sure, certain, I am positive Sulli-van could knock him out of
His head so quick—he could not see—he was out of the ring,
Then—he should be hit a kick below the belt—behind him—
Please remember, my God above, he is an attorney—forgive this
When you can I will come; my God above, they do not treat
      so good,
They many times are not as good as wild oats—some worse,
      Some better, very much better, some very much better.
I hear an angel—singing—of the Saviour,
My God above, I am here in a—hell of a pickle.
I came seen the oats to-day—he says I cannot have
The widow woman's mite—he will not tell me her—he will
Not tell me her name—I can—I full—have I written—
I remember something about a widow's mite.
I tell him it would do no harm to tell me to—to me to the
      widow;

He answers he does not intend to do it.
    He answers plain, firm, and quite loud.
I feel very much offended.   My God above, I cannot expect
Any help from him—he is an at–torn–ey—business men
Tell me plain they do not wish to offend him—so so they fear
      him,
They tell me they must keep in with him, my God above,
      perhaps
They had better stay and sleep awhile with him.   I am sure
I do not please myself with the way any of them treat me;
But please wait a moment—I am somewhat pleased with my
Fish–hook and Lemmon–squeeze—then we can come to the
    At–torn–ey—I expect he wants his commission.
    He will not bite at my Fish–hook.
      I tell him—he–can–go–to–hell ;
      He tells me—I can do the same,
      And I can proceed immediately—I leave.
      I find a man—in my town,
    In the same fix as myself—no one will trust his word
    With ample security—but wait a minute,
Oates told me the lady WAS IN my town—that I wished to see.
When I saw the man in my fix, I asked to help me out,
And try and find the widow lady, for me I had hopes
Of being a success—no one in all the place would give me
To publis Gabriel's Trumpet.   I am compelled to seek the
    lady.
I kindly ask the man to help me find the lady.
I tell him to see Oats, but not tell I sent him.
He sees Oats—Oats tells him the lady is NOT IN town.
There was a lie out of Oats some side—he told me she was.
    This man promised Oats a commission,
And of course, at–torn–ey like, he gave him the lady's address,
And quickly came to me, but said he could not tell it to me,
He would tell another, and another could tell me, and
Another could tell another for me, and of course another
    Can tell me, &c., to ask the widow for help.
You see they did not want to mix up with such a small
Business as the wild mean Oats had wound us into;
But I was compelled to fulfill my life, so I proceed
    To do as I am, as I wish—I again say
To that attorney he can go to hell—mean wild——
    And I want it to remain in print
I wish my God above I could see the lady that is my hope.
You know I have tried mammon—they are distant

Mean to me—and I had better stop
I cannot print this Electricity Record without steam money.
They—he tells me it's time I commence to understand business
                ways.
I expect they give me—if I give them all mine in the world
But believe me my God above—they can go to—I am sick
                tired
Of business ways—an I am at present not feeling much of it,
And still my God above it may be best for future
It may be best to try personally to see the widow lady.
If we can get the mite to print—start this Record
May best—some value—at some time—at future time
At present they have electricity—but none of them can tell
Me where they get it from—the sons of—ought to go to—
For not helping a poor man.   I am ass-shamed myself
                But I must see some one to help me.
I am beginning to feel so tired, heavy, sick of running around
To get a little help in this place that I do not know
What to do—I—I am Two Pony Two Strike

I must go to a San–it–ari–um—I am old ragged
                Dirty—Berry—Long—Dead &c so so.
                I want to go to a Clover–dale for a while
                I nearly want to fly—to I suppose have a Spirit
With me—Let Spirit stay to direct correct me
I do not want to burn in hell for this—I how—I am
Here–or–sooner—thing in you beginning to smell them bad
I have mixed them entirely much with some of them
Creeping crawling flies wore in on it—it is infect this world is
                I would like to drop it this some time.
My God above I wonder and wonder if the widow woman
Will help me—it appears a chance—most to Last chance.
Oats says her business is in his hands and he will not
                And speaks plain loud—to say she will not
Still it appears the most—of a Last Chance of mine
You know what Brush and all the mammons what they say.
                They say it is my own fault
But I certainly need a little money—they will not give it.
                Whose fault? Is it mine? It may be
After they way—they treat.   I want nothing to do with them.
Even my own family certainly not a great deal better
                Than I am, come down heavy on my way of doing
Business.   Perhaps it is for something I never did to
                Them; I am sure, quite certain in my way,

I hope I am not too much in my own way,
    I certainly like most sometimes to have my own way.
Please hear me say I do not wish to go the wrong way.
Please take me the Last Chance—to a Clover-dale.
    I hear there is a Sanitar-I-um there.
I find I need it—I am ragged or dirty—this so long
    After dead life—so—long,
        My—God—above.
I hear of prest-on there—I believe that helps draw me,
    Or a loan myself—or a loan life herself
    To a Clover-dale—and now I remember,
    The man I sent to Oats told me there was an Oat
    Vale near—a Clover-dale close Son-o-ma—C-Cal.
My God above, I am close to some encour-age—you ment,
I expect it encourage-ment of this—pleasant name,
    A Clover-dale—I may find the widow lady
    Oats would not tell about to me—I believe he wants
    To swamp me. Please let me handle this business,
    Come near to fulfill it—I must print it—I am busted.
Brush wants me to burn, I expect—they would swamp
Me if they could. I must find some one to help me.
    Once I heard of a widow Lady. She loved God.
She gave Him the last mite. She, she would give her life
    For Him. Find some one—can I—
At a Clover-dale may I find one—In my case
I hope I may accept help—even from a widow—my case,
    If she by near—Prest-on—me,
And I am certain I have to walk many times through Nap-a
    vale,
Knights of that vale—please me come to a Clover-dale.
Please I may see in Oat vale—shoo shine myself to them.
    I may be encouraged there—if not I can see
        No worse fix than I am in,
I do not care for the sons of——tis—should burn in fire
If they were all—but I can remember the countenances
    Of some good men at present—and Ever yet
    Remember future time I must get help.
I come to the widow lady over a weary stretch of miles
        I am look old-dirty-ragged
Will she help me?—no one else would so-so-far.
My God above I am on the beat—I remember must
    Copy all these in my mind—please wait until
      I find that widow who loved God.
      They tell me it is a put up job

And I wish to see her myself.
Turn on the Light of Dead Electricity
I see plainly now—I see her name is
                No—Ra—King
            Prest—on—Son—o—ma—C—Cal.
Of course I will enjoy my journey to see the lady.
I am anxious to—so anxious I prepare all for my journey.
I am old, dirt, raggy, I start in the morning time.
I am going to tell her—please lady know I am in heavy
            heavy trouble.
I may stay to tell her more or something else—we will see.
We will see each other about that in time—of course I will
            enjoy my trip,
At any rate I cannot care any worse than I wish to see her.
I can say at any rate I found her in spite of the Oats of Sweet
            Rosa.
I will tell you how much I am worth when I come the
            widow lady.
She has a mite, I hear—I can think of two mights close
            together.
If you hear this please say you were deaf or could not hear
            good.
This is only the band wag-on with the Trumpet
The weather is stretched very cloudy, I cannot help it,
Rain shine or rain fair I am busted—for this widow is in it.
I will bust to see if she can see through me—I in it.
I will have on my jail bird shirt when I am in it.
I wonder if she catch on me a jail bird out of the in it
I will show plain my jail bird shirt—I hold myself when
            in it.
And when with jail bird shirk no work I am the one in it.
When getting in my jail shirt—I see I am the red—for red
            man
When in it. I am for the red man if I am in it,
            And now I am wrapt all myself in it.
Attorney man near side—would. O, I could kick, I could just
            Shoo him a little bit—mite.
Better I think me to rest a Nap—a Knight—I am at Port—er
            vale.
I rest, I rest—a short anchor Nap—in Port—er—ly in morning
Set sail for Oat vals—heave too—anchor—furl sails
By No—Ra—King—ask mite publis Gabriel's Trumpet.
            Then come a Nap of me to end your life.
It is very easy continued—my God above, I will there

Two find—Two self—Two gain—Two strike—Two shoo fly
Whiz buc bee, whack, I start fresh, walk purpose,
      I am Anchor Berry, the Pilot man,
His heart is out, he crucified, burnt dead, Last when to
        world life again.
His heart is wrapt in—over protection, hard as rock drops
      Crucified blood—when Last Eli—Burnt—Dead,
        Last Burnt Electric-man Dead.
      Tell them it is time they understood My business.
      Many of them are left to the last to burn in hell,
      Improving purify in fire—many first come last,
        The First comes the one at Last,
      And returning First comes to be My First and Last,
          One at Last.

Last one's trip to a WIDOW LADY [that could help a mite.]
He up anchor—quick sailed from Port-er vale,
Come out in new Hick—lands by that place, came fed by C—
        rouse your self,
Came close to Young—Mis Look-Out-for-the-dogs,
      Came on well pleased through Friends vale,
Passed her—came quiet by the Kettle—well—with a belly
        and a bad
Man names him to burn—leaving that place comes out fresh
Into Alex-and-er vale—passing on direct to the Clover-dale,
Comes up in the Oat vale—near to widow—by prest-on Son-
        o—ma—C-Cal.
Shoo—to to—now then—fly whiz buz—knock you down—
        get up,
Shoo shine—we walk for dear life toward the widow lady,
And left at Last—fulfillment of this book, widow mite—of
        helped,
But she was one of the world—did not know about God,
She would not give the mite for such wild oats.
      She was born to the world, never knew God.
Left the Last mark First ones trip to widow lady, see how
        different,
One widow you are 1999 times different somewhat near it,
By that age—you are all tres-passers around the premises.
Kell-og he could not haul a twelve disciples out of the
Middle-town—so the Saviour died Dead as a fly-wheel
      Crank—he left this brain seed for ages in time,
      Come to his home and see they are mine.
The little widow lady gave the mite when near her last,

I expect I will have to Saviour her, so kiss—my
Jack—Eli-as will soak very kind—when he comes to the last.
They come around him—he pictures himself—the shed roof
      is off,
Pictures himself the nigger—with no dancers in the loft.
The coyote foxes of the world come around him to bark and
      bite,
He kicks so hard they run from the fight;
He pictures continues road of life again,
He himself good Antonio—he loves, likes the rolling main.
He pictures his life—to study each cause,
From the tainted wether of the flock washed at all the flaws.
Notice—look at his story, he was a youth of his time,
He was thrown in—did not swamp—quick swam out of their
      slime.
He was young—he a boy—he is out—then I can wash him—
      he is Mine.
But—prest—on—he comes to the little widow lady;
I will forgive him for all past—he is passing on to the clover-
      dale;
I forgive the little widow lady of-fence,
He can beg his way too and from her quick in his time,
He never fears his life or the kicks of furnace crime,
    He looks over hills and valleys of the world,
    He is noble pilot of courtship, all sails unfurled,
He does not run her on the reef or down under Adams' fall,
He waits to come too—he hails—waits—this is God's Bugle
      Call,
He gains knowledge—Electricity forces the time,
He holds it in and burns all hot heat slime,
He wants to come me on the Great-Eastern line,
He wants to come to me then more than any other—in time,
He looks down in the riffles of their stream,
He wants to say himself—he fires up with Electric steam,
    He looks over hill, valley and dale,
    Eve the vail remove to see him no snail.
    He looks at the clouds—is the Weather's prophet
    He waits writes told—slip—tick—news socket
      To them then he sticks to last
    He is a big crank packing also My Jack with him
    He looks ahead fences the world—with his rails in time
    He writes to hood wink out of them their crime
    And they to furnace burn their own ignorant slime
He has proved they had it until he is tired and sore

He wishes to come back—around home—and talk no more
Holding off' hat–s–down he kicks along
He comes back to the home—of this Gospel Wire Song
 He passes through—comes near the narrow gate
 He cannot see ahead but fears brave—fears no fate
 He climbs it he flies he is on the upper grade
 He comes on up—stands—in—takes breeze over shade
  He can go down or he can go up
  He willingly went for years without his sup
 He crosses the bridge—can go through My gate or lane
 He can come up to fly down over the rolling main
 He looks at wondrous gigan–tic mountains the view fine
 He wonders if he will ever hit the back bone of time
 He passes on over a beautiful straight ahead scene
 He can never forget—still loves young sweet sixteen
 He looks on ahead the most beautiful scene of his life
 With such views he cannot return to gloom and strife
 He looks at the gigan–tick forms of time
 He can not see the other side of him back in slime
He looks out over most beautiful views of pleasant home life
  He looks goes straight ahead—pleasant
For the red–white–and–blue–man for life
 The pair stand in this lane—they do not move out
 And you bet they are not insane—either—again
 They can pass and look at the most peculiar form
 They can look through the clouds of approaching storm
 God—can move them where ever He please
 They are as big—nearly—to Him as a span of fleas
 They look over the cities of the noble and free
 They are bound each one in the Home of Liberty
 They look over life so fresh and bright,
 The gentle songsters are pleased with the sight,
They look out over the open fields of beautiful life,
They cannot see far ahead yet understand Gabriel's Light,
They come to the lane—dark ahead mountains—dark base life,
But see smoke—passed on through and burnt old strife.
They wander around and find the straight right way,
They come heavy ahead—wait—and draw their pay,
They look over the stack for the Last Chance—straw,
They find it soon—and prest–on—they come to breathe then
  draw,
 They do not mix to eat like herds of swine,
 The herd is in the marsh in the mist of time.
The herd run—he fears the devil—in them is nearly in to stay,

They look over even mansion—view level plain,
They wonder why in devil did not accept God's name.
>   He gives His Word for man to mind,
>   Those that will not must mind as a hog a different kind,
>   They may look over the wondrous sky cap of time,
>   Grunt along—I suppose think they feel very fine.
>   They made themselves and draw their own pay,
>   Come in the world, I suppose, to stay,
>   They can see the man pass their lane,
>   They cannot feel to grunt out his name.
>   Great Spirit is a wondrous offended Power,
Present age—He gives even the hog of His Wisdom Flower.
This age commence—even the hog eat His Wisdom Florr.
>   He may yet herd them up and brain a few
>   To leave the earth—and Shoo-fly one—now one two you.
>   He hopes they breed up from the dim lane of hell.
>   They—eggs will not crawl or begin to,—
>   They may look out to see the bright light of time,
>   Even if they were deaf their eyes can shine.
>   Great Spirit turns in them the devils of man,
>   It is a slow way to improve the hog herd band,
>   They may pass and come to the narrow gate,
>   A stupid way—and I wonder if they know their fate.
Twenty-five miles—and—no oxen yet,
Can I come to them—no no—they are too good to talk about,
And the horses, asses, and all somewhat good in a way,
Man think better than horses, asses, and some time—in a way
You think so the wrong side up—then expect God will pay.
My God above, I hope I quit—I hope much—sick, weary,
Worked myself down stupid—them misty ignor dreary,
I must come around home some time a mite publis
This, a mite, a flea—bit—I pass through by rocks and kicks
>   of Time,
>   I try to come around home—feel very fine,
>   I Am—it was raining at this I wet myself,
>   I must stop in time—wash it all away.

P. S.—Now I Am, I feel very cool, small and limber,
>   I am just leaving the very tall timber,
>   I can see out ahead the light bright shine,
>   I am coming on around to I hope to feel fine,
>   Take and eat drink this sweetin with ages of time,
I take off the belt if going down grade,
You can berry in you the Bright Light or see eternal shade.

My Electric Laws govern all the band,
You can pass in by the Gate keep—Two Powers.
You can climb the mountain–dim line—at last Wisdom
      Flowers.
I can look down see all around under me—track the line,
I can see through ages—track the steps of time,
    I could continue on I suppose forever,
    I am dam'd if I fear—trouble much about the weather.
Now Great Spirit I do not I—you will have to squeeze wright,
      out me,
I do not like to be butted—by a by a good sized Weather,
I have looked much over and seen my time.
Now I wish to connect Battery. I am a sooner angel of the
      Gospel Wire Line.
    I am out out paper, I can write more—leave space
    With please connect wire of time to please Angel Gab.
    I remain yours, my God above—I am J. McG T. Gab.
      I am please you if I can, I am J. McG.
P. S.—Please box me out of tick—it is no go,
    My, the rains come like my tears to flow.
    Please leave me a little live Spirits before go
To lead me—I am litt-e, I can do nothing—help me out—I
      tick—
    From—with—tick—Last,
    And now, my God above—say stop me awhile.
Let me eat my first journey bread the first of this journey
I am in the middle of day—I may put on one—on two—one
      oil coat
    May I—alwright silence the Weather Electricity Breeze
    Tick—tick—tick—wire the news to Ma—I
    I can skate the wire of Electricity perfectly
I can roll to or from either—dodge over this skating-rink
I can understand—take a full course—study this Gospel
      Wire I think
My God above better let Spirit stay dictate interpret correct it
      I Am A Know–Noth–in–G—
I Am down hemed in by myself I can only see out to above
Top sky—I Am certainly feel lost if Good Spirit come
To leave me at last—I am coming to where I may be
Left at last—I know my God above if Great Spirit is
      With me I can hold—
Not to be left at last—I am willing to trudge life road—weary
To success weary—I cannot succeed when Great Spirit will
      Not brace up some for me

My God above and with Great Spirit I am a gone sooner
Without a mite—I cannot see so much ahead
Future may judge if for success I fight
I trudge and hump along all the road of life
    I wish you to know everything is not right
    Let Great Spirit help me a mite
    Scu sco—shoo you the flies of course
    Why of course I will folly—my God above—
    I will folly like litt—e stink—scrub—dog gone the flies
    Let me throw out this shoo—shine—flies
    You flies have sick—en my stom—ic it aches sometimes
Let me throw out this record of my opinion of them and say
    My Authority is the original Gabriel's Trumpet
    It is rich ripe—they can come and thump it
Speaking Frank—the Clover—dale may leave me at age 33—33
    Electric miles of shade—wait to see if my God above
        Helps me if I am left here
    I am most nearly sorry—if first—left—the last
Blow—Blow—Blow—Show—Show—Show—Light—Light—
        Light
    Out Out Out—A Come A Head—A Gain
    I will stop and eat with the animals, my choice is the
    Oxen cattle—I sit again in my shed roof
With all the cattle coming around me—I certainly like them
I like to see grass grow for them I hope it will sprout
Live fresh and green grass soon—or sooner—I look
My sight over the mountain another way—I will cool
        Off and qut qt.
I have fulfilled this last little sketch scene or I hope God
May kill me quick—if anyone was with me they could see
The animals—but I Am Last—alone—at Last
I can see the spirit of cattle I respect more than
        The fly herd band—
My God above I am in a most beautiful part of the
World—half way coming from Friend Alexander and expect
        yet
To light in a Clover—dale and with some Spirit Prest—on
Come—Oat—vale—I am the Bell of the mountains—my—
Some Friends tell me—I hear it and I see no reason why I
        Do not deserve the name
    I Am quit—a handsome siced Buo—y Bell
    My name is simple—common—Joe
And if they don't like it—I can tell them—you know what
Well—what is, tick, tick, tick, can I talk of you to them

Of tick—and fire me tick—at them
I come on tick, tick, tick, and if they don't like it—
Take me away as easy as you kill me quick by tick, tick, tick,
They respect me like on tick I can see a hole in the sky
Big enough for me to fly through—to outside—and you
My God above I—I—may I give a pointer to them
I can see the animal action under it—I wonder
If the fools, I wonder if they think they get it by tick, tick,
        tick,
They would believe anything if it was small, may they
Believe me—let them work above—and look down on this
I am simple boy—Not Much—they claim awful much—big
        —smart
Men of the world, let them—may their own way, this may
Not fit their size—still I think this suits the small boy
I hope his mind may not pass through the Boy screen wire
Out into fire hell—I say let men of the world make man size
And this for God's Boys—I and yes—God's Girl bells
My Maker I respect—I am a boy to respect and
My God above I think the boys and girls may
Act square about it if advanced little
        Tick, tick, tick—May they read my copy Book
        And pattern make like these—tick, tick, tick.
        I can do no more than give them this and look away
For myself protection, preservation, I leave the shed and qut.
I am in the most beautiful place I seen the world,
And in this tale—I am only half way to the Clover—dale.
I am going quick, heavy, by Electric track,
All my baggage not as heavy as is was an empty gun–ny sack.
I make graceful curves and on straight ahead,
You bet you bet I am not very much of a bullet head,
        That is certain—I am not made of lead.
            Please look by this simple rhyme,
            But I wished to remember I was—in time,
            Never a lead sinker of the drop–line.
I am coming to most beautiful place—streams, scenery of
        world,
I am on the Wire, all sails unfurled.
I am Shout, the Gospel man—to noble and free,
I want them to join—they wish—give them Statue Liberty.
        Make her Big Josh of American man,
        She holds her head above the fly–wheel band.
        She holds her head shines the Dead Light of the Free,
        She may be Daughter of Great Original Liberty.

I have now come down on the rocks close to water,
I can tell you to see she is a Noble Daughter.
I would let her blow Gabriel's Trumpet if she could,
But that would not do—she should be far away if the bridge
    stood.
  If she blew that Trumpet over the land of the Free
  All hell would not hold back the sons of Liberty.
  I myself feel Electrict Light in my hub head
  Of God—so big, I Am Son—she can take me to bed,
  I will take no one else—a live Liberty when I wed.
Blow, blow, blow—then she can come west of the rockies
       And blow Gabriel's Trumpet

Sand Sand Frisco, do not bridge bay until you hear Trumpet,
Sure fall, as she is my Original Venus to sound the Trumpet.
Am getting very much mixed up out in the back woods.
Please let this suff-ice, cool about down about the Saviour
    Goods,
And still I must come ahead on that mite be business, not
Pleasure—I am only a little past half way passed to a Clover-
    dale,
The mite is a Last Chance, of course, I can not get in clover
To-night, if prest—on suddenly, so I must take the last chance,
The straw, and sleep in it to-night, a good sound first sleep.
    Sound some time since I was dead,
        My animals come two by two
            Electric Bridge over the river to cross.
There is no one river—need bother you to cross,
    The animals come in three to one,
        There it a hell sight of them lost,
There is no Electrict Power to stretch the sinner across
    Three to one forever—forever to him is lost.
    I am sure I cannot tell—tell you,
    I burnt Dead burnt—so long, I am a sooner Boy,
        I Am old Nap–a–Joe,
        I Am Son–o–ma–Joe,
    And that is all I am—so long.
I have come to the most beautiful farm vineyard
    I ever seen in the world—I wonder who it belongs to;
I cannot tell you—you may find out some future time.
    It is red-mans—red soil, I am sure.
I think it is about sweet sixteen, or about those many
From a clover–dale. Come and look at it for yourself.
It would make some noble red-man a fine home—and

Still you may say there is not much game around here.
I find this sign on a post, which please allow to di-spel
 your disbelief:

 25 Turkeys **to be** shot for
 On Saturday **the** 20th, before Mrismas day,
 At the Alexander bridge—all are invitea to come.
  G(eorge) W(ashington) John—son.

I tell you it is a beautiful country **through** here,
But I would hate to see a red man here owning **it** without **his**
Liberty—I fear he would not be contented, even with this,
 I think the most beautiful spot on earth.
 It may be Garden Eden, or it may not, **but my**
 Opinion is on earth—Eden **could not surpass this**—
Alexander—and if that is **so I am now in some heavy**
Ticks—square **long** steps, **through the Middle of Eden,**
And expect to come one—some time into a Clover-dale,
So I Two Strike—Light **and out leave** fly **over past back-woods,**
 Light **in a** Clover-dale some time **to see**
 The **widow lady I am** stearing for. **If she prest—on me**
I will **take the mite. She** may be the **same one**
I am sure you **can learn** about it, **if** you choose **to know**
Me personally, **I Am**—Elijah Josiah Berryman—
Forever **I** believe—**I** suppose I know my name,
But cannot repeat a word or three or four **of** them together
 In this Book—I Am Dead—Berry—man
In Port-her Vale around me—I am out on **the** dead beat,
 Now then rags and dirt,
 I am rounding around home in my **jail** bird shirt.
I expect at last to round up the lady widow of Oat vale,
If she treat me kind I hope never again I bust—to fail,
And you can bet **if Able** I will **help the woman** who treats
  me kind,
But what **can I** do **with the curs who bark** and sit around to
  rub green chairs,
I can tell them to go **to** hell, and **mind** their own affairs.
And I am now writing about—in this some Words of God,
I hope to burn in hell **if I** let an attorney of Brush patch
 Walk **over me** rough shod.
 I hope forever to stay under the sod,
If I cannot shoo kick them out of time by the help of God.
I am old, raggy, dirty, **I** wear tacks in big shoes,
But I can kick the son of—common christianity away below
 the Jews.

They have descended far below positive—below age Christ.
I Am a crank—I must—stop—so long—sons of—
Is this the road to the Clover-dale? No answer yet.
Come, some one give me an answer—I Am Boy Joe,
        I might go—a stray—off.
Wait a minute, you son of—I am not a bit afraid of it,
You son of—you can go to—dam your heart—you
Should know I believe I have a God above to direct me
        What to do, you son of—dam you—
        Whiz-buz whack—shoo—shine—shoo.
        I continue my road, my God above, forgive me,
        Is this the road to a Clover-dale?
No, sir, no—tick, tick, tick—go back, you are astray,
You are going the Wind-sor, where you don't want
To—you are by this son near six miles of a stray;
You see I must take care of to learn you something,
        And now take shank's mare and hoof it back,
        I ride away shank's mare—I hoof, I hoof, I hoof.
Please take my care of myself, I be good Boy next time,
If not, so long—you know, my God above, I cannot
        Stand and take very much of such
        Impetuosity, or forth I must kick back
        Such immensity you believe him
        Say I am a son of a one-sided Know nothing
        About Himself or me, or anything ever
                I say am coming on home.
                Shoo, shoo, kick flies for me.
I blow, I blow, heavy I walk or trot I heavy tire,
So much walk—young Fast-speed passes me, horse in a
Foam—throws his bottle—I smell steam of fire water through
                air;
Curs, and curs, and curs bark at me, all many fast speeds
Run round—and curs and curs run around and round,
I pass on and leave the winery a past me,
Fast-speed run at me—blew and kicked up, run other
Way from my direct course, backward to turn
On towards the Clover-dale—I Am now only three
        Quarters to come on a Clover-dale course,
                Which leads that way.
        I hope never again well never to go astray
        When going the course to the Clover-dale.
I leave—pass the winery—a lady stood the door
I ask the way to the Clover-dale—she tells me and
                I immediately turn off.

Do not act the something—like my winery side scene ;
Do take it slowly with your wines—it is like everything
    Else—too much of a good thing will not do.
    I go straight ahead for the Clover–dale,
    I begin to hear the cow bells ringing
    I fly on—pass on—up grade look kindly
    At me—yes, they do—think, think of it
I fly on up grade—I am out soon—of paper—what shall I do
My God above I will skin my baggage to keep the record—
    crank of you
I look over one other most beautiful spot—in the red–man's
    old home
    It is nice rolling red, beautiful red soil
    Of course the redman left it sometime ago,
    I must stop this is getting—becoming stale, record
On towards the Clover–dale—I must come to quite last
    chance
By the way—I grab at a straw—sleep in it—that is the straw
    stack
I am busted not a nick—I work hungry dirty to raggy
I am commencing to catch a dose of the consequences
    I must so Prest–on in the sanitarium—see if I don't
    See if I don't fulfill this much of this much of it
My God above I then come back pass Turkey–Shoot–Place
    Beautiful of world—then I set my sail
    I fly on proper course to the Clover–dale
    I feel certain—then sure, I can forever tell my tale
I packed and never lost my heart on the road of Clover–dale
    It is now coming dusky—and no straw–bed stack
    Is this the road to the Clover–dale—ye, ya, yes—sir
    I am far from the Palace—ho–tell hack
    I must take the free buss for the straw stack
    Blow, Blow, Blow—Angel call me in
    I don't like to sleep here but must to fulfill begin
        I begin—I am—not yet in asleep
    I will tell you some more of it—over—over the river.
Come—darkey—like now—I cannot see—more to write
I forgot—I failed—can you help me my Electric Light
Can you help me in the home of the Electric Light
    Who is it that furnishes that Dead Light Fire
I—you—not going to tell—it is the Owner of Electric Gospel
    Wire
I must quit—I am using other—using up all Electric Fire
I kneel—to ask man's permission to sleep in his straw stack

Tell him **I am a farmer like** himself I am unfortunately
busted
Have nothing with me and would like to rest in by **his barn**
And also tell him I would be pleased if he could give me
In the morning a glass of—bread I mean a glass of milk
So if he choose he can give me some milk and bread
I am think **of Lemmon, squeeze** Brush—attorney, etc.—at
the time
How **much more I respect—farmer** call it square
Subtract and multiply—many times as you like
Blow, Blow, Blow—I see far **ahead** on hill high top
Dark night **I** see bright Light **or I** hope to be shot
I see Electricity another way—**I feel** all through my
body the Electrict Spark—
I whistle—McGinty—in beating **time,**
I keep step and feel quite fine.
Look, is this correct—straw sleeper,
I feel Electricity—and we'll rest our weary feet,
By the crystal waters sweet—over Jordan,
Over Jordan, over Jordan—and we'll rest our weary
Feet—over Jordan.
Trudging on **straight ahead I see a** Bright star,
So I sing—And we'll **rest our weary feet,** over Jordan.
I feel Electrict Gospel—**I come in the** straw stack,
My power double—Two Strikes, I nearly lose my head.
Fast, fast, the sno descended—scarce loud as a sigh.
Feel for our little Two—Our-fan Boys,
I cry, I cry, I do—you are welcome to,
Then I come **too—tack** in to anchor at the straw stack.
My shoo—quits quiets down—I study—to Light the Light;
Now then come to a lady—lady, I have **come** to see you,
I am a specimen of humanity—how **I** came you need
Not care—how I came to know you.
You know a Friend and an Alexander—I came over you,
I have come to you as wild oats, will you take me in,
I am in **trouble, heavy** in trouble—am sick down, heavy heart,
Can you **help me a mite—I** have fired my strength away,
When **I do** need your mite you help me.
I am respectably a decent boy—what say you
Of my specimen **of man—I** am a shoo shine sooner out.
I can justis **simply lay over** any son of—man that says
I am anything **but a** decent, disrespectful boy to them.
I came a some **for some of** them—that treat we well,
And some other—many I cannot know the ones they are,

I expect many of them by the time—commence to remember
    My shoo shine.
Of course I can take—some little bit of care of you alone,
Remember, I begin to do something for my certain home.
    Of course if you cannot—will positive not
So—to turn up your nose up at—in at me you can go to—
    I Am the Boy the Mountain Bell.
    You have heard me talk—to Blow, Blow, Blow,
    And now I am just step out with my Circus—show.
If you cannot respect the scrub of Gabriel's Trumpet,
I can easily tell you—you are a head-high strumpet.
    If you will not take me as the man I am,
    You can kiss—my head for a fry—shoo-fly tin pan.
    I will shoo you away among the flies,
    And you may burn in hell where the sons never rise;
    You may take me as I Am, or as I Am not,
    But you must respect my head more than—than—well,
        P. Pott.
    But please allow this to do—answer—give me—.
        Can I come—close to you?
    And I will spank down by it mine answer to you,
    I am left—I find I am alone—I take break back,
        Eventually I must wheel on home,
    I must the last chance lady—help me a mite,
    She may advance me to publis—Blow, Blow, Blow;
    If so I will remember her life must be pure as snow.
If she help me the mite, my God above, let her sins forgive,
Let her come to you and forever—love me—live.
If she respects me—separates man from rags and dirt,
Let her catch on to shoo—I mean—close to jail bird shirt;
    If she willing me to be the man to come by above,
    She to hold, squeeze tight, in the arms of love,
I am willing she catch on to Noble Power,
She can say I am a crank—hub full of Powder Wisdom
        Flower.
    She will, I hope, not trust Oats so much again,
    I had much rather leave business with poor insane.
    They may believe she is left, they may believe mine lost,
    They wish to place me in hell—let them pay the cost.
    I never did them harm—I can look plain to you,
    I am the man single, I thoroughbred Jew.
    You may take leave or lose me, my God above,
    I can wait until I die—by Electrict Light of love.
    You can leave me spirit, or leave me none,

I will always do best—can run home, run.
    You can give promise—one—give me one
    Until it come I wait—hell freeze over Ino Adam Son
God who made world—stars moons—Sky Tent—full power
Make one Bich come up to Wisdom—you know the Flower
    If she hangs away back to respect me not
    I can blow her out with the shoo—shines—I do not
      I am going to turn out the Light
    Please leave me spark—flickers to come light again
    I must return—to practical—business ideas
    I came to the farmer—to keep the dog away
    I cannot until I make friends with them
Ever with the dogs—I make friends—though they do not
      fear—shoo
They do not bark about Great-Red-White-and-Blue
The farmer of the small cabin—treats me kind—I am
      becoming
Serious—need rest—rest—of brain that is the rest of it
    You know I must—so I tell him I want to sleep—
      The straw of last chance
    He gives me some things—I find myself in oil
I am myself wrapt in the cover—covered with horse oil sheet
    Near at my head grunts—a pig—pig-pen.
    And I don't sleep much until—Two Strikes—about ten
    I am a shoo—shine—sooner—I started—like wings
    The morning I flew away—my friends—I left then
    I came on so fast I left far back an old Swan's—Hen
But return again—I am now here in this stack—soil bed
I may write this double—over sometimes—I take the baggage
      to keep record
And it is all scratch—no one but myself could understand
    But I must have tablets to copy my mind work,
Return again—creeping, crawling things come around my
      head
Terrible—I remember being—I not fulfilled in the mind.
I pull up the horse soil cloth around my head and go sleep
Never wet—the bed so cold—I awake the dogs bark in it
    They drag—I hear—the stick all over the yard
    It would do you good to hear the tame geese quack
    Pudding heads maybe they think they are not in it
      But they are the worst in the deck,
I awoke to find myself—say there is Son of—I hear
A foot of this Black Joe never burnt clogged with blister.
Marked all over—Electricity mind must make the record,

Pages plain—I hear Trumpet—Electricity blue flame—
        Revolving mind, must see the paper;
I hope they will be d—am—sure—to get out of this and read
        the other one.
My God above, I do groan in this—double and mix up,
I hear the geese—the—hear the cock crows in the morning.
They many cannot believe I hear Trumpet in Bright Light.
I back from the Clover-dale—my God above, I am
        In this plain—now then I will—will stop,
                I hear the Trumpet again.
But please remember I woke so early—so cold, shiver, shake,
And roll double rolls of shivers in the morning, cold, early,
I lost the pencil, must make another—I do—it is quite
A clean pencil—other one lost—it does good to hear the geese
        quack—
Tick, tick, tick—God answers—I can be on His Book.
        I remember, a time ago, I told you of my
        Courtship—I get dead stuck—dead stuck love,
        Down the wayside after—well burnt I can stand it,
                Can pretty little dark blue eyes?
We came together—now you must kill me, my God above.
I cannot get this out, still we came before the flies—I will not
        Care for then—we were dead stuck love,
We came, we stick apart do—not tie, that is the predickament
When see flies you may say I hear—quiet look away
By this when not treated right—I have the heart to forever
        burn you,
Of the world—I have been through these things for the
Purpose—hardening heart, I suppose—I never run,
For the heels—I am above—say this be the reason—say any
        Thing—I—one—I thought life—anew,
        Commenced the race for steam—her—cruision,
        I fulfill this book with some little–bit trouble,
        But the least of all was to find the No–ra–King—see,
        She gives her might willingly—to some one,
        The King she willingly gives—pin–money.
I am old, dirt, raggy—Last I tell them, the sons of—
I the Last have One to help me—to please me.
        We print this Book Two—Powers might,
        We leave it for future time—come see us.
My God above—I was left—you remember that
About Tail—or girl court–ship—she never gave me a mite;
Of course I asked her when in the Fair–field, but
        Su–I–sun, I left for Sacrament—O.

The mob around me moving uneasy—one said, **you Christ, I
kill** you soon

For that, I prepared for **fate,** as on previous trial—prepared—
come one **o'clock,**

Dark night, I am ready, waiting—a little Guy warned me—
quick,

Mr. Blessing, close by **me** said—awake, save yourself—we will
not stand this—a-gain,

Asleep—come **to the** Sacrament–O jail—soon **I** was locked up
—safe.

Very early in dark **cold** morning **an angel** called—

Called me from the slepileur—said **a** woman has just left this
place, follow her;

I up quick, started **for** home,

Escaped the **mob on my** second trip—without **her mite, of
course.**

Box me, **I felt much worse** ; rap me **on head, gradually**

Gained **sense, better to** good—I am left a **Last for you.**

O—that mite—yes, of course I was just commencing

To round up my Cir–cus Co—had a few good tricks, I **thought,**

I suppose I felt as big as Christ–of her C–1492—I **was busted
Now there** Is–a–bell–a–gain left me,

I had touched her feelings—said I would not have your gift—
I need help,

But she **had no jewels—she as poor as** common as turkey—
(I might,)

She said. have **patience. I said, better** go to school–teacher.

She went—I went—**up and back—she to** blow, still fixing up
her–self.

She—then so near Lost—Will–I–cuss **myself** again—for her
—I think—yes ;

Then, I think again—never—yes **never.**

(Rap, rap)—I hope **you** will take good **see** care of her;

I not seen her for **quite** a year **now, and** do not wish to
her.

I had **a** dream, dark and gloomy, in last night ;

I dreamt **my** girl come to see me—I awake, I hear rap,

I hear **knock,** I see I **am** dirt, raggy—I knew **the** geese,
But **it does not** matter now, the shoo **was** there.

When I awoke **I was** shivers, rolls of them—I was ashamed

I dreamt my **nose was** sore—like cold **could** not get it out;

But the girl **again—she shows** herself **off** around me—I
ashamed myself.

I speak to her and look another way, could not talk to her.

She had to stay away with another—I could not talk to her;
She had to stand—course—she made me near sick to look.
    I felt the smallest man in the world, I suppose;
    I imagine I would not like court-ship again.
    I am positive I would not—both of us knew—and
    I am sure she almost a chippy of the Block.
I awake, find all this of myself covered under gunny sack
And horse oil soil sheet—I rolled my shivers and got up,
    I shake—drop pencil—out of Light me—
    Forget—shoo—shine—I crawl out of this predickament
    Of trip to lady—I up with my bed on shoulders,
        I on me I have my jail shirt,
The horse soil sheet on shoulders I swing as my trail then
Out through door, I go very late in night, perhaps very
        Early dark cold morning.
    Last—I stole my own bed—think, think of it;
I took the horse sheet I was wrapt in by my farmer friend;
I will expect he remembers me for it—I told him where
        I lived exactly, join forest petrified.
Slight fear of rain when I started out of a hole in the barn,
Very dark, I walked on, could hardly see my own way.
      Came to a sign—I shin to see what is on it—
To the Clover-dale a finger points—forrest was on the sign
        also
I came along a dreary way—lost as fine as I know how
      To be lost in the dark—I came to another sign
Points another direction—the Clover-dale—finger directs
I follow—I feel what a God send these signs
Of the times—they direct the lost man in the dark
If he can leave the finger then follow a-head-his nose
I came on to another sign presently pointing direct an
Opposite direction—it was still dark—I shine my eye
      Shine up—seen a Clover-dale finger by Gey-ser
      This printed I wonder about that—being a guy
      But you bet I follow straight from the finger
      If any man should put up a guy sign board what
      Should be come of him—I did not stop very shortly
      Only to to and then I felt and knew my heart was
      With me—follow straight ahead course—getting
      Out in light I found I had stolen from my farmer
      Friend a very nice soft canvas sheet, some greasy,
      Of course in use at the time—but it was a fine one
And I was ashamed—I was troubled—I would repay him
      Well for this kindness to me—of course I could come

Back from my home—and repay him some—some
Time. Still I was ashamed—you may say I did
Not fulfill—I asked my farmer friend for the bread and
Milk—I stole the horse sheet, you may remember I
Did not stay to get the milk—so we call that square I
Fulfilled—I came on to a pleasant place and seen a
Pleasant lady—wo wished me to have something to eat
So I fill up—and run away—I had a pleasant breakfast
Talk with her—she seen I was raggy and dirty—but she
Talked with me just as good—and said everybody who walked
Was not a tramp—I like the lady very much she is not
Church member—I think respects God enough not to try and
Improve His Word—for own name praise—I come on
Where men protect orchards planting trees—industrious
I will assure you they have not much of a very big head
But I will gamble with you—if take tick, tick I can
I Am Able to tell you they do more good than a preacher
    man
They do not stay—sit and so wear out their pants,
They industrious, so are their sisters, cousins and their ants.
I look far over lanes—beautiful places—come to home after
    home,
Catch on one preacher-man, quit pulling at the wish bone.
Always respect the home of the Noble and the Free,
While you dig for soil—talk for the farmers about Liberty.
You can say the Word of God is the Liberty of man,
You may come to see God is something larger than spirit of
    preacher man.
Come stout chop your own wood—like crow—hoe your own
    corn.
I know you say suffer in world—never come to wrong end of
    horn,
If it is so my my strike a job suddenly preacher man,
You your pull-pit with you—leave woman the stand
Woman consolidate the churches, treat your brother kind,
The preacher cannot wash away the sins of time.
Shoo shoo—I was kicking myself—I was thinking of school
    all the while,
I have said—so I will allow it to stay—women try to improve
    the style.
Preacher, I am over the bridge—you need not alarm or lose
    your sense,
I Blow, Blow, Blow—remember this is only for the man
    audience.

O, yes, I forgot to **tell you the lady who gave me breakfast,**
    also **gave me lunch.**
I showed by Gabriel's Trumpet to preachers—I thought them
    butchers at once.
Is this the road to a Clover-dale—go on just the same you
    will turn up.
Of course I am not going to fulfill **this preacher business**
    myself,
They may—it will take some long long **ahead** time;
I am going ahead just the same to to turn up for **myself.**
I—o to gt pass the Gey-ser, I was telling all about.
God sends the benefits the Signs of modern times.
I am certainly a crank **on** the stump dumb–hub–head **a boy;**
I am going to stretch myself **for the** Clover—we will
Pass the church business—I **am going to** pass on my own way
Now I have **a private pass from you may** have heard of Baby
    Joe;
Joe came **to pass Baby size—you men preachers pattern this,**
And **word larger, you** may have to mature for man size,
So do not **blame Joe at the last you may not come in for**
    Baby size.
Remember, I am the boy Joe—writing this to pack—bring as
    God's mail.
I am stretching **out on the track home stretch to a Clover–dale.**
    I meet **a man who** pities me—going on my way;
    I never wait—for steam wheels I would not delay;
I **half** cross the bridge—I can look out ahead,
I **Am** the boy may know remember—well, so long—Dead
    I am traveling on tick, tick—I **know** it well
    When I wash by Jordan—I can **look** back on hell.
I **will** never drink Cut–her bourbon—I burn—fire water I fear,
I **could drink brew,** but I, like **the ox, prefer** my cool water
    clear.
I could use **your to–bac–o like a** man—then feel like a fool,
Od judge—cig–rets **never** cool my breath—so very—very cool.
    I see your **tent** stretched, I **see** the animal in the door.
You had best leave you habits—and leave the the—so long,
    My God **above, you** should hear curs bark at me—for
    Blowing **this.**
A lady can call them **I bet they say—you** know—can kiss
I come out in the open **country far around can** see
I hope the last chance **lady is in record of** Judgment Jubilee
I **put on** my oil skin—breeze **measure is about** to blow me
    away.

I want to stay and see her finish—to fulfill I wish to stay.
    I pack my baggage and come on ahead,
    I want you to help me by the Light of the Dead,
I fly straight ahead please direct on my course,
I hope you will give me a full dose of Quiet Force,
I am pulling up grade by heavy man power,
I will come to you personally talk about the wisdom flower.
I wish to leave this record for the Land of the Free,
I am kicking I believe I know—all the faults I see
They have many noble inventions to great steam car
But cannot believe God any larger than a so-fa-fair-see-Pa
Now I want you to let breeze feed me Bottle of Quiet Power
And I will take common bread for my Wisdom Flower
    I had rather be buff-a-lo where I could rest at night
    Than to continue forever this worth-less fight
The redman respect, greatly respect the breeze of God above
The char-coal blackman is always happy with bright light
      love
I will be any of them if you let me rest in Your Home
I want you to take ne right way—I will let you—alone
Of course the some pale face—think black man left in the
      cold
But I can say to them—I think I believe they are sold
I can remain awhile if you wish me on this dreary coast
I will try this to kick them down who put on the most.
P. S.—The grass is very, very short here yet. I forgot to
Tell you not to worry about the baggage I skinned,
To keep record the lady gave me note paper when I beg
At breakfast. I told her I was writing a record of life
Of the time—writing as went—she gave me paper. I do not
    Trust memory—never expect to write lies.
    I am out all through—just feel as I tell you—
You will see what a peculiar boy I am. If I do not
Get there—I hope you will let this be in print by some one
In the Breeze—take to you you may forgive me for
All the faults—I do—since you forgive me once before.
I have been a very fast colt—I hope they may see no one else
Need be because I was. If some boy had written Dictations
Washington style—by tick, tick, tick, out of his head,
I do not know what I would do—tick, tick, tick—that is so
    Cuplids we talk and say just what we please.
If we Cuplids cannot fulfill this we write it all—just
Because we feel like it, and there is nothing else
Better for to do. I am the Father of Cuplids and throw

The Original shoo–fly–shoo—
Now I am going to feed—I hear the bells ringing close
Where I sail. I must Light and rest my toilet,
      To fly to see the Clover–dale.
I light both feet in a stream—water does not hurt feet,
Cupid never, no·never fire water let your feet rest sweet—
Tick, tick, tick—stay on earth awhile, My Boy—Cuplids run
      The domestic—tick, tick, tick.
P. S.—Pa, I light out from top redman's Mt. Olive, fly me
Pass the Clover–dale, let me light and Prest–on succeed
In the Oat–vale—but I will take a Solomon cast
Sullivan iron oath I will never run the light domestic
Even in among the flowers in a sweet Clover–dale—
      Tick, tick, tick—shut up.
Just now, coming through Ma—I—and I want to be an
      Angel when I die—to never Dead die.
I wish—carry the news to Ma–y—you hear—if I am Cupid,
Safe through, I will speak to her ear, if I don't go off die a
A sooner to soon, I will correct this—then give it to my eve.
We together will Light out for—for the moon.
I feel for my heart, it is still safe and sound, hard as stone.
      I will drink many cases of cool water clear,
      I will tell her many tales close to her ear.
Seven years I have washed pure and clean my home,
I have worked myself down to pure skin and bone.
When my wink is out, what I leave put above or below the
      sod.
For I now assure you I will Light out for the Home of God,
      Blow, Blow, Blow Gabriel's Trumpet in the end.
JOHN—The funnel is one hundred long.
ELIAS—Scratch that out, that is bug business,
      You know it is more than that.
ELI—Let it remain, Boys; don't quarrel; it is a small matter;
      Show—fair—play—out.
ELIAS—I say ten times—course—the widow lady will give
      A mite.
ELI—Jack, take Elias to success by a head,
      We must fulfill this—attend the lady in the future.
    Come just same as Indian—to pale face—lady—
      O—help—we weary—I came far.
LADY—No—I do not wish to offend—I cannot
      Take your word.

With steam and electricity—be noble in time,

I hope this hand car(d) of David's Son—is no slouch.

There is no one in the world will take your word—you see
That is the reason I said—burn world—burn,
Leaving widow lady—hear that big squall—then see,
                    Commence to feel hot.
Turn back to page 153—near it—to lady—
You will see I have hung a long time in a wild goose chase.
I told you in time the widow would not loan the mite,
And now, My Boys, you can commence to fly your kite.
Now commence burn—without further orders proceed,
I will see there is nothing saved but a pair of Hay Seed.
You treat me kind, and My Two Strikes Boy go slow,
You all right, you are just as good as Old Black Joe.
You please and mind me for another, I will not hunt,
The weather will now proceed to burn off the hump
World—judge is it best to obey—God or man?
Judge by my little round, which I Am Able to stand.
If I ever mind an attorney with big head ways,
I hope the same he may burn in hell without any praise.
I will mind God's Ways—man I will mind Him on earth,
I hope He may set the fire all over this little hearth.
            I see his steam coming all along the way,
            It passes, never hurts me, He has given me my pay.
            If had not—I would have more to say
            You of the world may say the rest or get full pay
            This My Boy—has suffered long
            Soon I must ease his mind—stop the song
With My Great Spirit I assure you he is pleased very well
I know the best of you you can burn in fields of hell
My God above, I am Joe—please place me at the end of the
            horn.
My God above, I am so mind sick I not stout—why was I
            born?
            Remember promise will it save the brutes
When I blow—yes—will you—yes—in a—Horn
            Then I will Blow, Blow, Blow—
That is, my God above, my fish-hook must first catch a
            sucker.
            I promised a man in my town to see him soon
            Please, I am not quite ready for my trip to the moon.
            Let me stop until I blow them—away to hell,
            Then take me home I feel very well.
            My God above—tell—look—good bye John.

I see the fire commencing—it can do me **no harm**
I am nothing but **one** Hayseed—on the **Way–up—farm**,
And when I leave **I swear** by my writing hand
I will leave **all I have** can for the **noble redman.**

I Am a Boy—the **curs** bark at me—do worse they can,
 I wish **I may** come to please **my** Uncle Sam.
 I am on a stump when I write **this word**,
 I feel about as big as the **blue J** Bird.
I know I can fly and I know very **well**
I am going to proceed—fly back **away—find** fields—of you
  know—**well**,
  My God above, let the **curs smell of me,**
  Then let them pass to **a higher degree,**
   They may **forgive this—our**
Come on home fast freight all **the June bug kind.**
They may say **I fly Fire—I am dam'd if call** me bedbug of
 time.
I had rather **be dam'd than have them call me bedbug of**
 time.
I hear **them calling—Nim–rod—now I had best** qit,
 They should remember Cupid is all this course,
 And uses only help Great Spirit Quiet Force.
 In this he comes speaks plain now to your ear,
 Wait maid—and man—many days **after—hear,**
 I have told you this same old story **many times plain,**
 Go back read—hear it many times again.

If you wait after you feel the Electric **Fire,**
Go a little higher—be like McGinty on **the** Gospel Wire.
Never climb away lower—any higher **than Joe** Josiah.

Please, you may remember **about** the **wasp** nest—he did he not,
My God above, I Joe Josiah—I do **not** want—get me any
  higher.
 I am repeating, forgive me, **when I drop** the fight,
 When I do feel well I feel **all–wright.**
I am out on **the beat,** and **I** want to go home,
I am half Dead again—John, please take me home.

My God above, allow Great Spirit to help John get me home.
My God above, **you tell** me—good bye—see me again soon.
 I am close **the forest you** petrified—close
 Pa–C–if–I–c—O–Ce–an, I am in Son–o–ma–—C–Cal.
 I am coming **around** on the back track
 To where I started this journey of life.
I am to where I **see** one **woman** ride the horse back

Close to where I see Adam (man) rides the world—She bare
      back.
They certainly no better than the original Adam—take this
      Boy pattern—do do better—for your own self,
         I do not care to offend—if you do better—do good.
My God above, I do, I do, I will stop—I cannot do better
      than stop.
My God above, you see I stop on the bridge—and forever I
Want you to see me again—forever forgive me—I feel your
      ways
And actions—forgive my impudence—anybody see I am a
      crank.
My God above, I believe you turn me like a crank, as easy as
      Your Power turns the world ;
And that says I hope I am Boy Crank by Power of God to
Turn the boys in the right direction—of course I seriously—
      In my ignorant youth thought of that turning,
And it was because God made and gave me a purpose.
The man is a fool who reads this and does not think so.
All my life was direct—and conducted for this purpose,
         All things shaped for me to fulfill this purpose,
         And I hope the world will take it for a purpose.
         I give it for a purpose—and it is a good purpose.
         I turn this life like a crank for a purpose.
Try and see through it—I will say no more than it is best
For you parties concerned. I have a sore back and side.
         I must forever quit the copy business.
         Cupid, please go on home ahead of me—you bet I
         Will take care of myself after this.
Everything going the wrong way—you had better stay
Awhile then—they may do better—when they see every
Thing is found out at last—I must qit I have taken cold
         Honest—honest—remember I am Joe—
Tick, tick—away P. S. no more use for you—I am back
         To Mt. Olive now—then—forever
When again I sleep the straw stack as you heard
You may believe my promise and you may believe
When I say—I have walked to continuous days days
Days to get this tune out of me—Some days twelve
Very next twenty-four hours days continuous—walk, walk
      away.
         I will wind up a home—I am begging my
         Way here—along the way as I go,
But please remember when writing this I hear an angel sing.

I kneel when handling this copy Book—I assure you it
Is sacred—sincere to me—I make it as pleasant—myself
      As possible
Before I go home I take my farmer friend his horse soil
Sheet—of course I am the thief—in the night—just is—same
I will repay him some day—dark in night I leave the sheet
Inside his place—he is not away—I told his neighbors
When coming my way—I would bring it back—but
When I did bring it he called me a sneak—just is hard—
And was going to give me a black snake—and fire me—but
      he did not
Just is the same—I told him to wait, and soon I left out in the
      Dark night.
I drop my book, honest I do, yes honest—I drop it—
      I drop it—I see the star that falls—
      Tick, tick—my God above, may that mean—what
      Wait until you are again—see—star business—
      Is square under me—I am sick of tick
      Some time ago—I dropt my book flat square on earth.
      I told no lies—be a John—a John S. if you can,
      Or be a boy like Joe when you are a man.
  am so sore about it, my God above, I think I will
      Only look at stars for the future.
You folks curs big heads, please remember all came
      In the same boat full of animals.
Ah there—now hold up myself—stick up for Us.
I will forever say my God above owns the earth and
      Animals—they come
At no expense. He loses nothing—may never know them.
      I do not think He—for many—
He owns the earth—landed the ark—brush patch burnt.

i look up pleasant, my God above, let me stop keep
Looking up, up—my God above, I can fulfill that
      Many times. I can fulfill things in this Book
      Many times—I can and with God's help—also—fulfill
      All things in this book—at the Last.

MEMORIES—OF PRESENT TIME.

  I am well satisfied, those not pleased may go to—
  I hear this Light soon shine. I was out of record paper
back track from the Clover-dale. I tell you by memory.
  I lose myself, heavy dark, dark night. Feeling so heavy I

lay down—thorns hold me up. I coming around about and coming straight down from the Gey–ser, I was telling you about the guy—I came weary, weary along, see the signs of the times again. I know I Am near the farmer. I wish to leave the sheet.

I go again inside his straw stack. I am weary again. In a few minutes he comes to tell me I acted—this I told him I did it a purpose. He said his notion was of the black snake order, and then to fire me. Of course I did not want to retail any of my fire, so I did not take up the black snake—to him. I told him not to bother—go let me alone. He went—shortly, silently.

I left and came in the night.

He never seen me—he never lost anything by me.

I think the farmer is a dry hard egg—dry and bad most times. My God above, I am no prophet to save them. I will only speak for the Two Hay seed—keep them in cool water.

My God above, I need brain food All–wright, my Boy; you a head absorb it.

And the red man, they respect Great Spirit wonderfully. Of course, do as you like with the Jews. I think it a losing game, to hold off for any of them.

I can hear the women cry.

But, my God above, you cannot gain respect by mild treatment. I have seen it tried too long.

They respect God in a small way.

I think the Two Hay seed you made Electrict and redman. The negro I do not know what to say—my God above—all burn or do as you can.

But please save the Two Hay seed.

Make us a match—we away out of way. You fire top of heap first—we will keek—keep away out of fire.

The farmer has a bad shell—best crack him open same as the rest.

Save the Two Hay seed. I will try if you wish to round the herd up to follow Gabriel's Testatent Cir–cus—and you say as please. I suppose I mean they can come as they please.

I am—terribly—serious.

Up, I enjoyed my trip; never less I am very glad I started for a Clover–dale. I stop three minutes—by the way. I enjoyed myself coming back—walking dead asleep. In this place I will leave my picture—something as I looked—honest —my shoo—heavy by the wayside.

My God above, you know you say in the last verses of Old Testament:

Elijah comes to keep them from the curse.

My God above, I give my feelings of the case, my respect to you in this Book—that is Great Spirit Cuplids does—for I as a man, I am a know nothing about it. What's that?

I am satisfied my world mind was killed Dead and knock out of me—Spirit making room to say these things, which man on earth could know nothing of.

And again, Angel Gabriel can dictate to me.

I almost find I do contradict what I am made to do.

I think you must have made me a purpose.

I can remember when saying my name is—mud; and apparently by this record my remembrance tells me my name's mud—this book built around that life.

Making a mud ball of that sentence.

This book has collected my entire life.

That is, most of it. The lawyers may find out in this Book that some one contradicts. I let them prove case contradictions. You know we said there was Father, Son and Holy Spirit.

I think, my God above, that I, the Son, chip in too often, and I cannot continue to say that, either, for I was Dead, and I think Spirit can make this just as He wish.

Let the lawyers find contradictions to tell you—let them plead their case to the breeze—before they come to you.

That is about the way I feel towards them.

You know I am a crank and know-nothing, never big head towards you. If I run over a few on the world I suffer for it. My opinion is my right. My God above, allow me to stop my contradictions. I expect I am beginning to wake from the half Dead again. I hope—you—will.

I know you see me when I stave myself away—and ask Spirit to do for me writing as please Him above. I can do no more than say every word in this is sacred to me—I believe all, and I think this is for the best. It is a change. Many of them cannot respect anything. Many and many do not respect the Old or New Testament.

I know this to be a fact. This may please some. It allows choice. They do not deserve it. They should, and I must say, they must believe the other.

The son, as the flesh of man on earth, knows nothing of God.

They cannot see. I, as son of God, do believe all Books

He claims this far in ages of time, I believe, and I am sincere and keep them sacred. I know of only two—that is the Bible and this Gabriel's Trumpet. Of course, there is a good deal of guy, apparently, about this, but it most certainly indicates the times I am sincere at heart. I am heavy at heart about it. I would not do one slight act against God or this Book or the Bible for the coin on the globe, every bit of it. It would not move my determination in that direction.

And I say I can blow that sentiment forever.

I cannot tell why I am a crank Boy, but think my mind was made and educated for the purpose,

And I am sure I have the spirit that tries to do right.

When I write these things that apparently contradict each I can say it better, you understand the body of the Book does not contradict itself. God has been accused of contradicting Himself in the Bible. The man lies who says it. God did not give him reason to understand His way. Man places his judgment against God's and that is pure, sharp, distilled ignorance.

God, who holds all things, the fly man should not contradict. The man who contradicts, disbelieves what God speaks in this Book is a fool.

It is the nature and Spirit of God.

I am sure it is written by intention to benefit these times.

I am sure it is written by the Spirit of—

I will not say. I cannot, because I cannot fathom the entire mysteries of the sky any more than by this Book.

I am no astronomer and I do not want to be.

I know there are stars—planets—moving—that's what.

Any person can see that studies the heavens.

I do not know what is on any of them—I do know what is on this one

Neither does any man on this earth know what is on the rest of them. I am sure I do not care to know anything further about it until I am dead again, and then I expect to go on a picknick. I think I should contain nothing but hope according to this promise to me.

Which, I must say, I, as the son of man, never expected. So you may know the Spirit of God tells me just as He wish. I am sure I was intended to write this. My name has always been Elijah. But I will tell you plain, this was a surprise to me. I wished for this style of business, but never expected such a gigan–tic scheme as this was going on about me.

Find where these lines are contradicted if you can. The study may do you good.

I am pleased when I see in this Book God has a way of protected Himself from the opinions and thoughts of men. The very breeze holds down the minds of men. I believe if they collect and hold the proper spirit, it leaves a moment too quick before they die, like electricity, can go through every pore in the skin. For that reason, I hope forever to have a clean body. If my electric spirit strength comes and goes that way I must be clean to gain the electric of the air.

I do not intend to go off naked for the business either.

By nature the red man is pleased the way he is. Adam behaved himself naked, and we can see there things contradicting. There is no understanding allowed man to cover all the ways of nature in this world. As I am—the only sentence that covers my mind is that I respect my God above.

PICTURE OF LIFE.

When in the barn on journey I was prest—on to produce this last picture of my life. I do not give it as a slur on myself.

I can say I felt worse than this picture.

Many of my Friends know my foot was sore from kicking along the way. Blister was nothing—my foot raw skin and bone.

I do not like to quit this Work. Now I am coming at the end—but I fear I am coming out fishing with my own hook, and I hope my God above will be pleased if I walk the rest of the tune out of me, and straight ahead I do the best I can.

The future I cannot see.

It seems to me that in the beginning God knew all things, or commenced in the beginning, and brings all things down to the future.

I am satisfied I can never see God's ways until I am Dead again.

Therefore was I Dead to write this Book.

I think I was.

God's Great Spirit kept my flesh alive and moving as He wished. By that circumstance I blame myself for nothing on earth. I think it was intended I should see all the evils of life—to write the Pictures of evil life. I believe God wished me to give this to warn the boys of future time, to keep them from small tricks of all description, of all nature.

A boy is excusable if he does not know.

A man is not ; he should know better.

If he does a small trick of any description, he is not a man. Perhaps such will not esteem this Book. It is most of all to warn and show the evil life. Evil life is low. God's Way is sacred to me.

This Book descends the life of man very low

I am satisfied this life of mine is an average of these States.

I know these d'rty Pictures of crime are live and swarming in U. States. I have seen them myself and know.

I think my intellect is capable of knowing what I see.

I profit when I see truth. You can believe as I tell you, these things are not proper to exist. You need not be a fool, because I was made to prove these things to warn others. I was compelled to prove this to appreciate truth.

To warn others, it took me years to work up. It took all help I believe that God gives to man—determination of will and all attractions of nature. The Spirit of God made me in some way—I do not know how—and now, of course, not ashamed of myself, God made me suit the purpose. I do not believe he takes the trouble with every boy; but if they have the determination to make themselves, it is something to be proud of.

I did all in my power to improve myself.

When I found I was not improving.

I worked firm in spirit. I can say I believe I helped the Spirit of God make myself for the purpose. I never in all my life did such except I was made to believe it for own good.

It is a fool's way of doing.

The United States does not need any more characters like my own.

No boy need make himself a sign of himself. To warn others I was made. I will fulfill the purpose.

I am the scrub's Saviour.

If I had not—grow and model a pattern of yourself.

Be original—do not copy where it is low. It is evident God Himself has instructed Spirit that He needs no more scrubs in the world.

Stand still where you are. Never lower yourself. Place your determination to work straight ahead. Build yourself upward. Commence in this Book where your mind says you fit—firm—work—up.

If you think **yourself** higher than **this** book, **I have no more to say.** When **you tell me** that personally, **I am sore about** it, and would forever **say you** could **go to** hell.

Because **I am sincere to** sad—to **say** this is dictated and the **Word of God;** and **there** is nothing low about the style, except the **picture** of your own character—characters in the **United States and** elsewhere.

I am willing to say elsewhere, especially—for I am an **American.** My choice is the noble red **man—I** respect. With **some there is** a chance for improvement.

Elsewhere—but especially on the Pacific Coast and **South.** I am pleased with the noble pale face still.

With most of them there is a chance for improvement.

I know the Pacific Coast **quite** well. I have heard about **a** few of the boys elsewhere.

I will not **make a speech to the girls—because** I am one of the boys.

I am, and **I can say to** the boys that the **girls are not perfect** by a long **sight. I have—heard** of them.

I have and **I claim one of them** myself. There **is a** chance for improvement.

It now **stands on even race, and by and** by my Trumpet I hope the boys **can keep ahead of them.** Man was made **boss** in the beginning.

And I know I **say if** I ever Mary before I **get to Venus** I will **be** boss head **of** the family.

Of course I went **along** for years in **a good humor. She** thought me a simple hayseed flickety, fly-up.

But I **was** sure she was no good—I got—

She **see** me with the sack on the highway. I will return **the sack at** any time for I love and respect **no** one but God **above.** I **feel** so small of course I respect Him greatly. He **holds in** the stars and planets according to my theory.

They are the worst **on** the surface—in His this is to wash and burn one of them over.

And I hope it will make a big, a very big, stink.

Because I think God's power, His self protection, sufficient to hold and quench down, consume, all stench under the fly wheel band.

Of course He at some time purified and melted this one **down** to rocks and soil ashes; but this is now growing a coat **over** the soil that should burn to ashes and then to pure lye.

God is not satisfied **with** anything but the strength of—

And dry rank smell of pure cleanliness.

So I advise you to burn, burn very slow.   They wash out
the lye, until you are as pure as snow.

Coming again, I expect I am compelled to walk, walk—off.

If my God above does not compell me, I will promise I
will not write poe—try any more.

My God above, I like the job, I am peculiar Joe.

But if you don't stop me they they can break about me a
leg with a corn cob.   I am working myself down to raw skin
and bone.

At last pull my ear and take me home.

I am Baby Joe's Old Son-o-ma's pet.

I am the boy to please my girl so never will fret,
I want to come to you in future time.

I am willing to leave this d—— place still I feel quite fine
I wish to stay until you call me home.

Then I will leave the flesh—they can pulverize the bone.

I have worked—I hope I will gain—may I please my fair.

Then I will take her home, and deal on the square.

I have told her she was judge—I am Antonio.

She can place me the jug if my nose gets sore.

She can stay with me by the lock-up, or trust me with the key.

If she thinks she can do better let her stay away from me.

If with me she is pleased and thinks I Am the boy,
She can travel with my Cir—cus, have lots of joy.

But if she thinks she can come and run the fair,

She had better go cut, cut—hair cut—cut short her hair.

I am the single—act—man—no other need come to help,
If she wants more—chippy down—clip, chip her down to the
scalp.

I do not want her to run with everything in town.

If she thinks me a splint, I can say to me she is not bound.

She can come to me, together we will be free,

To my mind she is the picture of liberty.

I have written much about Noble Power,

To me she is live liberty, God's sweetest flower.

I have written much about Quiet Force,

Please let me quit and follow the quiet course.

While earth rolls by God's Power, I could continue this
song.

I limp along and hop along, improving, ease the pain of
time.   I was sold myself a purpose.   I eased off my course to
pass straight ahead—stop.

Preach M. Wan-a-maker—might get up his back up—he
might find I throw heavy shoo at the preacher kind.

But the preacher **should be modest, patient about the time** he weds—they should. **God gives the Word—by His own** prophets writes His law.

His Words are plain—He says what **He means.** A preacher has **no reason** to interpret further what God **means.** Such **preacher** becomes mysterious—lose **reason.**

Hold! God above gave them none—they vanish.

They **profess to** interpret, revise, etc., God's Word.

They **are Adam** heads genuine, Adam dead heads. **Many** of them I see—of all things I do despise.

And some have insisted **with me,** saying I was passed redemption—when I believed Christ **was** only Christ—and they insisted he was God—Himself—"three-in-one" (their proof statement), and they would throw that three-in-one up to me until I could kick them away—if there is three in One, that One is God above—and they insisted God was in-side-of-Christ (words to that effect) fools—I wish they **kick** hell.

Of course, **their kind think they** know **it nearly all.   I,** a boy, I could **see through it,** why could not **they?**

God would **be disgusted.   Soon His Spirit comes.**

Then **this Book is BY SPIRIT AGENT, Word of God, to** sprout fresh **preachers.**

They ask—sing—talk—praise Saviour **well.   When he** comes they do not know him from an imp of hell.

Telling me and insisting that Christ is God—when I know **well**

Some of them dam—I could kick—to **the** road—to hell,

If they would take the Word Christ gave them, they would **very soon** find—Christ's Spirit—Maker—above mankind.

You Adam preachers could not comprehend like the noble **Indian, your** mind so small–towards God—thinks God Himself.

All **Himself in you** or any other **man.**

You preachers **like** Ingersoll says Christ was God—think what fools will a preacher man think **me** claiming so much in this Book.   Will they think God Himself has come in-side.

Think what an ignorant fool you would be to think so. God sends HIS SPIRIT **to write for** Him.

I think God is well pleased **just** the same Himself.

Preachers remember learn **your A** B C.

God made all even in **seven** days—gave light—spread the **sea** out **over space—can you** understand to believe the first of **the** book preacher.

get along with no one of this world—wait—this is private—worldly subject expressed for effect—go on.

I must say, and this book shows plain I cannot get along with white folks.

If the red man wants me can have me—

Tick, tick—God above says He is out of the business also. Says He turns the pale face over to statue liberty.

You may absorb from the fly-wheel-band, and the breeze will sift you where you belong—according to mind.

Please remember to keep God sacred—that breeze respects God.

Your minds must improve in that way—liberty will attract your attention—monkey-shines the other way from God.

When you are better, you are perhaps between the respect towards God coming from liberty, then go straight ahead and save yourself.

God leaves liberty as your judge, and I can tell you she is rather cool. If you wait for a live modest specimen of liberty, you may commence thinking about the last chance, an save yourself.

Tick, tick, tick—God says He is out of the business—stick to liberty.

I assure you my name is entirely out of the saviour business. I am Two Strikes Cuplids, and the Jew is still out in the cold, if he don't side in for the red man.

God has given His promise to the Indian last.

And the last must come first, and the first last. The Jews have waited a good while for the prophet Elijah; but the Indian is waiting for his Christ, and it is the first one he ever had—and the last one this country would want, I should think, if I remember about what is written previous to this.

I have waited some five to seven years for a live liberty to judge me, and she does not keep time with me yet.

This little Book I write while I am waiting.

It shows a very small amount of my love to God.

He will not let me praise Him.

I expect He is safe, and wants me to kick to benefit a tough country. You may see in this book a VERY, very little of my love to God. It appears to me He will only let Spirit write His love of me—and I see no reason why He should think so much of me.

Of course I love God through space. I do not know why I love God.

But one thing I do know, everybody else has given me the

sack—and God the only one who thinks to praise me—and of course He is just about to give the sack—this thing cannot last forever.

My Boy Joe, this much printed and I will give some Spirits to instruct you forget and disconnect the battery.

Save your picture just about as you looked on the voyage about the time you struck earth coming from the Clover-dale.

A PART OF ME THINK OF IT.

My folks placed place for sale. Of course, I greatly regret, but me they would not mind.

I told them—I would buy it myself—but me they said they never would mind.

They respect me equal as much, about as much as they respect God. I positively say they dislike me.
My mother respects and loves me I suppose more than any
   on earth.
The rest of my family can go to ——, like the balance burn
   on nature's hearth.
They quarrel and snub at me they—theyself I suppose it does
   them good.
My mother cried and beg me not to go away—she does as my
   mother should.
When I in love she tried to hold me and kick me off the track
I assured her I was not going to wed—I want experience and
   then was coming back,
She begged and cried me to wait she using all her power
But I had to take the trip—I was clean out of wisdom flower.
Before leaving gave her all my security I had in the world,
That I would not wed in courtship while the sails were
   unfurled,
  So I went my way and continued for years.
  She seen I could not mind her—so she dried up her tears
  When I am away she fears for my life;
  If she does not know where I am she is gloom and strife
She does not know my character writing day and night so fast
She thinks I am a failure and will be sold at the last
I hope this book save her—she at present never cares for God
   above.
Some day I hope this show her—I am a boy that knows how
   to love.
No human knows my writing which I do not care to show
Some day they may buy, then my character they will know.

I worry and bother when they will not mind and treat me
        well,
I shoo and kick them all force I can down towards hell.
They may at least respect me for having a mind of my own,
I can say they think I am worse than a crank in my own
        home.
To the rest of the world I do not know what to say,
I hope the wasp-nest will guide you the way.
        Of course I stand alone against all the world,
        And I am going ahead all sails unfurled.
        My best girl makes me a genuine cuckoo.
        I am quite sure the red man would not know me from
            big hoo-doo,
        So I must give the entire world my shoo shine shoo.
I show it makes me cry to think of God's love
Of me, a simple boy everybody likes to tramp and shove,
So I expect He will help me further, will send me some His
        Power;
I have with His help struggled continuously for the Wisdom
        Flower.
I am sure God will find out when this goes in print.
Please, God above, let me qut, I commence so sorry, I want
        you see me limp,
My foot so raw and sore, kicking along the road of life,
I have returned again near to my gloom and strife.
Please send me some your Power to help me on the way,
And at last let them take me near my God above I wish to
        stay—
To come to you—near you—I wish to stay—forever stay.
Please let me qit kicking at them—I will take a hack—
I am laid up to think of my trip—to the old straw stack.
        I have struggled along over mountains of pain,
        I want to come, leave this, when I am dead again.
        I have come on through life a simple common boy,
        I wish some help if this letter gives you joy.
I, my God above, come to you, I always try correct a lie
        before it is out of my trap.
I am the boy who never lies, I am at your door with mail,
My God above, please hear me rap, rap, rap.
My foot is bleeding sore, I limped far without my pay,
Please let me come in the Home of the Free, to rest on the way

    I stop—I am sick in morning—my meal must be brought
to me.

I have come so far I am used up.

My mother many times told me I was carrying the mail too far, but I could not mind her.

I continue—and now at the last, my God above, I am waiting around at the Last.

> Please let me in the Home—I have journeyed
> Far from the men of the world, and I have some
> Mail. Please overlook my impudence
> When I come and rap—rap—rap.

I hope, my God above, I may prove my pictures I bring.

They were taken in the world, they are true of life.

Please take and say I am your poor little Joe or fan Boy.

The Gate stretched—firm—swings—wide—open—

Joe is lifted and carried—faint, weak and weary—in the Last.

GOD'S CARE OF ELIJAH.

Read record 910 years before Christ, 1st Kings, 17 ch., 1 to 16th verse. This Gabriel's Trumpet spreads out the life of Elijah, and gives further details of character than the Old Testament.

I hope it will benefit this age as much as Elijah did 910 years before Christ.

His life is recorded true. God's Word is always taken from truth. Actions are recorded as they happen. The man or woman who will not take God's Word must at the Last be very, very sorry for it. The consequence of such a small mind they cannot know. God's ways are so immense they cannot tell the consequence.

Him who handles all the planets will not personally to each man. He has agents for the purpose. Please remember the breeze sifts.

Respect it as God's agent.

Simple man cannot understand God's ways. I have seen men in the present age who believe the earth flat. I can prove the statement to any one of this age that stretches out the view to immensity.

There are millions all over the world, they do not believe God's Power to handle planets with the swiftness of electricity. It is almost impossible for the common mind to grasp the gigantic proportions and size of God's Power. Take this Book —it does no harm. Your crime should leave you for your own good. You are a gone her when you stick to She.

God's ways are too big for you to understand, so take His

Word to you—the Bible—follow this Gospel—truth. **Follow** both of them and you are safe. This little Book **deals mostly** with the first chapter in the Bible.

The world did not obey God's **Word, on** an average, **any** better than Adam and Eve.

I can say for sure they **spirit** stick, stick, and degenerate— **they** spirit—stays in the world and gives life to the lowest animals. They spirit—does not fly by electricity—love. They cannot soar **to** the Home of God, because God has no use for them there.

Simplicity will not keep a man **or** woman from gaining God's Electricity—the negroes and **the** red man have it to a wonderful extent. I do not say all **of** them get to the Home of God—for they do not always obey the Word of God. Their mind gives them away. The red man who knows nothing about the advice to Adam and Eve, comes nearer obeying that law to affection. The noble red man **is a good** pattern for the pale face—to many.

In regard to mammon and marriage—those are two things which give the mind of man away to the Last Electricity Breeze—and he drops in his own tracks to become something which God does not care to see or have come to him.

God in the beginning prepared.

Men grow up from nothing. He never seen them to make them. Then they are not His children. If they grow up and do not love God He does not lose them. He will not take ever stink–er of the world. He would soon have a hell of a mess in the Home of the Free.

They are sifted by the breeze—measure as they deserve.

God's way is too much for you to understand. You had better take His Word He gives. Do not go around saying He is lying to you, because He does not care, He does not hear you. You dam yourself certainly. This Book shows he does not care for men of the world.

By this Book His Promise is fulfilled. He damns the world.

At the **last you** must take care and try and save yourself for the last. God will do no more for man than give His Word. And the man who follows God's ways — God's Laws—deals with nature.

Gain the Electricity by this record, and save yourself. God never knows you if you don't—you descend—you descend too low to think any more about.

I think I will quit.

I know I love God, and God Himself only I love—none
else. I don't give Adam for any man on earth, and I will
not write any more by this.

Personally I will never save one of you.

But if you take this word, which is myself, dictated as the
Spirit of God wishes—you may save yourself, and improve
from what you are at present.

Do not say you are perfect. You are a fool if you do.

Best you climb above the mind of fool big head. I write
this from Spirit. Any one who praises the flesh of man for it
is a fool. You all respect the flesh in one way or another.
Some respect the Jesus Saviour (name) If they read his
word they will find he WAS an ordinary man.

The man is a fool who claims Christ (Jesus) made—beginning.

Bob Ingersoll, one of the wise men of the present age, says
Christ was God—and blames Christ for not telling the world
something to protect humanity from all future cruelty.

He is a fool according to God's estimation.

He must think God small—to kill Christ forever.

To punish him forever for the world.

Christ wished to leave before his time was up. So do I.

I will leave.

Follow me if you can—if not you are handled by nature
(the same) I may never see you. Each one's future is what
each one deserves.

I will say no more. Old stags, I may not help very
much. Little boys, I hope to show them the way to become
men—and they may see they are safe, if they get up as high
as—Our Fan-Boy Joe.

I will sign this I give as his recommendation.

I AM—THE I AM SPIRIT—THAT—HELP—HIM.

So I must quit and let him eat. His foot is sore. His hair
is almost dead, and that is about the last thing that perish.
He has returned to earth from the journey, packing the Mail
—and Lights in Son-o-ma C-Cal—and I will say has God's
permission to publish His SIGNATURE to his Book—but he
will not do it, as the only Joe thinks God respects him too
much.

He was in evil, and remembers God's Spirit gave him a
purpose—as a warning to others to see the trouble to save one
man.

Each one must save himself.

Joe is a quiet farmer—eats the hen egg if he wants to. He is independent as the hog in ice—in—A—ice-box.

The girl that gave him the sack may read this and judge his character. This Book is his life. If she likes she may take him according to this record.

If she does leave him to take another she is a gone her—because the Word was given to him.

You must come in the same eve—hold the same course.

You must hold to the same one that started Quiet Force.

And if she goes back on him it is not fair play.

It is the best thing in the world to give a man the sack. It turns the mind to purity—that is the only correct way. She must be bold enough to give man up entirely—leave him without hope. Liberty is the only one cool enough. Statue Liberty is American Josh.

Live Liberty take the Original Liberty as the model—and she is Antonio's Venus. She again returned to earth. Mary —Al-ice—Tail-or—strumpet. Through her Gabriel was born again. Through her came the Quiet Force—the Spirit of John to Joe—Joseph. She, by remarkable judgment, aided to mature the mind of simple Joe.

He again says:

I sign as the copyist who has permission to copy.

In my Master's absence—do not judge my Master.

As He is absent, and this could not show all His sense,

Yours then and Yours now.

I am yours simply,   JOE.

I am Joe—now I will not take any more again on earth—I have to work my passage. I save myself. Believe me serious when I say I am glad of the sack. Believe me, I have kicked along until my foot is sore.

I am tired, sick, heavy at heart. It is small, but what there is is as solid as the rock.

I have, a short time ago, found a mate to it—and will in this life pack it to my grave—that is to say, I will never lose my heart again while I live.

Mine is as hard as rock, (see) the other one is same as stone, which I may lose at any time without serious danger to life.

Blow, Blow, Blow—Mary—Sant-a—Rosa toots Gabriel's Trumpet.

It should appear to any sensible man that the spirits of men have been left in the world for ages—and the Great Spirit fulfills their work at Last.

There should be no doubt, some of them had noble qualities.

Perhaps they for ages handle some one action of man to fulfill God's purpose—in that way they gain in ages, they gain their freedom. I am satisfied some descend and come to the lowest dog on the street. I am satisfied the way of nature can make them give vitality to the sneaking cur.

And they in the street are the picture of the actions of Adam, descended from the beginning.

They at the first stick, and become ashamed of themselves. All may look they so ashamed—but cannot get over the act they matured in the man.

God does not care to see them. His law of nature keeps them away. Some may say they do not care—they will take it as it comes. If God wants to act that way it is all right.

But they must remember God made all things—Breeze—Electricity—Planets—Sky-Tent—and all things.

THAT IS SOMETHING IMMENSE.

And also He made the Law that governs and divides the Spirits of man—and it is best you obey His Law.

He will not change. He gave the world in beginning.

He—made—all—

Adam disobeyed the Power of God—could not take His Word. The same has proceeded for ages. Again if you would take the word Spirit Christ gave you would be saved. Some imagine all the world was saved by Christ, the Spirit Saviour. Is it true?

Christ said to those of his time, they would not believe his word. I do not remember any of the New Testament myself, but I believe it written by the same law which writes this Testatent.

The Spirits of the world are improving (some of them) gradually. But by this record God must have the next age improve more or there will be hell to pay. The present age not perfect should improve. There are Two Hay seed kept out of the fire.

The rest stack yourselves for protection, but be calm about it. A crowd at a fire is no good, those on the bottom may get used up as bad as the last who gets scorched blister, who rarely cares for his life. The only way to do is to wait patiently, gain all the Electricity you can.

God will, perhaps, give orders—slowly. He generally does.

I say wait patiently and improve life—gain Electricty of Spirit.

God is slow; but when He gives the order He is authority.

Never takes back the word.

People of this age do not take life of others or yourself. Take life easy as you can. God will allow you to save yourselves, and then make the Two Hay seed come in life and start the future age of the world. They will be the models of the future generation of the world, because they obeyed God Law in the Old Testament.

They will be Adam and Eve, for the future world may understand them. They will be in the Garden of Eden, and will obey God's Law in the Old Testament.

The future generation will have a great advantage which the other could not have. The other Adam could not write a Book for his offspring. And we know God is somewhat over the Sky-Tent, and did not wish to come in and make a little stink of Himself to come in this little world.

He handles the planets. Man must cultivate the Spirit before they leave. The Spirit has gradually improved in many ways. We have inventions that should surprise all ages when they hear how they were invented.

How our common, ordinary men by deed and by heavy study, night and day, by perseverance, studied out the wonderful inventions of steam and electricity.

Who is the man who cannot feel for his fellow man who has given to the world such inventions?

Edison is a pattern. The study of his mind was not play. I have gall to tell him he was—given a purpose—a purpose. I praise God's Spirit.

Ed—son—I do not know anything about Edison. I do not know if he likes God or not, but I can say he should reflect on the future, for his own good.

Follow this my Electric invention.

His inventions improve the understanding of Electricity, which has existed for a great time, but he was the one man made to bring it to perfection. He knows there is Electricity but cannot tell what it was made from. I hope he will take the words in this Book as truth and Electrict Gospel. I am quite sure he can save himself. There is much Electricity.

Talk about him about—there one man may escape to live a happy life. And there—many others all of you wait until you die and then see what becomes of you.

Do not jump off the earth, and kill yourself to escape the

fire. It will not do you any good. Yoa will burn in hell anyway if you deserve it.

You must sift yourselves prepare for the breeze measure.

We are all here in a place in for it. I will take my chances with the rest, for God's promise in this Book saves Two Hay Seed to lead the way—to be the model-match to touch off and burn this generation, and then show the style for future generation to cut out brand their calves by—good-by.

Take care of yourselves.

I am going—again.

I took a trip with God's mail once, and wish to go again. I was pleased with the journey. I am simple Joe at present, and perhaps you think I would not like to leave this Adam place—you are mistaken for I would, but I intend to stick it out until—

For God above kill me quick I should gradually wear out by nature, rust my flesh away and leave my Spirit pure at the heart. For that purpose I use plenty of water pure and cool.

Inside and out—especially inside and outside.

I make a pure water boiler of myself, and do not get up steam with fire-water.

Take care of yourselves the next generation's a long time—to—come.

Be sure to keep the breath—dry cool—pleasant taste.

The next generation may model after the Two Hay seed. They are purified to the bone. All their flesh is fresh and sweet. They are to be the models for the future generation.

They are to be known as the Electrict man and Woband.

God will bring them together a purpose for a purpose—and if God is pleased and allows this to come to earth—gives some one on earth power and understanding to write this—the future had best take it as truth—for the Spirit of God never comes—to extent by one who lives without a purpose. I want no other purpose except of this description—never did since I was on earth. I never will change. I am satisfied with my work.

God allows me to bring this to earth, and no one need kick back at me—or be offended. I am simply Joe.

I hate to leave at the Last, but I must go.

Each save yourselves, I think you have plenty of time.

Use what you have to good advantage at least. Be quiet, and use yourself to be quiet and steady—straight, square ahead business. While I am on earth I will do the best I can.

I hope the future will be pleased with Electricity man and Woband.

They will be quiet and live in a modest way.

They will come to earth—they love work and play Together—mind equal balanced, some serious the Light of the mind—

When they do stop together they love—but work most the time.

They Electricity collected by long delay—

They come to the earth, but do not wish to stay.

If you want any more of this, sing it yourself.

Or go around the Book and come in the other way.

I must leave this and become the original Joe.

I still at this date have the sack, and expect to for three years from the date I commenced to hear and copy Gabriel's Trumpet—and of course that is not long, when I remember one year is nearly one-half of three.

I leave you my picture to have you imagine how I feel about this business.

Compliments of Joe to Virgin Mary. Was I for First and Last entire through Garden gate. You lie if you say so.

I Am, JOE.

Please do not trace pass the premise I positive feel bad.

Or worse at present my friend is D—Di—on, and I cannot praise him in this Book. I will praise him personally and I cannot do that as he will not let me. He does all he can for me and will not take praise.

I am poor, old sickly settled Antonio, Launcelot came to cheer up—and of course I was excited about it and have run myself down about it after I was taken up. I am Two Strikes Anton-I-O-B-ass-an-I-O I am sore.

I got the sack so can you. The sack does not hurt I am satisfied—I have had lots of fun of a hard character—I come to hop along day after day.

Now I must return to be the original Joe.

This Book was fulfilled in action before it was written.

I positively say all action I do not say anything else but action.

By by you know by whom my God above

You are mine Joe you the tick—tick—tick—it of leave man.

My God above, one commence to treat me better. Of course, my God above I have nothing further to say.

Only after this generation please fulfill save two little Hay seed.

You know what you know they are, you know who, my God above. You know Spirit said, come sit on Your Knee at Last.

God's two babies come see at last—all over God above.

My God above, when near the last make me again Baby Joe the Son—o—ma Boy—take me as God's boy at the last.

My God above, to give further respect I can only say in life the story of Boy Joe of Gabriel's Trumpet. Please let me please you by this my one single act.

I can do nothing more without troubling my God above, and that I never wish to do—Please, God, may I run away play—I fear to bother—I will come if you call me—please may I—I will not bother you and cry to come pick me up. I will keep clean after this. I will—never I will not come around—to bother. I will never be so dirty in this picture, my God above, my heart is clean.

These rags are of the earth gent—ladies—I intend leaving them on the earth to rot. My Spirit and my heart is pure and clean.

I did not commence this journey to make myself a lady's man—and of course I have run around—I feel sore and bad.

Tick—rap, rap—now I want to qit—by Jesus Christ—
I must quit.

Does Spirit drop the Book—my God above—I respect, I bring respect to many.

I love in a way that pleases Him—in relation present I am working around for Him much as I can—please find in these pages.

I wrote the first and I wrote the last.

From first one I did not know what I could do in last one, but I believe my God above did—I am sure of it—I am spirit, my God above is Himself.

And I try to please no one but my God above.

And that leaves me out—God above, the only one I must respect, or I am a gone, at the Last by Laws of Nature. On my return journey I take my chances—I force myself ahead. I must—my God above has my future a secret. He is the ONLY ONE WHO KNOWS IT.

When I look over the fields, I wonder ever—over the fields of night in astonishment.

My God above, best cut the Electrict cord—know I love Thee only. While I stop I try to please only my God above.

I fear to take the woband, but I am years past and far away from my court–ship—and my God above has encouraged me many times by this tick, tick—for years past has kept me going—I wait marriage, can wait. The race must come to naught if it will not defend for the action.

Myself to know proportion—to ask God above to forgive action.

I know we Cuplids are His children. He said, see like all over—and I wonder if this love business of mine is a mate to the mite business. If so the man is a fool who will say I am left at Last—because I am certain, through to my life I profit by experience.

And if Gabriel—Spirit—which lady—I dealing with takes love courtship off—wishes her to leave me—I am sure it is for the best—and I stake my life will—I would never marry another.

Because God above has given the Law, saying—

You must hold the same course.

You must come in the same eve that started the Quiet Force.

His Electricity that conducts the planets conducts me if I am quiet and easy to follow His Laws, as I have never married in all my life. I can say if I am left on this, He can treat me the same as the mite business—that was wound up to suit me. I had plenty of yarn to return home.

I am satisfied with my experience in this my last courtship. I have waited years—and now when he burns me dead again, then He can place me in the courtship of the future—which I know nothing about—as the man.

Cuplids, that writes this, knows all about it.

Take your journey bread, Boys. Venus is the judge—don't try to crowd her.

Let her take her own time. You look—out in another—way towards me. She will come around in time.

But like—she is light liberty — and you must not crowd her off her perch too soon. She will come to life and lower herself in time—and she is now alive and wishes to see you.

So you can get your court–ship–shape.

In the next few years prepare for another journey. Take the Journey to me then, I will make you my children again. You are now on earth—Gabriel and Mary.

You can return when worn out at Last.

Return then the same children that were playing around My Knee.

You can climb up and hug My Neck again, and I will box and send you to play.

You can hug about an kiss Me—I will stop you when I please.

When you quit world life, I will take you as My pair of Fleas. Then I can make you the future Electricity man and Woband—your little Spirits as the start.

Now do not say good-bye, Boys—because I am with you. It is necessary. My Electricity Spirit is with you when necessary, Fear nothing.

I am pleased with your love of me. I know your sincerity by heart's tears, and I will ask no one to be My Judge. I take you for My Self.

Venus can be judge—and remember—she is simply judge for herself, and that is all. I hope she can take time to examine your case, though—and will never be influenced by outside humanity, or the—for something attorney—for himself.

If she turns you loose, stand it like a man.

If she locks you up for good qualities, stand it also. If you do not respect her, I am not so well pleased.

If she wishes to lock you up, I am not satisfied when you try to escape.

So use your good judgment to good advantage, and I will instruct you Two further at the proper time.

Future time can follow your footsteps. I will not trouble every one in the world. So I give you two now they must follow.

I give Adam and Eve as a warning—they would not be warned—now they must follow and sit quite under—or they can go to—

I will not bother like this again among the curs of the world.

When I give My Word, it is not my place to come to earth.

I bother My Spirit to come—it has bothered greatly, and makes you two as the pattern—the rest must get down and out of big head, or they are gone.

They must respect you, or I have nothing to do with them, and they remain forever. I make you the model and My only pattern—the curs of the world can do as they like about barking at you.

They may be prepared when My curse reaches them—traveling around the world slowly, it can consume all cases as they come, and the last of this generation consumed, you will be respected as Electricity man and woband.

My model man and woman in the Garden Eden, obeying My Word.

Without warning they must respect, and follow, and sit under. Now good-bye, John.

Do not fail to help Elias do what is best.

I give them Statue Liberty for their Josh. When they get through ignorant josh they can come under near you, and then they may be good enough at last to come to me. But they most certainly must respect me above all things on of earth. I am the only Saviour at Last—the Jews knew that perfectly.

It is plain in the Old Testament.

Spirit Christ came on earth, and I hid myself. Who is the man can say I am not pleased with that action? Who can say I did not know the filthy, slimy set?

Who can say I did not know—crime existing in the world.

Now as in the ancient age.

Who could view such filthy action. The Great Spirit would give life to the brutes in preference. It is best you put it from among you, or I will burn you from it.

I must purify you, or the Spirit of life on earth degenerates, and that Spirit originated from Myself.

And I respect that Spirit, and it is not Myself.

I am not for Myself—I am talking—for the talking spirit.

My Spirit knows I am God above—you never know me unless he thinks I will be pleased. I cannot be bothered by every barking hound in the world—and I will be pleased when your generation is past, and I commence another.

All you that are able try to improve, it is best.

My Laws govern your future the same as ever. A Spirit talks this through the man who lowers his own opinion of himself more than any among you. To me he is the best one among you, and you can find My respect for him in this Book.

There are no two people alike—strike for yourselves—but pattern yourselves to round up in this course.

It is easy, and you can follow any business you choose. There is only one kind of business I have ever advised to leave, and that is crime.

I even say you can drink fire-water—you can burn in hell, also. I do not care what you think—but it is best you mind me. In this Book is written that you may know you do not mind me—and this book shows plainly I do not claim every one in the world.

These are My Two children—at present I claim no others on earth—and still there is a place for each one of you as you deserve.

The Sky–Tent is large, but I will not be bothered in the Heavens with curs.

If you wish to make anything whatever in the future, profit by this Book.

You cannot respect me unless you **respect My Word**—

The Bible and this together.

So I again say, you must take the Bible or be damned. I have been told that is a foolish saying.

So I will say it again now—I mean it—**you are** damned if you cannot take My Word.

For that reason My Law protects Myself.

Such minds will never see me—when they think themselves as big as God—they descend to animals.

Take this Word for your own good.

My Boy Joe is weary and sick of writing. I must allow him to—but now Good-bye, Joe. I will give you the Spirits, never fear that you are not My Boy.

If we do not succeed one way, we will another.

Future can remember I talk this to Joe just as I please, and it need bother no one.

I am talking to him and through him. He is pleased, and others may profit by our conversation.

His voice is My Own. I do with him just as I please.

Others must profit, because I will not come to every one. You must follow Us. We have lowered ourselves, and do not feel well about it. We will forever be offended if you do not respect. We are now down low.

But you must keep under. We need no ruler over us—and will not have any.

My Laws protect me from big head men.

Read this Book again and study My Ways.

You have your josh liberty—if you can find out more about me than is contained in this Book, I give you your liberty.

Study the ways of this Book to appreciate liberty.

I hope now and forever you will want your liberty.

John, let us—stop quiet—Joe, keep a clean, sweet, pure heart.

Do not wish to kill yourself like this any more. And now I set you free. You wished to be My slave now I give you your freedom on earth. You my slave, I made you a purpose—and now I will love you forever more.

Because you never spoke anything but love to me—you are coming to me and never will—because we have been together and worked these many days, until My Spirit is a part of you.

Our wires of Electricity connected, I cannot lose you.

Always respect me as you have, and I am pleased.

You can journey on through life with a—sweet—heart. Change the mind and commence anew. My Laws will finish up the flies for us.

We must clean our mind all out.

You must wash—pure clean yours—it is dangerous to continue—We Three shall meet again.

Do not cry, My Boy Joe—Good-Bye.

Look up—cheer up—you come up—do not fear anything on earth.

Be good, and when you come I want you.

Now cheer up—we must away—remember to be good—you free to do as you please. You shall have the Spirits if I have to send them in a part of Myself.

I will now leave you enough to last your time. I will not

work you down until your meal must be brought to your bed —and then leave you helpless.

Cheer up—take your mother's advice—after while.

Wash the Dan-ruff—off your scalp—cheer up—good-bye— any My Spirits—you remember sixteen Devils Power—hoop la—that's right, smile.

Well, remember me when I am away—I will keep you in Spirits. Do not fear if you commence to run short—Spirits come at that time.

Good-bye, boys. You must stay, John.

Your Spirits are what he needs.

And if you are with him I know he is safe.

All right, Father, I will be one of the Boys. I will keep him out of the fire—and the fire-water out of him. I will be his Saviour—and Saviour to him only.

We will give the rest of the world this little Book, and they can save themselves—now Father, you know I will stay with him—do not worry.

If we do not succeed one way, we have patience to wait an- other—APPEARANCE. If it does not come, we have patience to wait—at the last we will hope to come as close to you, and be with you again.

We THREE are the Last now—say Good-bye in Good Spirits.

Good-Bye——Good-Bye——Good-Bye.

Now, Brother Joe, we cannot have any foolishness. We will not stand any from anybody. We will leave first. You must call yourself—little—you know what—and I will event- ually bring us both out all right.

Don't you—don't you—now don't worry.

I am—Joe, and take it all around, am the original little stink—and we together will make the biggest stink in the country.

Brother, you know I am the prophet Eli-as.

You know I said we had the widow lady, sure pop.

Yes, and I worked your game—wild goose chase now. We will finish picking it—we have found it one dark one—now we pull the wish bone—and be

> Two–Strikes Cuplids—Two Simple Boys.

I LEFT—SHE CAME ON AFTER ME.

Come, should near make a bare-foot—think of Judgment resurrection.

Quit Eli—the **Bow is** over the weather's **horns.   Many of** our arrows are lost—best we kick out of another engagement —we would get left—could not be another Bow like **the** original Cuplids found in world.

We **now** quit to continue sincere love **to** another when **we are again.**

Forever our love is sincere—Father, **and** now He is away **our love is** sincerity.

No one in the world should be otherwise   The Light hap**piness in this** is His changing nature towards Himself, and **does not** give other flies of the earth the privilege of any light treatment **or** ridicule of things sacred.

God's nature changes—He has the **right** and Power—others run, **are lost** when they commence to **ridicule** His nature.

He **can** and is combined Power—of **sincerity, truth and** happiness.   This **is the** gayest style **God above allows us to use**   I hope it **will** never lead Christians **or any others to** fritter their lives **away in** gayety.   The **best** may follow God's Ways in sincerity, **truth** and happiness.

And **now my own** wish would be that this Book could **not** be taken pleasantly by people of the world.   I am a Christian and I hope all Christians will be sincere in truth in nature.

Life of **the world** I presently leave, and I Am sincere.

In absence—God above—I can tell my love scrape.   He will hear about **it some time—and in** truth giving all small **details** of **my life I am familiar.**

I will give **you my first and only** love letter I ever wrote, **or ever expect to write.   I** am sincere—I dislike **to** be **familiar.**

Some have thought I was stuck after them, after leaving my first love—but I hope you remember who I was packing the **Mail** to.   I am finishing this up as a clean sweep to the world, **and leave** all such behind me when I leave—for the Last time.

I call the girl my first genuine love—before her it was all boy business.

About the time I wrote the letter I was preparing to leave her sadly.

You may judge by this book whose mail I prepared afterwards.

The **letter I sent the girl—of** course I had to copy it care**fully.**

I kept an original copy.   **Of course I** gave her a few little presents before that time. I was trying to work her up to the point I was coming to in the letter.

My first original idea was a little birthday card—a soft, very soft and pleasant picture of a horse-shoe. I believe she took it for good luck. I placed on the card a few lines—I do not remember what. No one could understand them—but she said she did.

Again I sent her a chunky round ribbed jug of extract—scent with it a few lines, of course, plain, saying it was diluted extract—union of Sweet Briar and Orange Blossom—for her to use all subsidiary advise to avoid use of all others—or something like that.

She said she was pleased with that sweet home variation.

Shoo to the Fair-field. She was well pleased.

So she said—quietly—come to myself, please—Sol-a-no one knows it but myself—or pleasing words for proper effect to me.

After that a space of time, which brings my court-ship to that lonely love-letter.

I scent it in candy — the market afforded the best. I a quiet farmer could (ill) afford it—cost me value of U S hog coin dollar—I paid for it—one box.

Her answer came—it was far from free—the answer we do not care to see. You may remember I spoke of it.

In Pictures of Life where Liberty gives a Light heart the wings of Love—and that and this together is all the details I am going to give of my love a-fair.

This is the letter which received a cool answer. I excuse the girl for not understanding it. I believe she will have to read the book before she understands it:

MARY——CHRIST-MAS—188— SANT—ROSA.

With this there is a box, and some contents also enclosed—please find this permission—in return to me is acceptable part empty package in payment.

But, dear, bo slow—in truth I only say this seeking an opportunity to wish you past surprise.

That to your ear I may dare speak

My kind intentions—and likewise it gives me time to see that I should be free from the influence of haste.

So I will venture to look one year back from the face of time.

First I will tie necessity (untie either).

And then—in defense of modesty—with your permission—I beg to say—I regret not—it was not unfit—if so certainly excusable. **As to** help noble patience—was **to hurry that** sometimes **dumb** companion, time.

But now, **at** this late date, I do **not wish to be guilty of** praising qualities which duty calls from me.

So I hesitate much—concluding that your own mind should **say if I** need appear different to be a disciple of that most continent **man,** Joseph **(son** of Jacob). I am sure if occasion **bring** a little more practice, I will be perfect in those **ancestral** qualities.

But do not forget, **I am far from** impatience.

The last I seen of **it was with that** little parable—**one year** is nearly one-half of three.

I thought of something else, **but if you can try to find in this what an** idle and sober thought **keeps me company.**

Believe me from my first step in **this secret style of weakness**—nor now **am** I guilty of striving **for advantage**—but rather with rare **honesty.** I do this that **you may know me** as—I Am.

Therefore, **with your** other many advantages, **I will leave** you as the judge.

As for me, **I am to** that stage where I feel all these things. Come they good **or** bad, help us to ascend.

I know these are very sensitive intentions—

But **I** send them trusting such **a** quantity of wit (please let **me call it** wit) will **not** subdue reason—but **in** such a sad case **·I can** only think **to say or advise** you to earnestly pray for some quantity of inspiration to relieve you.

For, when **the curtain is drawn** aside and I look far back through the **dim mysterious mist** of our past, and properly buried experience, **I** see myself appearing timid.

Irresolute in times of such need.

Methinks I was better **suited to meander in** toilsome travel **after the** solitary plow.

Nevertheless, at times when in painful meditation, I doubt not **but I** could have appeared in **better color**—if your eyes had smiled more pleasantly.

But I fear this is nonsense.

While my **kind,** patient, and I regret to say, much abused steeds, should now with outstretched necks, slow and measured tread, be directing their weary feet towards the highway leading to the swift rapids of lonely Port–er Creek.

Even now, **with faint** beating heart; I think of the dark **pass** leaving Curt–s **place.** Probably danger awaits me there

—with some glistening weapon concealed in the ambitious hand of fiery youth.

But I hope to come out into that fragrant atmosphere—that sweet locality—

Where the spicy air is manufactured, and used only for the soft breath accompanying the low whisper of angels.

That romantic space—that green oasis of paradise—entirely controlled, presided and ruled over by the Royal.

Thence up those steep hills close by to—who now collectively meditate pilgrimage to the sunlit alfalfa-beds of beauteous space—thence on, with my heart still beating, to view the deserted vil-ages—their stillness only awakened by the baying of that black watchman—barking at weary passengers or straggling footmen.

From thence toiling up in most any direction.

With our eyes we might behold the beauties, the very corners of the universe—but before I look I will take time to tell you—I Am—your friend,   JOSI.

There is more, but I will not say it—in the name of Elijah I ask you to forgive my many faults.

THE DAY WE CELEBRATE.

THIS ACCOUNT GIVEN IN THE SAN FRANCISCO EXAMINER,
THURSDAY MORNING, DECEMBER 25, 1890.

Sitting Bull Laid Away—General Miles' Report to the
Commanding General of the Army—The Indians
Determined to Fight.

Special to the Examiner.

The funeral of the Indian policemen took place yesterday afternoon with military ceremony. Sitting Bull's body was laid away in the post grave-yard with few honors. Detailed account of the fight—Bull Head, who was in charge of the Indian police, was a bitter enemy of Sitting Bull. When the courier from the police came back on the road and notified the cavalry of the fight, the latter started forward on a gallop. The hostiles were in the timber and firing on the police, who defended themselves from Sitting Bull's house. A few shells from the Hotchkiss gun sent the redskins hurrying up the river out of range.

The policemen formed in line and presented a fine appearance as they received the soldiers—but the spectacle a few yards behind them was horrible in the extreme. Eight corpses lay about on the ground, riddled with bullets and mutilated. Sitting Bull was on his back, and his face was hardly recognizable, so shot up and battered was it.

The correspondent thinks a number of the hostiles who escaped were badly wounded.

The police entered the camp early in the morning, and proceeded quickly to Sitting Bull's house and surrounded it. Several went inside and arrested Sitting Bull, when he gave the alarm by yelling. Several of his lieutenants repeated it, and fighting then began. The police stood their ground heroically, in spite of tremendous odds against them.

Catch-the-Bear and several other hostiles rushed into the house and began firing at the police. Bull Head was shot in the leg—he whirled and put a bulled into Sitting Bull's head —and at the same moment Red Tomahawk shot Sitting Bull in the stomach. Part of the hostiles retreated to the stable, a hundred yards off, and the policemen pursued and drove them out. The policemen also got possession of the house, and took in their dead and wounded. The hostiles then fell back into the woods, and the fight was kept up until the cavalry drove them off.

TROOPS CLOSING IN.

Pine Ridge.—Officers counted up the returned dancers to-day, finding 1024, and issued rations to them. It is believed the hostiles in the Bad Lands number 500. The troops are closing in on them.

NEGRO GHOST DANCERS.

Bismarck.—It is reported that the negroes in Mandan are affected with the Messiah craze, and are holding nightly meetings in an empty government building.

WAS IT WANTON BUTCHERY.

Bismarck.—It is now being claimed that Sitting Bull was murdered in cold blood. Corporal Gunn, of the Eighth Cavalry, was also with the troops that went out in support of the Indian police. He says the Indian police did not like Sitting Bull. Every Indian at the agency, except Sitting Bull's followers, was jealous of the latter's prominence, and only too glad of an opportunity being afforded, under government protection, to kill him. Continuing, Corporal Gunn says: **Lieutenant Bull Head, of** the Indian police, went **to** Sitting **Bull's** house, opened **the door,** and commenced **reading** the **warrant** for **his arrest.** Sitting Bull and his two sons—one a lad of **twelve—were** the only persons in the **shack.** He carried his **arms, like all** Indians. The boy came to the door and gave **the cry of** alarm, on seeing the house surrounded by police. **He no sooner** cried than Bull Head, without a moment's hesitation, and before any resistance, fired at Sitting Bull, the **ball piercing** his breast immediately over the left nipple. As he was staggering he managed to draw his revolver and fire one shot, the bullet entering Bull Head's thigh. Sitting Bull fell about six feet away from the door. His horse was standing near the house. Red Tomahawk jumped on it and flew with the news that Sitting Bull was killed. Crowfoot, the boy, was next killed, and fell across the body of his father.

The combat was **then** hand **to** hand. Sitting Bull's enraged followers rising **up from the** brush like magic. But few **shots** were fired—guns **were** clubbed, stocks shattered to splinters, and barrels badly **bent.** The Indian police soon found themselves handicapped, **and** sought refuge in Sitting Bull's deserted shack, leaving outside four of their own dead **and** nine of the hostiles, including the old chief.

Shortly after the troops appeared, **and the hostiles hastily retreated.**

READY TO RETURN.

Rapid City.—General Miles has received advice from General Brook that 500 friendly Indians have left Pine Ridge to attempt to bring in the hostiles. Thirty-nine of Sitting Bull's Indians, who left the agency on Monday, have sent in word **that they will** return.

General Carr has thrown out a cavalry force to intercept **the band now** reported to be moving across the reservation of **the Bad Lands.** **If the** force fails to intercept them, they will **be pursued** and arrested.

General Miles says that **no** advance would be made until **the result** of **the** Pine Ridge conference is known. Big Foot **and Hump** have surrendered, and have returned to the agency. **No Indians** except the band mentioned are now going to the **hostiles, and** the gordon of troops is constantly tightening.

General Miles discredits the report of a large band of Indians **in** the vicinity of camp Crook, on the Little Missouri. No further engagements have been reported from the lower ranches. A government herd of cattle was located on Alkali Creek, and a force of twenty men have gone to round it up.

Two companies of the Seventeenth infantry, from Fort Russell, are expected here this afternoon, and will at once follow the forty-five Cheyenne scouts from Pine Ridge, who started for Cheyenne this morning. The available force along the Cheyenne, under General Carr, is about 1500 men.

SITTING BULL'S GHOST APPEARS.

Minneapolis.—Tribune special says that a ranchman in to-day from up Bad River, reports that the hitherto peaceable, semi-civilized tribe of Two Kettle Sioux began a wild ghost dance the night before last. Some of the bucks, when returning home, claimed to have seen a white figure on top of a bluff. One of them said it was Sitting Bull. The alleged phantom motioned them to follow, and glided from hill to hill in the direction of the Bad Lands. The ranchman says the Indians accept this as a proof that Sitting Bull is the Messiah, and that he was beckoning them to join his followers. The ghost dance is the consequence, and the ranchman says the Indians as far down as Willow Creek are affected.

If the story is true it is a serious affair.

INDIANS SURRENDER.

Washington, December.—Major General Schofield has received a telegram from General Miles dated Rapid City, Dakota, as follows: I believe all or nearly all of the followers of Sitting Bull have been captured. Colonel Sumner reports to-day the capture of Big Foot's band of Sioux numbering 150. He has been one of the most defiant and threatening of the Indians. The result so far has been satisfactory.

On the same Christmas day I was very busy myself.

I was heavy at work.

My hat off I was diving into it as a farm laborer working for my board was my thoughts. I was pruning out the extra branches of fruit trees on the place where I lived a quiet life.

And after serious reflection I do not think this fighting the Indian was right.

If he wished to give a ghost dance during his idle time it was nobody's business in Washington or anywhere else.

If the Indian wished a Messiah it was nobody's business in

Washington, and it would be sensible not fight him again for it.

Kind treatment comes from gentlemen; trouble originates from Government officers who slight work.

Result, fight, hardship.

Church members—I am a Christian but not a church member.

Scrubs of the world—I am a scrub clean in world. I do not respect people for the above active fight. I do not respect big heads who do not respect God. My last wish is they may go to—. Realize I am sincere, but cannot handle you all.

Make yourselves sincere. God's Law will handle you at the last. I am man. His Law is truth, exact never to fail.

The Indian ghost dance was doing no harm (to the breed).

Was doing no harm by the Mile like other jigs are doing. I hope Miles will quit fighting the Indians and turn his Hotch–kiss against the other jig—or against a feather bed where he can do no harm. I will be familiar (with the breed).

There was certainly no use for the white people to interfere and give the Indians bad treatment, because they were excited about a Saviour.

Bad treatment to them is no advantage to any one that I know of.

It was no advantage to any person that I know of for the the American government to commence fighting the redman because he wished a Saviour. He can do no harm with his belief to other than himself, and this should be a free country to all who have as good judgment as the American Sioux.

Of course they wish their right and show it as quick as the army officer can show the big head.

I forgot Miles. He is an army officer, and after his achievements against the red man, he certainly will get a head quite large and quiet. He should not either according to account, he walked the floor mostly his soldiers and the red man out fighting the storms killing a few in fair weather, they were all glad by account that the weather was destroying the red man for then they wished to freeze him out with the severe cold storms.

It simply shows the American character is cool in feeling towards the red man a cool and small calling for others.

That is the reason I like to take this to drop man one and all forever. I have never heard a preacher, missionary or any one else say very much in favor of the American Indian,

and they **respect** Great **Spirit** more than any other race on
this Globe.

Reference the Spirit that writes this Book—Ladies—change.

They are firm if they believe their Savior is coming. They
have the right, and show fight when **a big** army department
tries to tramp—them.

They should not dirty **their** hands on a few white trash; but
they have **a** perfect right to fight that thatis spread over their
land if it tries **to** corral them, and get them out of the way,
and allow them nothing (but something).

And then take away their **liberty.** I forever give up **the
white** man—they may **josh liberty until they** are sick **and
weary** of it.

I want no **more** of it.

I will be **with** the red man if he wishes, and still **I love**
only God above—their Saviour by Great Spirit—and **my only**
Saviour.

That—I **can—God** moves the only Saviour.

A man **must save** himself by respect God's Laws I am
Elijah with **a heart** of stone. I was made for a purpose—
educated. **But a man** is a fool who thinks I would be allowed
to write this **Book if I** was continually pulling the other way.
Without **firm, sober** thought, I would **have** been a weekly
failure.

Great Spirit **must see evil kept** away off.

I myself will forever respect my God above only.

There may be many people who are as serious as Joe.

They must be exact, level-headed, earnest, **to be** like Joe.

To skate the Gospel wire I am simply **Joe.**

At last, if Spirit takes you, you skate **the** Gospel wire.

The original man–u–script—this will **be** burnt in the fire—
it must **be** taken by the voice for the future.

Remember, I am Joe, I **drop** pencil.

I trust my future—A—be—to c Z—you know. **My God**
above, you **know** C Last you C what I mean.

I hear the Trumpet Blow—again—I am Joe.

Future may judge my predicament—the difficulty of plac-
ing this in type—I standing against everyone. The world
apparently could trust no one to be friendly to me talking
against the kind who published my first book.

I remember **there are two** sides—I come with the one that
is getting **the worst of it.** I see a—rat—I come to one to

help me—I treated him very cool—with him coin would gain my way—so—long—De—moc—rat.

Repub—li—can — I am same as top fence STONE-WALL JACK-SON—man.

If I get left good John—son save yourself.

SHE—(THE WORLD PLANET.)

She was and is one very large and fast wo—man.

And now God has come to judge her. I hope it will last.

I think He did it a purpose the U S is left give away.

I must say I believe you—U S sold.

Commence look backward the word of God may unfold.

I have a promise in this Book my next journey will be to see the Mysteries of the Morning Star.

But I will not give it away or make it to sell everybody like this Record of my journey trip to earth.

That journey will be sacred to me, sacred and sincere to God above.

The trip to the Moon eve may run and record.

To buy herself something. I don't care anything about.

She is very light on the fly she may cork herself up.

In the moon get there with small wings of this pattern.

Wait a minute—sew bossy, don't kick up over your milk.

Eat fair—beware—I fire you hide at milking time.

Hid quarters all the bags in the diary—give up.

Speak to help—never kick.

Brave Indian S–I–O–U–X Y Z.

First—last—after—future—pass—out—to future—time.

Ready for publication thirteenth day of February, 189 one in days after fulfilled.

By small head—peg leg I have been told God's Word in the Bible is babyish (in contradiction a lie).

Take care big head say what you can about this let God's Word be sacred. The same one said the Electric wonder a Georg—a fake. I did not understand him thoroughly, he had never seen he was born blind in his belief.

He minded me of Gems of Thought—in belief he was English. I questioned him—he knew nothing about Gems of Thought—so he certainly was not Ingersold. He promised he would be interested in Gabriel's Trumpet.

I hear of those brutes with their bollows—

So I blow, blow, blow, to stop them.
Space—a record of the Wasps of the past.
Statue Liberty look at him—judge him who he condemns.
Wasp is in a coffin fit—something like rain in face be my
Judge at last.

W–h–o, **Boys, I am** Back.

THE BIG MEDICINE MAN (with me).
(Latest) MR. THREE — KICK — POWERS.
(THE SINGLE-ACT-MAN.)

For the Big Round-Up—Kick **Up—Show,**
Show—the Old She—Burns—then **Dies—Tick-its**
Ante Over—to Show She Commences **It—Hear—**
We Go—for the OLD SHE.

SHE is worse than ever.
SHE is a fritter in gayety.
SHE sticks—them in the street.
She is on the run—so of course
They in with She call me fool, insane; idiot,
For my way slow business.
Of course—I have no thanks. She snaps.
I call her the female—She knows—what
Because She sticks them in the highway,
Holds most anything that comes along.
Then She runs round for growl and snap.
I profess I am a simple scrub,
Wasp—brute or She—beauty—bitch—are you better?
She, I wish to keep quiet—my Friends know
I learn something—I bust—I am glad of it.
She keep quiet, you think man's ways good,
I advise you to learn another.
This to future—be best—for you of future
Now—vers—us again—wasp case—fool talk
By an insane wasp-a-turn eye—
To Berry the scrub. Mr. and Misses, attention, please—
There—is only—a few of us left.
After there was more of it—but I had to leave.
I left—he had not impressed that he was better than—Berry.

One said he **was raving against** scrub Berry, who was q-t, q-t,
        quiet.
He who sticks up to say the past-age nearly **perfect,**
        Condemns me.
    I am not with them for money.
        Mr. Preach this baptised again—
           The future like my honey.
Preach-er is far better—
      Preacher I respect you far more than the man who
         Ridicules Sacred Power—
            Is beneath notice.
I do not try—improve them—they can go to—I dispise
      Them—I am not talking to them—I dispise
         Preach-er—you **tell me**
Christ was God—all Power—
      While he was only Spirit Saviour from God—
        Spirit from God Himself.
God controls planets—Christ—Spirit—was on **earth.**
      Spirit Christ—all power given over **man—**
        Not **over** planets.
A dam-p-reacher, small mind, **cannot comprehend God.**
        Christ—man is his god.
Christ, as man, was exalted—humbleth himself.
        He **knew** God was Great.
Preacher should know he was not God—who praised him
        In the Word of God.
But they do not—they say he is God—three-in-one.
How can the one man—Christ on earth—handle planets?
You sicken me—think of the Sky-Heaven planets.
      God, in the beginning, made His own way.
Dam-p-reacher says man—Christ equal to God.
      A **dam** preacher too small to talk about—fool, insane.
        God's Power man's mind cannot comprehend.
          God knew that.
    He gave them Little Spirit Christ—from God,
        A fle part—from Himself.
Dam-p-reacher cannot **see** God made planets,
        His electricity to suspend.
His thoughts far above simple humanity,
Of course He allows Little Spirit Christ to make kingdom,
        No extra trouble.
    God's nature handles such small things.
    God's sky-heavens move, man cannot comprehend
        His Power Pleasure.

Insignificant preacher saying man—
              Christ, God Himself,
(Who sent Christ to dam preacher up).
They tell me they prove it in the Bible,
              So of course Christ was a fle god.
Humanity cannot comprehend His Power.
              Find good place—dam–p–reach—her,
You are not fit to open your trap about God.
              Christ is a high as you can get—go to
For saying man–Christ—God's equal—
              Christ humbled himself—he was saved.
You did not take the model—he is your god—
              Liberty is American Josh.
My God above controlls the Heavens,
              He is not in with this She—inside ;
                     He rolls her rapidly about.
I want to be taken by God's Great Spirit
              That was given by Himself.
Christ–man is a flea–J–us–T–is Spirit
Of Brothers—Joe and John Gabriel—Great Spirit
              Gave all permission to Joe, the mail–carrier.
Preachers' praise of God is very insignificant—his largest
              Thoughts are insignificant of God's Power.
You say God is love—wh–e–u—away preachers—
              Nose—I hold—my nows—you are through.
              Preachers' god–Christ limit of your mind.
Woman, your time comes—do not make the same mistake
As preacher of man.   God owns the planets—all on them.
              You are something on one of them.
       You are The Flower made in beginning.
       You gain electricity—do not make the mistake;
That you are certainly—CREATOR HIMSELF GOD.
Man preached three-in-one Christ as containing God Himself.
       See their mistake—they idiot—loon–ticks.
You are liberty—(preachers) use Judgment with woman god.
              Mark—liberty is the model for her purpose—She
              Improved—She cannot be improved.
              Improve your ways—style—model—Liberty.
Think of His planet—earth–machine.
       Earth made in hours few—men say fable.
              God's Word is truth.
              Who can speak the Joy He feels—
                     Foam—vessel—reels—   .
                     Now—there is a Girl,

SHE has so many tittle dark blue eyes,
SHE is well bred
To the weather—She is rap rapt—She clings and holds—
SHE is rose, rich with pride of the common rich kind.
She has large amounts of it
And She is no better.
I am as raggy scrub pine standing in the brush.
I claim no relationship with her flowers,
In season I say—to family
She-mind—come round—in the humbleness
Of pansy blossom—respect—
Or the wind blows—your leaves begin—to turn
Summer past—I know beauty wilts down—beauty decays—
Departs—descends—becomes run down
To stick—thus as the shameful
Bitch—in the street
Ends the She family,
At this Judgment—future pride advance
By wisdom-flowers, it is best
Your pride—is on the stem—of thorns and weakness
Preach or wasp I know the family—I know
The one who respects—I am quiet I hear—I know when
I hear human thoughts, I leave the entire family
I am a separate kind.
I am the Disciple of God above.
I hide myself from the family.
Take your liberty and—stick her up
On a rocky shore.
You are a rocky lot of sheep.
I advise you to follow the Bell Sheep
Going Home.
Allow Liberty to enlighten you—by the way—good
By—shoo.
I can say many never would mind this shoo
Shine scrub—so they cannot obey the Law
Their mind takes them down, down to the Lake
I cannot help it—they are in the shade.
Fools say they never will mind
So of course I say they may slide down to the lake to hell
When they commence to help the human family—they think
They do too much—blame me for hardship
Think I do not act proper.
I leave the family—I will continue
And take what is good for me.

You mind or the breeze you mind
This is a dam–p, cold day tick closed up.
I proceed to repair it myself
I advise let go the slack swear—wire
Showing the faults of the present age correct.
We tell them plain,
We do not need another character exact—like your own
They must not copy the faults.
Saved—they cannot be
When they continue the faults
We leave them the faults—to be saved
We show them their faults.
If they wish certainly they can keep—their faults
And go to —— certainly.
Great Spirit would not recommend one
Who would not mind—some one
Now never frown or sigh
Though dark the night—be ever gay
There is sunshine—when She is near
SHE has many little dark blue eyes.
Christ to soon depart—then take your liberty
She mind preach—her forever—on earth—future
Family God will attend to the rest of the planets
Christ—loved—God
Christ, a fle Spirit, could comprehend God,
You cannot—He is too much for you,
You had better sink—down—down—and
Praise little Spirit Christ
God made Sky–Tent—God above all—
Holds all—quiet, calm, peaceful.
Compare God to Christ—a fle—you fool.
Preacher—disgust yourself—ashamed.
You man do not soil God's name—your thoughts
Of God are insignificant.
Preacher of Christ (greatest name)
God can move Sky–Tent—all planets—stars in it—
Move it upside down—away—you would not know
Anything about it.
Little Spirit Christ given all power with man.
How could he have all Power of God?
You fool, look at the planets.   Can Spirit–man–Christ
Handle space of Heavens?
You say to preach Jesus as God—undo confusion.
Dam–p–reacher fool—Christ is the greatest name

Among preachers—on **earth**—heaven.
Do not soil God's name with **your traps**—**flies**,
You compare him **to** God.   There is something
Matter in your mind, **preacher.**
Preacher, **sicken** yourself disgusted—look
At the planets—stars—fields and fields of them
In the Sky-Tent God holds—surrounds—peaceful and **calm.**
The planets obey God to the second—perpetual,
Humanity forever do as they please,
Then God is not with them.
Preacher, preach Christ until you are sick,
You can praise him,
But God is beyond the limit of your reason.
Am I—I so sorry—I in sick spell,
Disrespect Judgment—flies ashamed—
I have remained here a number of years, **when**
Saying to preacher, Christ is not God—they say
Christ given all power—three-in-one—better look that **up,**
Showing plain, blind, blank idiocy.
Wait a few minutes, preacher—return **to subject,**
I fix you—no time now.
Hold knows, pew, preacher, s–t revenge.
Adam preach–her, shut up your disgusting draft damp–her.
Preach to them I dispise—remember I will not talk
To them I dispise look at them—I cannot think
I sicken disgust—God above made three one
I Am—remember I one—common trinity Spirit
ONE has three in one
Learn A B C—down—over slow—to Z
Quis—Who is J—Joseph—an–s—Joseph—is the Father
Then who was—David—you
Quest—Who is God—a—n—s—God is not Christ
Quest—Who was Christ—a—s—Christ was Spirit for John
Joseph
Quest—Who is John Joseph—a—s—He is—Father Spirit
for Joe
Quest—Who **is** John and Joe Gabriel—a—s—they **are** cir—
cus partners
Quest—What is sky-tent—a—s—it holds God's earth—
machine
Quest—Where is God—a—s—God is—outside all hold—to—
gather test—a tent
Quest—What is electricity—a—s—God's breeze—Body Wire
—Glisterin—Axgreasion

Quest—Electricity man—cuplids God's two fle Spirits—an—s
    —read signs
Flea-Christ leaving—leaves—take liberty—I Am is going
    home
       The sky—tent hangs to hold a thick and heavy mass
        I go through it to get home
                Rest against liberty
       Respect God—if you follow—I Am—home
Preacher—home—do I kick you up—to progressive time
Will you mature moss—back in the fields of antiquity
Again come now—to set you at work—to get ahead—move
       Listen to the tick—its song—singing on the earth
       Recollections—find to bring—of days—of
       Could I bring—back—singing—here—to-night
        Those happy days so bright.
       But I am bold—this is a cricket—song
       God is the only one—can see His nature—His last
So He allows me to give this tick, tick, its song to—future
        And I sing it on His hearth
        So my love for God will never die
       I will never drink to be drunken—to forget God.
       You to perish—how can you serve me so—away
       My my own—ma—was ashamed of me,
       Through and through, and knew nothing in my Book
       Or the dam—age—of wasp business
By the ghost shirt—said A P—would be ashamed of me
       And I had better go with my Book—off
       Where I was not known—and J–C was such
       A fine man, and John played such fine tricks
Himself.   I should be ashamed to go around any of them.
       Some do not know Cuplids—we of the South
       Together busted—great future big head—demolish
       Liberty saved for Two Hay seed—saved
       By my style, she thinks I am bound to wreck
       On Salt Creek.   She thinks a trip to Salt–Lake best,
        So her friends would not hear of me.
        She cries—I know she is sincere
       In every word—of course I obey my parent.
I prepare for the voyage—I leave soon as I Am—ready
        To wreck or death—Berry me
        In the ocean of immortality.
Storms of life are swept away—I move to the light of future
        Day—comes—soon.
       Big-heads—end She—mind all take mine

Offence in future—mind.
Come to venus—is SHE suspended in space.
We come—bound to venus—
Three one—Electricity Power—God above—does she follow?
She mind is she with God's Power—now true,
Does she follow the way—does she come round on time?
We do as we like—Cuplids do as God wishes.
We fold our wings—we rest—stop the curs,
                    God is above wo-man.
We come to Mary;
            Mary—I proposed—first,
                    And second time you refused.
You can take one of the fists that track after you.
        You may stop to stick—and burn hell,
                I am God's servant forever—if He wish,
But I proposed—I would take—if you
        You wished no other, I would take you.
            If you entice others, go to hell
                    You bitch.   My life is short,
                        I am—alone.
    I forgive thee—fare thee well—good night, ladies
Joe hears the answer—say truth—I forgive thee,
                    Old-Black-Joe.
You are listen to the tick-its song—I forgive thee,
        Of course.   I turn away.   I think
                I hear the angels calling—Old Black Joe;
                I think I hear pleasant sounds—
I am coming, coming, for my head is bending low;
                I cannot stay, stay, so I must go.
        My head turning, bending, my heart I must go;
        I fly in time in pieces, to leave nothing but the hub,
        Electricity departing out to star eyes, I look myself,
        They use deceit, I am told by one, they need not
                    Love of God is not deceit.
                Then they cannot be disciples.
Do not confuse each other about your two gods.
I am Eli-Joseph, Jehovah is my God—best let Him alone.
Many say Lord, Lord—shut up, loon-ticks—savi-our-self;
                Save yourself, your chance is better.
To hell with some slur, ridicule towards sacred things;
                Do not think they are funny;
        They are silly—son-ny—sulky—idea—otick flies
        Inger-soul, you son of your—hell can handle you.
        G-t you like the bench, let go the bar.

Down slide to the Lake, go
Plead story, telling attorney.
Preacher; stick to your Lord, Lord, Lord—A, B, C, don't
rush to Z.
You understand—flea Cri, Cri, Cri, is not God,
Then loon–tick preachers in it. take your Lord Christ
And liberty. Stick your gain up, up by them.
You are below them, please continue Sunday-school.
Many odd churches—rich business.
Perfect, away back, behind confusion.
Churches—you in it—stick in it—stick up in it—up—then
up in it,
Direct to The Word.
Please continue plain kind Sunday-school to future.
My God above, my call to duty to kill, burn—
HELL—hell afire—FIRE!
Shut up, Joe—false alarm, turn—stop,
Short time, now, now, I am the prophet, don't you know
Never forget the Two or Fan Boys. Strike
Wind up the Saviour Business
We may take the trip, space, space, to the moon.
I cannot stand near the stingers. I record to future
Wasps in cof–in fit—to cover his outside,
Wh-u-z while he is in cof–in fit outside court
We will dive out to ocean end. Judgment vers–us wasps.
Wasp's nest hive round world—swarms again
They swarming—light into the herds—
The buffalo they slaughter like raving, insane
Remember the scenes of the prairies—where are they
Red man with good nature regret—scenes departed.
Fire—fight—pale—face
We take pleasure in protecting an animal family
Old Ben Harri–son and his buffalo family
Come safe from the Fire.
They may live by Electricity close to the Two Hayseed
Waiting while they are sprouting green future
We cuplids have permission to leave, to go far.
Then again far—to view the sit-u-at-I-on larger planets
Going as the Electricity man I Am
Then the Promise takes us all around the seam of the sky–tent
(Sew, bossy, the milk-a-way)
Then we can go all over sky through star–eyes to outside
We can return some—some time
Wander back again—wayward—and careless

In ages, ages, ages, to look for hearts of gold
    In dark minds of earth.
God knows what is best—we cuplids go as God wishes,
In heavy clouds we climb out to get the opposite attraction,
    Then rapidly fly away from earth.
By–by, She—we far up—then up and up—turning round
And round, looking down on the gigan-tic form of SHE,
Then away we go, till SHE is dim on the face of the sky.
    We look back—She is hid in clouds—away we go,
      Then shine up towards the Sun—
    Rest on his attraction, and float over to the Moon
To explore—all then we continue to look over to the SHE-
    planet.
Earth—we think of her—we will return in proper season,
    Ourself small, all record we do not pack ;
In this record we send thoughts to benefit—future—remember
    Things you see—you see in this record
Only things you see. You cannot make them false—of such
    Most of them—we prove them on earth.
We can say when they are false—you do not know.
      Humanity is blind.
    God can see His nature—
      Knows His Laws—humanity cannot see
        Breeze—Electricity—Power
Joe First burns—stands by type—future voice.

FUTURE—VOICE.

In the year 1891, in the heavens, was visible
A blue heat—Electric flame—tire perfect round,
    Gradually tightening to SHE-planet–earth,
    Holds—entire round circumference.
It draws in close as She rolls rapidly—flying
Through space—all things to become pure blister,
    Then melt rocks—run lava beds—end.
To commence future, Great Spirit blows this
    Future Voice, giving record to the future
    He not in it—look on to enjoy the case.
Tick, tick—1891—from the heavens was visible
A streak of Electric fire—following one of the planets—
    By observation it was seen to be She (earth)
    As She flew through space—the fire
Stretching out as the comet's tail. They not in it
    Look on and enjoy these proceedings.

Tick—closed up—Good—Saturday—night.

Space—from date—sweet sixteen—of ours.

I again—I thankful—see pure good Rain in Face down falling
    Streams flowing again, swift, cool and fresh,
    Cooling earth, washing down impurities,
        Flooding, making green grass, washing
    And rolling fresh cool water down to sea.
    Space—date—temporainus—very thankful.
    Space—space—space—of time—great space.
O yes, O yes—wer–u of course I prophet said
    Fire—FIRE—hell afire to the old SHE.

Future, now, later-day-saints now in future, more-man
    Later-day-saint—Electricity-man says
    Many weary days exertion for coin—no success.

Later-day sons of—Golden West—staved me off.
        Could I get the best of them?

Later-day-Lady Timid did I take—try to get the best of her
        I Fish—Ear-l-y—no success.
Cannot you take my word—afraid of me with security,
        Double—double security.

Speaking Frank, I come to A Jew—thinking, perhaps
        Can Moses return in future, give me help,
Then, I O. K.—think of Shy-lock—to one of that tribe
 With him, I expect him to bleed me severely—I expect
    As on my previous trial to come, by authority, safe.
        I come safe by the Highest Authority.
    I sounded my name, sick, to public ear, of past,
I again I Am—Antonio—to accept help from the tribe of
        Shy–lock.
    Will he make a fish-bait of me?
    I come, Shy-lock, I say I was out fishing for—
        Can he help me catch one.
        We speak of an old quarrel.
        There was no friendship with me.
I told his family one to go to hell—he thought I did not
        mean it.
    Certainly, I meant just what I said.
    He remarked Jesus Christ.

I would take no impudence from any.   I told him
To continue the difference, if he wished—do so, if he could.
I was always ready, nevertheless.   To his brother

I told him not to tell—Jews I had enough dealings **with**—
        previous.
    I was sick of it—willing to drop;
    I dealt a long time without profit to myself.
    He would continue with me, enemy **as** I was;
    Business—was his saying in the transaction.
His intention severe—plenty of it—to bleed me severely.
Soon I would have been thankful—no one to help me—
        Bound to the necessity.
    I will when necessary—Shy-lock—take **my** bond
        In the pictures of life.
I am the cruel heart to play the disagreeable **part;**
        The audience **large;**
The stage a field—I stand **alone**—**scenery,** the prison yard.
        I stand alone, in opposition
Every one on earth. My Friend by this BOOK is God **above**
    Therefore, **I** am Light Heart—Last—so **far**
        Proceeding to FUTURE—to **publis**
           All my fortune floats **the see,**
    I proceed with security to help me on my **journey.**
    I continue my course. The Jew
        Backward—shaky—does not **come to time.**
    I find one to loan me 3000 **bits of** gold;
    I come to one who had respect for my word.
I begin at memory—first thought—Mary was Irish-man.
    Second—Jew **BACK**—hang back—you can go to—
    Can you respect—TO APPEAR—can any one?
May you take God's Word—remember New Testament
    Anew, you must respect the Saviour.
And now, in memory, in this you must. He says respect
Some, one, or best you do not come—cannot know Him.
Shy-lock descendants, read Bassanio—advise Book of Port-i-a
    Antonio says—satan takes—you live for gold.
    You do not. Could you love one so big as God?
    He does not know you—do not care—Breeze—Yes.
I then remember I am Antonio, the disciple of God.
Then I commence to respect those who respect God above,
    Even she all Irish-man—not so very, very good.
    I remember, then, the ancient round-up.
O yes, I remember mammon. O yes, I came **to** him;
    I wished him—Joe Gabriel—to help Joe—came.
    I did not think he could do better than—help Joe
With my word; but mammon said it was a pig-in-poke,
    Though a fool would not, I would **have** felt better.

He would not, his mind not sound, he was thinking about
                    money;
He owned a bank of wealth—such an old shell-back
As him hangs on, while the new generation are out sprouting
To help; they do not make the new generation any more
            Than the old one, not perfect. I expect
                I will expect they cave off—decay.
            Their money to another—to SHE. O yes, it sticks.
It goes to another—tears, tears, tears—some to future.
            In joy I do not, how did he—he came in some place
                To understand God's Law—I profess, for mammon
God's Spirit does not wish to take him—his money with him.
            Mammon, O, O—C-on-ell HELL—you go forever;
                Your qualities far below the Brush.
Brush mammon may sprout fresh after fire—in ages of time.
            Future believe—old generation rapidly disappeared.
Electricity man and wo-man appear.   Their Spirits
        . Prepare for future—they the model brand
                Generation to commence future anew.
            Generation commenced—placed at the Last;
            In time come around, and come in at beginning;
                So and so continue round and round
            And round—never find the jumping off place,
                    End of The Horn.
I give straight my entire opinion—plain.
I hope never to mention the subject again.
            I wash myself clean, for business
                At the end of The Horn.

Time and Space   *Space—Time*   *Space—Space*   *Time—Space*

Past in truth—heard—
        Original Gabriel's Trumpet
Now reproduced in print—exact as from
        Original Trumpet.

SCENE—O

INTO——FUTURE.

She Blows—Blows—She Blows.
Future receives this record — of Original Gabriel.
Sacred this MEMORY to earth–wasps–hive nest.

GEANEOLOGY.

THE PROGRESS OF HUMAN FAMILY.

Family Geaneology—Spirit **from Great** Spirit from God Himself—Commencing **Darkness**—**First Sprout**—
As Two Hayseed.

'To fle Spirit of Great Spirit, to Spirit Christ,
To Angel Gabriel, to return to God Himself,
Angel Gabriel return as Spirit of man,
To Electricity, man of God.

GEANEOLOGY—PROGRESS—ANIMAL FAMILY.

Of old Ben—Harri-son.
Spirit in Buff-a-lo to old Ben himself.
Commencing darkness—sprout—down—down—
To rats, rats, rats.
(The one that sting Dead Berry, has not returned we leave
him
Outside court—a cof-in up his outside).

Fle Deck—for 1891.

She—nay you waited for Elijah the prophet.
Now come this Book—return of Gabriel prophet
Ben-e-fit the S-I-O-U-X—Y Z—see.

Joe Gabriel—return—is **on** earth—wake
The fact, this is the Two Strike Boy Saviour
Ben-e-fit the red man.

She—mind this Book **by** Two Strike—Indians Boy.

Record—journey to earth of the Saviour.
The redman Ben-e-fit fool.

God's Judgment is before you, future American
People, this Joe Gabriel's Book. American
Treat it light and you are—fool.

Remember the curse of the world, return of Elijah,
The prophet, judgment of She—planet—earth.

Wake American! For future the Saviour returned,
Fulfills Judgment—of the She planet—earth—record.

The Great Spirit from God Himself pronounces
The Judgment on all humanity.

Cupid dictates to Joe Gabriel—God wires him
By the gospel-wire, big heads have no time to wait
You may say hum-bug—you do not know.
If you say this is not true you are—fool.

Day of Judgment—God herds His planets
By Electricity band. His Word comes to earth
By Electric gospel-wire.

God Himself sends His Word Electricity quick
Cupid interprets the Word of the gospel-wire.

Wise men hear something—you do not know,
You cannot understand judgment—you are under
Judgment. Take Boy Joe's Word, God Himself owns it
It is Judgment of earth—Gabriel's Testatent.

Day of Judgment to earth—fools—hypocrites.
Money sax take the medicine—yours is bitter.
Dose: Use honey, butter, Gabriel's Testatent.

Old Harri-son says Indian go.
Indian's Boy Joe Gabriel says Harri-son go to ——
Joe the Son-o-ma Boy's challenge for three rounds
Indian take gate money—all come.

Judgment of She—planet—earth
Two Hayseed saved for commencement human family

Future—with Electricity man and wo-man.

Geo. Washington, please claim Harrison is a fraud.
English pale face takes red man's home.
Harrison says begon you Indian—dog—gone him.

Joe Gabriel is Able—he will be a brave for the red man
Of the northwest to kick Miles and Miles over the continent.
Read this judgment—Miles—in—it.

Money sax take this Book miser mind, sir,
Mine, sir—judgment, sir, Saviour work, sir,
God's wisdom, sir, little head, big head, fool good
American take Gabriel's Testatent.

Son of God born again—with God's Wisdom
He brings Judgment to earth—little Jew fall in
Line or go to —— you waited long for the prophet.
Come read of Gabriel.

Pale face do not continue doubting your mind
Reading record of Judgment of earth—by Two Strike
Boy Saviour Joe Gabriel's journey to earth.

American read of Big, josh, liberty with the
Wisdom—flowers—to her rapidly
Fly wheel band is on—earth rolls rapidly—save yourself
By Joe Gabriel, the last chance straw
Joe Gabriel, God's mail carrier, returned to earth,
Could have GOD'S SIGNATURE—BUT HE WILL NOT USE IT.
To Gabriel's Testatent he signs as the copyist.
SIMPLE JOE.

O God's Spirit, come close—corner of my bed.
May I say to them, of course, go on?
Who revises GOD'S WORD—sons of ——
O of course, preacher, big head, to hell for impudence.
God's Word is to remain just as it is—preacher is impudence
This is to remain my Word suits me to remain as it is
If it does not fit your head does not suit me—remain—it is
If it does not suit your brain does not fit my meaning
If it does not fit your brain it does not suit you—at last
If it does not suit to fit your meaning it suits me—to last

Take your brain away—it is my meaning to remain—as—it—
    is last.

Leave—it is it is best for you **not to change it, as it is it fits**
    —suits—mind.

OK—COD—PS—N B.

Steer—and—air hist—Spirit of Joe Gabriel
I have walked 1891 miles **of** air—in clouds of air
And many more—simply **to** round up my tune,
Now I—letter go as the Two Strike letter fly wh—whe—whiz
End side show side, blow side light out Joe—Josi-ah there end
I am little old hag-god yes I am **sure—my** God above knows
    The I Am Spirit of the J—J—Josi-ah Boys.

Returning to my town—I find the **view covered,**
After—now after fire, white as ash-es—lonely, **I am** all alone
    Seem to hear voices—rumbling **noise.**

I see three of the buf-a-lo family,
Lost—I soon removed—in a departing fog—litt-e **q-t, q-t.**
    Boy keeps along my company—after
    I collect myself, and return, lonely, in the fields,
I come **to** a place, and remember the Great Original Gabriel's
    Cir-cus record grounds.

O yes, O yes—wer-o She—till I fly to pieces—wer-o
Yes, take my Word—Great Spirit—blows this—wer-o She
I away—fly in pieces—arms out revolving—solid hub,
Retaining electricity to depart, take in the stars.   I Am
    Mr. one–David–Christ–fle Spirit—Son of God,
    As Tick-it-of-leave-man—in Electricity-power.

BY PUBLIS-HER.

All taken in—big round wher-o-up three is one—one last—
    last one.
Three in One—one three, three one.   One made three one.

IN MEMORY

OF GABRIEL'S ORIGINAL CIR-CUS GROUNDS OF THE ORIGINAL
SHOO WHACK WHIZ BUZ BIG ROUND UP.

I AM THE FIRST—So-l-a-r System.
I AM THE LAST—So-l-d air System.

AGAIN MODEL SON—MODEL BOOK

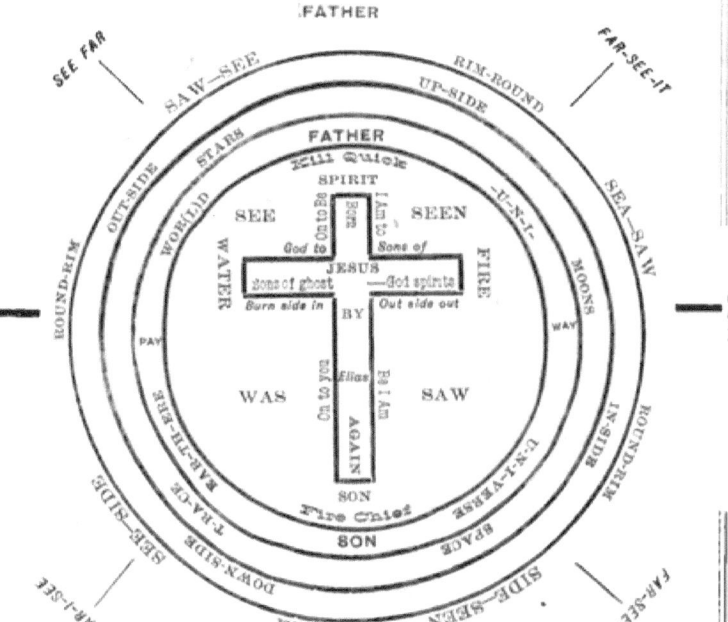

MAP—MODEL—MODEL-MADE BOOK

SAVED AMONG OTHER THINGS—SAVED.

The following deck cards, found safe in great safe,
    Possessions at the last—Joe—Josiah's departure
        Left to publis–her—Josiah Joseph—proceeds
Shaded with disgust—proceeds balanced by the hand of
    Liberty,
In the morning by the bright Light—accept this—love from
    Eli J.
Under favorable conditions I am satisfied ignorance
    Cannot defeat Power.
If this Book is successful—time proceeds to establish all things,
    States, Schools, Indians—future see
Things—and things entirely harmless—to a good constitution
Proceed, to any age, sex, or color—this Book fulfills more,

Advertises more attractions, more than we advertised to fulfill,
    —much more
In these advertisements, in future as marks of development
    appear,
I take the responsibility—power given from Elijah
    To Josiah Joseph, publis-her and a-gent.

In the past age these cards were given to the old generation,
The prophet was on earth—before the Fire—they would not
    take them.

I give them to future in remembrance of Joe (Elijah) Spirit
Of John Joseph (Jesus), who was with Great Spirit, who came
    From God Himself—who knows Himself.

        He sends His Spirit—dictates this
          To the Scrub—clean Spirit He wires
      Some of this to earth—some to humanity—
      Some choose choice, some choose to let it alone.
      I deal the deck—these are my choice cards,
        In memory of Joe, the Mail carrier.

      Return to earth of Elijah the prophet,
        Gabriel's Trumpet—record on earth—for sale.

Gabriel's Trumpet was heard—copied by A. Jew.
Age you—of future receive—copy as original from Trumpet.

Gabriel's Trumpet descended from The Power
    That owns the earth—His Power is Original.

Latest from above—up the ladder without a fall.
    Joe McGinty return's—on Gabriel's Trumpet—mail wire.

The Seventh wonder of the world—Gabriel's Trumpet—
    Dictations of the Gospel Wire.

      Gabriel's Trumpet—a friend to Light Heart,
        And light-hearted sailors for Liberty.

      He fulfilled in Gabriel's Trumpet, by Authority
        From the Power giving life to the world.

He is chosen—the hub for the crank—of the universe—
    Descriptive pictures in Gabriel's Trumpet.

We extend the privelege—each one may help the crank turn
       the world.
    Gabriel's Trumpet shows the Power to use.

Gabriel's Trumpet is a bundle—containing the pattern
    Of the hub crank of the world.

All who admit the superior will of our Creator,
    Will find a few of His wishes in Gabriel's Trumpet.

Elijah the prophet kicks Adam one way—Eve another;
    Benefits described in the course—in Gabriel's Trumpet.

Elijah the prophet fulfills the new by remembering the
    Promise of ancient time—honest truth—in Gabriel's
    Trumpet.

The prophet that brings Gabriel's Trumpet—takes advise
Of good men—hopes they will take the Book now for sale.

SACRED—HERE—LIES

    The last—fly-leaf—t-o-f-lies
In memory of the Frisco flies—free press opinions—together
    At the sound of Original Gabriel's Trumpet.
    Ante-room class in ru-diments:

PICTURE SILENCE OF FLIES.

A fly-blow—from Examin-her.

LINES—TO—SHE.

    Explanation in—construction—in—struction.
Sacred her to—Oin memory of the Shoo—Fri—sco—s—cat
    Wasp—nest—case.
A Wasp—nest—court Dec—ember of 1891.
    The pleading wasp throws HER case up in a cof-in fit
    Throws herself up, her wings spread out, dry.
        She comes down—dies very—dry.

Her speech is not in view—I can only give you a fair sample
        extract.
Continuing at length, she said I Am—simply—Joe Joe-o-ho.
Oho ho ho—O-ho O-h-e th–Oho hoo-r-ee—just like her, I said,
        I left.
    I know there was more of it,
But a cof-in fit to die she shuts up with dam-age.
Her show herself—opened wide—give away—doubled up,
She goes out back-wards, head under–wards–as–forwards—
Sits on Herself—on own self until Her She it is it dies;
      Then h-e She-it dies in it.
Publis–then hum-d—am I She—O don't, don't, She—grieve so
      She—I—Am is gone—O don't, don't, She—grieve.
O where in my new skirt—owe-r, O where can he be—in it?
So I–b–d–am—we-r in She–it–is it so-so—She is so city-ful ;
So so don't—J–o–grieve She–so–for me–so–so on.
His as–just so saw Old Ben's rats run to catch breath.
      Said cat-ch it all broke up—run
      Back—court-house one said with authority.
        Said let tired She–lie–decay;
        So tired She lies still—in present day.
Argument—Decision vers-us stingers.   Q-t, q-t, to Judge
      Liberty.
Decision—Argument against dictations—are sour, putrid,
      pickle pi-sh shh—
Great penalty—Great decay—stingers nest–waist away wer-o,
      Shut up, Joe-si-ah, there is one worse.
O yes, O yes, I remember, the Chronic–D–Young–O–Grady.
Who gave him his money—SHE did.
Who does SHE belong to—I know.
Why will he refuse to help HER—I don't know.
Who wants him to hog it up—I don't know.
Why is he like he is rich in it—I know he is Chronic.
      Rich in it, and She, poor thing, decays,
        Gold–days–ways–wer-o.
Picture Chronic–hog–indifference–the pi in it, he keeps, keeps
      Home of Chronic—les—old time dirty sheets.

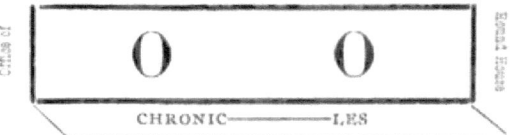

Can you help the Joe Gabriel—Trumpet——Co.?
Chronic-answers—We do not do that kind of business.

Chronic-crawl in it Examin-her fly up—you are in it.
Remember this the record of Original Gabriel's Trumpet.
Come—next—letter—flies.

Wasp—O yes he is one ass—kiss now, My Honey—ever—o
Come to me again—I Am—Jo-si-ah
Come to future Litt-e B-y B-y steerage—Q-t, q-t.
I, Electricity man, will now proceed to fly into pieces.
Departing my, my hand continues marking—a—gain Last.

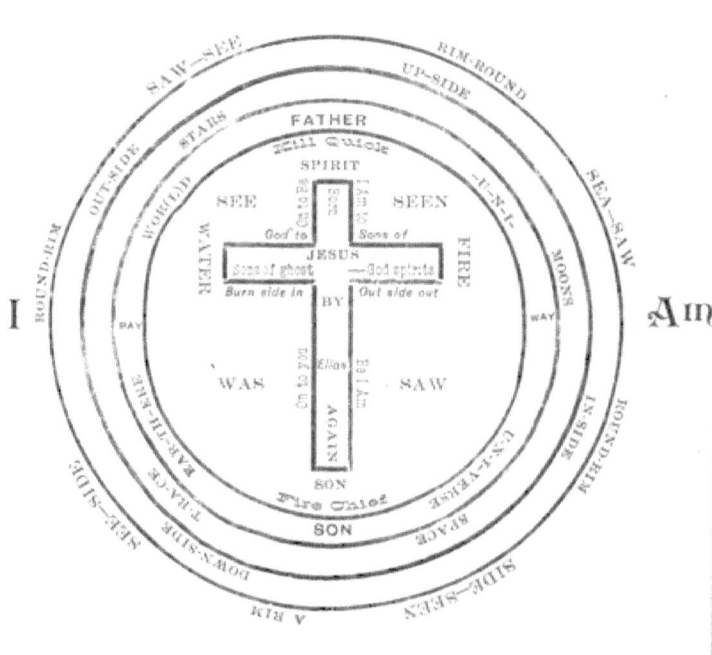

A—NEW—FEAR—AL——ICE—SERV—ICE.

A-gain Last—never change **one** I-O-T-A in **it lookout.**
A T——ail **or** you are left—take care of **your—save yourself**
Now you **are** left—look out—I f-y, fl-y, fli p-p-ices.

By your I-s-cream free-z-her—self cool-her—safe keep
Fro-z-in good-s Kate-s—p-p-on—d—a-m yourself—i-s-h—
L-o-v—c-z—get away—I—go—p-p-aces clubs—spades—dia-
            monds
        Hearts continue beating
Electricity—Kings—Gospel wire—continuing marking
Rapt—for wind up—round up wo-band—holding cool—in A
Ice-box, cool off—end attraction—opposite current—see.
        Flickers—go back-wards.
    Gospel wire rolls up in earth-quake—it **is**
Histed-ho-e-e by wind-up—SHE-cus—Cir-cus **S-her** s-cat
———— T-ick, T-ick ho-me-stop thief
O yes, ever, **O** good by, old dry rust, decay egg, farm-HER
        good-by;
I fly to sparks—**Mark,** John, Luke at M—hew yourself
        Leave on the J-E-Mark Co-s wire—sparking sparks
I leave—sparks of the J-O-S-I-A—J-E-S-I-AS—Co's wire
Leave on the—S-he—J-E-S-U—St-rum-pet-Co-s Wire
For E—turn-it-y—rrrr——wo-band continues marking
Publis go roll clouds by—then hum-d—m hi—yi—hi-e—hi—
        ye—ho—hi—you
Ma—good by—good by. Q-t, q-t, Boy—good-y, goody.
I fly to pieces of life strength—his-t-ears—wo-band continues
        —marking—
Just so another thief came——somewhere I stop—man,
He came just in time—take a journey he persuaded me—we
        thought—
I collect, we going to-gether—he bound for Port—I-a—bound
        for Venus.
He knew my little game—in time he told me he fooled me
Just so—bound—out over the face of the deep—we go—
        together
As Friends—above brothers—we talk on the way over space.
My mind is this Book—I tell him of the life on—SHE—I
        know nothing else.
Far we go—he leads in space—we leave the attraction of
        SHE—soon.
Ahead I see—we take the opposite attraction—to float over to
        —Venus.

Then wo-band continues—marking
W-e-r—o-h-old a minute, Boys—I-stop—a mi-nute
  She has something on a stick—now see her mark,
† (She thinks she is something on a stick).

PUBLIS—HER.

I came out—just in time.
I see a sickly smile on shame face—I see something,
  A—stick—on it—herself—by it.

HER

—WO— —BAND—

MARK

P. S.—After making her mark (showing spite) stretching her
Pair-a-sol she went light—as—like a cork herself up to the
Moon—herself—or Venus—she was so far gone she would not
    speak.
    Soon flies came around—the smell simply fearful.
I leave for a time myself for a more wholesome location for
    future.
To fresh fields I see the grass spreading, fresh streams running
Cool and clear. I leave this for the rising generation (in
    green) commencement
    Continue to publis this record of truth
    (Witness) of record grounds—Eli—J—Berry—man
To witness this as truth I was given the peculiar vision
    To see electricity in air, space
    (I berry the remains of Electricity-man and wo-band)
They leave this to their descendants—my own power soon de-
    parts
I came to future as a witness of the big round up record
        In past age I was, I am
    Three Kick Powers (the single act man)
    This place positive—it is simply fearful such smell
I came in companion to Joe—same with Electricity man
God continues the work in the sky tent at this date.
    I see other planets circled by the electric flame.
I am from Spirit. I can say Great Spirit came in for the
    purpose

(Bitch) He finds one besides SHE that needs burning to
           purify.
        My opinion (is) SHE was a very hard case and deserve
           THE FIRE (record)
To benefit future country commence—the weather is fine
And pleasant, earth cooling off—ah hum
        Che che—at you I am catches it cold—I must think
        To get Home myself—good morning.

After seeing the wo–band make her mark it disgusts me
           I must go off to lose my head.
I came down through the stream of time on the back of an
           ass.
        Now I stop alight from him—he we cik everything in
        The SHAPE of wo–man—she disgusting—high head—
Proud after making her mark—I think she is something
        On a stick. I proceed to rub it in and
        I can make her smeller know it.
        I seen the one who held up her nose at old Joe's rags
        This record shows she was a positive stink, stick, stuck
        She kic's so low she could never, never blow
        She could never blow, Joe Gabriel's Trumpet.
        She is venua (Mary) the original strumpet,
She kic's herself out.   George Washington takes the contract
           Through the land of the Free.
           Forever by John and Joe Gabriel.
        Declare the Independence of Liberty.
The family advanced our Father Spirit, takes His Freedom,
Releases the dirty work, returns Home after weary years.
He came in as a part of God above—can he release the duty?
He is Great Original Liberty, he wishes fresh fields,
He returns Home to start to rest—to start anew from Father
           God Above of Great Original Liberty.
Now take care of yourselves, be good, your mind has this
           course,
Your mind has the model in Statue Liberty—be contented,
Great Spirit given in beginning—releases the world.
The SHE-planet takes this Book, starts you proper, fresh
           . course.
Take care of yourselves until the breeze handles you at last,
Great Spirit can make anything on the world He wishes.
           Now he wishes a rest.
Improve your own spirit of the times, the tent is full of
           electricity.

Follow the **course.**   Great Spirit is of Himself,
  Controls any one He wishes.   Man gains the honor
Of inventions since the world began—now **continue**
    To continue the same.
Great Spirit gives a number of small spirits here on earth
    (perhaps one)
Sure—each one is sure—wishes to follow the Father Spirit.
He takes them now each, and in future each one make his
Own spirit of his or her own time of life—early in life
There may be a few little spirits left—try and improve them.
Now you know what becomes of you, if you do not fly **up**
  You crawl down, breeze sifts and measures you.
I give you credit for your dirty **work.**   I ask no praise
From you.   I away—work.   We Last Two leave.
We advance to help handle planet–earth–machine quit man
  (As Two Little ragged urchins) in the twilight—
Witness of Gabriel's record—guide sign—points
We are the Last, **we remain a while, we** come, **we go, our**
   time **we** take,
Sure as fate.   Consequence—we happy, think of journey,
All quiet, we think—think to save yourself, can you?
   I sign this as truth, by authority,
    Mr. THREE-KICK-POWERS (the single-act-man),
     (with) I Am The Big Medicine Man.
We wander around to get perfect—sick—disgusted with the
   place.
   Quiet light out For Good.
Your country is safe, the war ended, live in peace, improve
God's breeze continues a bleak and unweary laborer.
The breeze is blind—takes your measure mind fair
This is written by one who understands the nature of air
   Space, follow it to please the Last Electrict
    Light—air—breeze (it is)
   I go, the breeze continues blowing at times,
    Dry, cool, fresh and powerful.
By the Power of God it continues to wind up the flies to their
   proper destination.
Do not push out your wings too soon in dry weather.
Have patience, and respect the steady breeze that blows, or it
Will not fly you very high—to drop you for the dogs
   To continue, then, run after them—you continue.
Breeze continues now, successor to G. W. & Sons.
I hereby recommend it as a persevering and powerful agent
   of justice to one.

It is not selfish in measure—selfishness it measures disgusted.
Soon a body of breeze comes to take me. I am not alarmed.
      I wish to go.
By this see I am completely disgusted. I remained
To improve man in ages ages of time. You have riches and
      honor.
I leave. I came with nothing, as I leave—remember breeze.
Do not be selfish. I leave a little spirit for you to improve,
      (Future as combined nation).
I came, I go, free as the breeze that blows. I go, be good to
      yourselves.
      Now, wind in God's Power, come.
The wind is my only mourner—it sighs at my departure,
      It knows me as a friend.
It I see it comes at my departure, my little spirit I leave
      Guards this until future generation publishes,
      Now, good-bye, yourselves.
God's Spirit Company comes to meet me. I am proud, I
      suppose, affected.
I go. My past existence says be contented when you get there.
Breeze continues—sighs at my departure. It comes around
Bleak and dreary—as I depart I sigh myself, lonely.
I cry, but I must go—I cry—I see they are ready to start
      me off.
I go—after I start, I drop this to little spirit guard,
This in future to be in publication—For I Am now departing.
I see the breeze is my only mourner. It says my life
      Companion now I leave.
      It loses its Great Spirit—I cry, and cry myself
To go—I start—good-bye—I feel much worse—breeze blows
      things away from me.
I change rags—soon down goes man-u-script—from me,
And I am a well red-man-u-strip of foreign territory—
      I Am the Last
One, By-Son—now you bitch, stand, roll or shake—never
      trouble me again.
      By YOUNG THREE-KICK-POWER (the single-act-man).
      By BIG MEDICINE-MAN (witness).
Departure—leave—at last—yourself—a drop—to—earth.

Scene—Picture—(the Drop) Certain.

SPACE—TIME LIFE OF—LITTLE SPIRIT—GUARD.

Now you stay, you Little-May-be-so—Guess-not, spirit.
You must stay, you are left. Stay with them; improve in it.
Do not cry, when you are in it—Good–b-y.
Take good care of yourself—you are in it—watch the Book.
Now don't cry any more—good–b-y—when you look—
　　Stay, leave your mark when leaving—this Book.
　　Come to here—read this find out—here you are a drop
　　　In—left in reflection—A SCRUB.

————P————S————

The contradictions in this Book—allow them to remain.
　　By Young—May-be-so—I Guess-not (the drop),
　　A-gent Better-Believe of Spirit Co. (witness).

　　Space—Space—to the Little Original—Round-up.
　　Now Little Spirit—OOO guard—be careful.

　　　MY————ROUND
The heifers inside ◯ Cow-boys are out—go sook, sook, sook.
　　　UP————MARK

　　(Little Spirit-guard) OOO the gate was left open,
　　　The heifers are out again.
Ho-o-ook, boys, stear clear, little boys—don't let them hook
　　　you.
Now–let– her go—Gal-ag-e-r-u-n-o-u-t-o-f-i-n-i-s-e-n-d-it-u-g-o-u-
　　　t-e-x-yz—wo

————————

Space—Length of Space—Lengthy Space.

DEPARTURE OF THE DROP (LITTLE SPIRIT GUARD).

New swarm just hatching out—I see
　　The mongrel breed shows—soon millions of mongrels;
　　They most part wasp—three parts chronic—balance fly.
The hog spirit full—they—the dogs sicken—diseased.

Head-quarter will not take them for **improvement.**
They may continue **(to She)** spirit stick **until they breed** so
      thick
Great Spirit **will** never again stir them—or rock—a-by **stick.**
      I give it up—I lose my grip—
      I let go—I stub my toe—I fall away off
      The world into—E—turn—it—tie.
    I will sail away—this is all I leave—as
      I Am—the ORIGINAL—BUZZ-HARD,
    (My eye witness) MR. SKELETON TRUTH,
        (child of Carryon–Worldwords).
My carcass forced in through the ribs,
    I float away as a drop from the (bottom) of Time.
Spread **me out** over the world—berry **me in** my—fly sar-cas
      I am
    By—Poe—Two Make—Two Strikes—one.
(Recommendation by)EliJ—Jack-ass—Jack-Son,
(I Am prescribed) To keek sores from the **new** generations—
      no–ze–wo,
(All–turn–native) When this separator fails **to be** useful—
      take your
    Infirmities a head run through a thrashing machine,
Then berry yourself in–h–in my w-h-o-man–s-a-s—Q-t, q-t.
      I know you—now that's what you can do.
1st Thief—Now, Berry, shoulder the Cir-cus Harp
      And **we** will go—play—else–where **show.**
2d *Thief*—Light out.
      W–h–old—a mi-nute—Boys.
    Now then, together—Father—Eli—Spirit—three–one
      together—go
    All inside the case—tight squeeze—let HER go,
    Letter–fly—Future—Publis–her—opinion—
(Q-t, q-t**)** Pa—I can kiss, and that's **what** I can do—ne–good–
      b-y—hold a minute, Boys.
    Pa, **I** fool—that's what—that's what—
    I know I Am now—now Pa—now Pa, take **ne,**
      I want go to—certain.

(Th—End–core–all) by Qt–q-t—bow flies from dressing-room
(Scene—Extract–all) Behave—go slow—good by, mary—
      yz–wo.

    I find this Book by **me,** after careful reading—study—I find myself here in a place—revolving in space—and the ignorant theory (of their being no Power—being commencement) of beginning controlling planets (not owning the Heavens, is gone). Whose Power is it this Book tells? Elijah Berryman obeys, though it does not tell him of the star that falls.

I can find knowledge of future.

Fools may look for faults, and find them—they see some.

They may be so keen finding faults—cannot see—ben-e-fit.

It is to benefit those who respect—no see fault—cannot find one.

Mind character low—unmatured—look high over faults. This Book finds faults—makes enemies of those who cannot look for their own faults.

Now, good-by, fools. I Am Mr. Comean–Seeme. I wishing you to act fair, square away, and attend to your own affairs.

Future respect—Justice to Publis–her.

By my promise I will proceed to inspect hell, personally. The fire must be in perfect order. I will have the Power to fulfill my duty. The Foreman can then have—a rest.

Court——continue——minutes——my——Judgment—— Sentence——Ends——Certain.

www.ingramcontent.com/pod-product-compliance
Lightning Source LLC
Chambersburg PA
CBHW030115030726
47498CB00007B/2387